W9-CBO-236

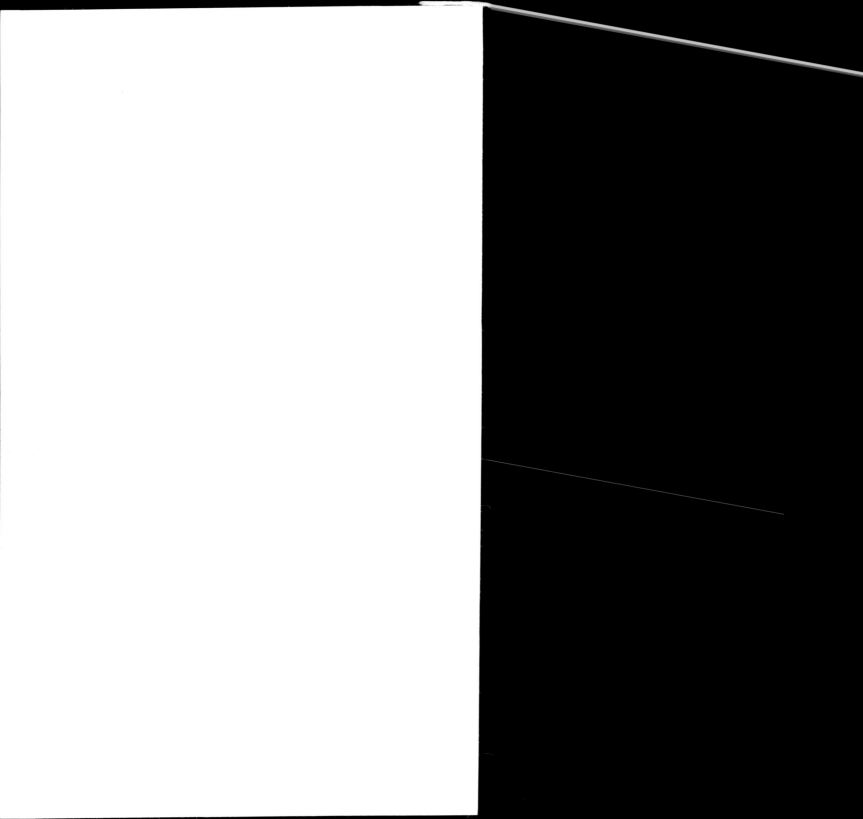

CLAIMING THE
COWBOY'S HEART

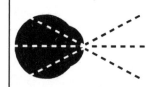

This Large Print Book carries the
Seal of Approval of N.A.V.H.

CLAIMING THE COWBOY'S HEART

LINDA FORD

THORNDIKE PRESS

A part of Gale, Cengage Learning

GALE
CENGAGE Learning·

Detroit • New York • San Francisco • New Haven, Conn • Waterville, Maine • London

GALE
CENGAGE Learning·

LIBRARY OF CONGRESS CATALOGING-IN-PUBLICATION DATA

Ford, Linda (Linda Carol)
    Claiming the cowboy's heart / by Linda Ford. — Large print edition.
        pages cm. — (Thorndike Press Large Print Gentle Romance)
    ISBN-13: 978-1-4104-6633-4 (hardcover)
    ISBN-10: 1-4104-6633-7 (hardcover)
    1. Large type books. I. Title.
PS3606.O7395C53 2014
813'.6—dc23   2013040742

Published in 2014 by arrangement with Harlequin Books S.A.

Printed in the United States of America
1 2 3 4 5 6 7 18 17 16 15 14

Fear not therefore:
ye are of more value
than many sparrows.

— *Luke* 12:7

To my sister, Leona, and my friend Brenda, as you struggle with so many challenges. Remember how much God values you.

CHAPTER ONE

Eden Valley Ranch, Alberta, Canada
August 1882

"I didn't expect it to be so heavy." Jayne Gardiner held the pistol between her fingers. She couldn't bear the cold feeling of the stock against her palm. Her hand trembled and the shiny steel barrel winked in the sun like an evil tormentor. Panic clawed up her throat like threatening flood waters. She struggled to push it back. She knew first-hand the destructive power of a gun.

She stiffened her spine. Fear would not be allowed to rule her life. She would learn to defend herself and those she cared about. She'd be ready to take action if ever another life-or-death situation arose.

Behind her, her friend Mercy laughed. "It won't bite." But then, Mercy lived for adventure. That's why she'd accompanied them on this trip west. As if ready for an escapade, she wore suede riding pants that she'd purchased before they left Fort Benton on their journey to western Canada and the Eden Valley Ranch, and her mahogany hair was pulled back in a braid.

Beside her, Sybil twisted her hands in the fabric of her fashionable pinstripe blue walking skirt. She completed the trio that recently arrived from England. More reserved like Jayne, she wanted to come on this visit to Canada to get over her parents' deaths.

Jayne had come to visit her brother, Eddie — owner and operator of the Eden Valley Ranch — and his wife, Linette, though some might think she'd come to put the past out of her mind. She tightened her lips. People who thought that would be wrong. She didn't intend to forget the lessons her past had taught her.

Sybil shuddered, causing the golden curls that had escaped the elegant roll to bounce around her shoulders. Modern wisdom said a woman with curly hair would be of gentle temperament. Sybil lived up to the expectation. "I hate guns."

Jayne sucked back an echoing shudder. Her brown hair was thick and straight, supposedly indicating a strong-willed woman. So far, she'd proven the statement false but she meant to change that starting now. "I hate what guns do but I want to learn to shoot one." She studied the target placed about fifty feet away.

The young women were in a grove of trees that sheltered them from the wind and provided slices of shade depending on the position of the sun. They were far enough from the ranch buildings to not alarm Eddie, Linette, or any of the other caring people there who saw no need for Jayne to learn to shoot a gun. Eddie had said it wouldn't serve any purpose. It wouldn't bring Oliver back. And, he'd carefully pointed out, there were plenty of cowboys around the place should it be necessary to shoot a gun. What's more, he'd said with utmost conviction, he didn't think such an occasion would likely occur.

Jayne had tipped her chin and vowed she'd learn with or without Eddie's help. It wasn't some foolish notion of undoing the past. She would not allow herself to ever again feel as helpless as she did on that horrible day. The events had been burned permanently into her brain.

The day she had in mind had been sunny and warm after days of damp sky. Her fiancé, Oliver Spencer, had suggested spending the afternoon together instead of abandoning her to her own amusements while he pursued his as so often happened. On several occasions, she'd objected mildly to the amount of time Oliver spent in gambling establishments. The promise of some quality time together, just the two of them, had caused her to laugh at his jokes, though, as usual, she failed to understand them. He must have thought her so innocent.

They'd been walking side by side along a street lined with shops inviting their business. She had glanced in one window and noticed a beautiful display of lace gloves and thought of purchasing a pair, but she hadn't suggested a stop because she and Oliver were discussing the future. She didn't want to distract him.

"We'll live in the house with Mother and Father. There's more than enough room. No need to own another house."

Did he mean she would go from being under her parents' direct supervision to being under *his* parents'? She wanted to be a woman with her own home. Of course, it made sense to start with. "Will we get our own home when we have children?" A hot blush had flooded her body at the intimate topic.

Before Oliver could answer, a man had jumped from an alley brandishing a gun and demanded Oliver give him everything.

Jayne had shrunk back into the recessed doorway of the building beside them and watched as Oliver emptied his pockets of quite a lot of cash.

"It's all I have," he'd said, his voice hard with anger.

The thief had jammed the money into his pocket. "You know that's not all I want." He'd waved the pistol. "Where's the key?"

Jayne had glanced about, hoping for rescue but no one turned down the street toward them. No one noticed the robbery.

"I want it back," the robber had growled.

Jayne had swallowed hard. People passed at the intersection a few yards away. She tried to call for help but her voice failed her.

Oliver had continued to say he had nothing more. He'd even turned his pockets out.

"Where is it? I can't prove it but I know you cheated. You took everything I have." The thief had lurched toward Oliver.

She'd never seen Oliver move so quickly. His arm slashed across the man's wrist. The pistol dropped to the cobblestones and he'd kicked it toward Jayne.

"Pick it up. Shoot him," Oliver had ordered as he and the thief tussled.

Jayne had stared at the gun just two feet away but she couldn't move. She'd never touched a gun, let alone shot one. She didn't even know how.

Oliver's head had hit the ground with a thud and he'd lain stunned.

The thief had grabbed the pistol. A metallic click had rung through Jayne's racing thoughts.

"Get up," the thief had ordered.

Oliver had staggered to his feet.

"I'm done playing around. You know what I want. Give it to me."

Oliver had swayed.

Someone from the nearby intersection had called out. "He's got a gun."

Then everything had happened so fast Jayne couldn't say what came first. A shot had rung out. Oliver had pitched to the pavement. The thief had raced down the alley. A crowd had surrounded them.

Jayne had hovered in the doorway, too frightened to move while blood pooled around Oliver. Someone had leaned over him. A man had looked up, seen her and waved her forward. Her legs numb, her heart beating erratically, she'd managed to make the few steps and knelt at Oliver's side. "You'll be fine. You'll be fine." She hadn't believed the words she'd uttered.

He'd caught her hand. He'd struggled to speak past the gurgling in his throat. Something about gambling and winning from the man who had shot him. Then his words ended in a gasp. Gentle hands had pried her away. Someone had taken her home.

For days she'd sat in a straight-backed chair beside the cold fireplace and replayed the scene in her mind. The skin on her face had grown taut every time she'd come to the spot where Oliver had kicked the gun toward her. Fear as deep as the English Channel had shaken her insides. Oliver was dead because she hadn't been able to act. Hadn't known what to do with the gun that lay so close to her. All over some gambling money. The world had gone crazy.

One day Bess, her quiet younger sister, had pulled a chair to Jayne's knees and taken her hands. "Jayne, I have always admired you for your determination and sensibleness. It amazes me you sit here day after day. I beg you to get up and start living again."

Jayne had looked into Bess's sweet face and made a decision. She would not be defeated by this event. With God's help she'd use it to grow stronger. She'd pushed to her feet and hugged her sister. "Bess, you are right. Never again will I feel so helpless. So useless."

Bess's smile had widened with relief then

faltered at the conviction in Jayne's voice. "What are you going to do?"

She had no firm plan at the moment. "I'll tell you what I'm not going to do. I'm not going to be a helpless woman."

That conviction had carried her away from home and across the North American continent to a new, inviting country.

Now she lifted her arm and looked at her two friends in the grove of trees. "I will learn to shoot."

Mercy steadied Jayne's hand. "Hold it like this. Brace with your other hand. Look down the barrel to the target." She guided Jayne into position then stepped back.

Jayne's arms lowered until the gun pointed at the ground. "If I hadn't been so scared of guns I might have grabbed the one Oliver kicked toward me. He might still be alive."

"Exactly," Mercy said.

"Or you might both be dead." Sybil covered her face with her hands as if she couldn't bear the thought.

Jayne wished she could as easily block the sight of Oliver's death from her mind, but it wasn't possible. Any more than it was possible to forget she was twenty-one, no longer planning a wedding, and not ever wanting to think of such things again. Oliver had taught her that life was too fragile to make dream-filled plans.

"You don't want it happening again," Mercy insisted.

Jayne cringed. "I don't have another fiancé, you know."

Mercy laughed. "Not yet, you mean."

"Not ever." Oh, she'd likely marry. Everyone did. But nothing on earth would convince her to again open her heart to such fear and pain and disappointment. Any more than she would ever again let herself become so weak and dependent on others. Though she'd only begun the journey toward living strong and free. "But you're right about needing to learn to protect myself." And people she cared about. Never again would she stand by, shaking in fear, while someone died. "I can do this."

Mercy repeated her instructions on how to hold the gun, aim it and fire it.

Sybil crossed her arms and looked like she'd sooner be anywhere but there. "How do you know all this?" she asked Mercy.

"I sweet-talked one of the cowboys in Fort Benton to teach me."

Jayne and Sybil looked at each other and shook their heads in unison. Mercy was notorious for sweet-talking men into doing favors for her.

Mercy saw their exchanged glances and

17

simply laughed. "Jayne, pay attention. Aim, squeeze and fire."

Jayne lifted the gun, steadied it as she squinted down the barrel toward the target. She closed her eyes and squeezed. The gun jerked upward, the noise of the shot making her squeal.

Mercy gasped. "You're supposed to keep your eyes open and focused on the target."

"Hi yii." A yell came from a distant spot.

Jayne eased open one eye. Through the trees she saw a man leaning low over the neck of his horse as he raced away. Her heart clambered up her throat and stuck there like an unwelcome intruder. "Did I shoot him?" Her voice barely croaked out the words.

Sybil fell back three steps. "He might be after us. We better get back to the ranch."

Jayne shook her head. "First, we have to check and make sure I didn't injure him." Her stomach turned over and refused to settle. "All I wanted to do was be ready to defend us against bad people. But if I've hurt someone instead —" The blood drained to her feet, leaving her ready to collapse in a boneless puddle. Much like it had when Oliver was shot. So much blood. Such a dark stain.

Tremors raced up and down her spine.

Cold as deep as the worst winter day gripped her insides.

Mercy wrapped an arm about her waist. "I'm sure you only frightened him and he decided to get out of range of your deadly aim." She laughed like it was no more than a silly joke.

"We need to check." Jayne lifted the hem of her black taffeta walking skirt with its stylish Edwardian hoop underskirt and forced her milky legs to take one step forward and then another. Mercy marched at her side. Sybil hung back then, realizing she would be alone, rushed after them.

They passed the untouched target, pushed through some low bushes, wended between tall poplars with their leaves fluttering noisily in the breeze. The wooded area gave way to a grassy slope with a faint trail skirting boulders. Allowing her legs no mercy, she hurried to the trail and bent over, looking for clues.

She stopped at a round rock that could serve as a seat if they'd been inclined to sit and enjoy the view. A dark, wet streak dripped down the side of the rock. Her heart beat a frantic tattoo against her ribs. "Look. Isn't that blood?"

The others joined her. Mercy touched the spot and lifted a stained finger. "Fresh blood." She wiped her finger clean on a bit of grass.

Jayne's eyes felt as if they might fall from their sockets. "I shot someone." She straightened and stared in the direction the rider had gone. "What if —" Would she find a body down the trail?

Mercy grabbed her hand. "It was an accident."

"Explain that to the man I shot." She pulled Mercy after her and signaled Sybil to follow. "I have to see if he's on the trail."

"Dead, you mean?" Mercy said, putting Jayne's fears out in the open.

"I knew this was a bad idea." Sybil's voice was high and thin. "Let's go back and tell Eddie. He can look for the man."

That sent resolve into Jayne's insides. Her brother wouldn't always be around to rescue her. Besides, he would be angry that she had ignored his directive to forget about learning to shoot. She squared her shoulders. "I don't need Eddie to clean up after me." She marched down the trail. But her courage faded with every step. Dark spots, some rather large, dotted the dirt. Once she touched a stain and lifted a damp finger.

"More blood," Sybil moaned. "Lots of it."

Jayne tried unsuccessfully to block the memory of blood pooling around Oliver's body. So much blood. Sybil had no idea.

They passed between two table-size boulders and turned by a stand of thick pine trees whose distinctive scent filled the air. The majestic Rocky Mountains rose to her right. Such wild country. Open and free. Had she spoiled it for some poor, unsuspecting man?

She could see down the trail until it turned and disappeared. No rider. No limp body stretched out in the grass. "Guess he wasn't injured too badly." *Please, God, let it be true.*

Mercy chuckled. "If we hear of some cowboy dying mysteriously on the trail, shot by an unseen assailant, we'll know who is responsible."

"Mercy," Sybil chided. "Show a little compassion."

But Mercy only laughed. "Jayne knows I'm only teasing, don't you? It's probably only a graze. No more than a splinter to a man who lives in this country."

Jayne's tension relieved by the absence of a body, she tucked her arm through Mercy's and pulled Sybil closer. "All's well that ends well. Now let's go back to the ranch and see if Linette needs some help." Her sister-in-law was efficiency on two legs even though she expected a baby in four months.

Sybil glanced over her shoulder. "I pray that whomever you shot won't be bleeding to death somewhere."

At the teasing, Jayne faltered. "Maybe I should ask Eddie to ride out and check the trail."

Mercy urged her onward. "Like I said, it's likely only a flesh wound. If the man needs help he will seek it."

Jayne nodded. The words should reassure her but they fell short of doing so. She couldn't get the sight of a large pool of blood out of her mind. The last thing she needed was another death on her conscience.

Who was shooting at him?

Twenty-four-year-old Seth Collins bent low over his horse's neck as they pounded down the trail. One minute he was sitting on a rock, enjoying a pleasant moment as he drank from his canteen and ate a couple of dry biscuits. The next, a shot rang out and pain gouged his right leg. It took two seconds and the sight of blood soaking his trousers for him to realize what happened. Then his only thought had been escape.

He glanced over his shoulder. Saw no sign of pursuit.

Why would anyone shoot him? He was

just an ordinary, poor cowboy. Except for the wad of cash he carried. Had someone followed him? He'd joined the cattle drive north from Fort Benton to a ranch in western Canada for only one reason — to earn enough money to pay the special caregiver the doctor had recommended for Pa. A man with knowledge of how to manipulate paralyzed limbs. The doctor spoke highly of Crawford, saying he'd seen great success with other stroke patients. Some, he said, had even learned to walk again.

Now he had to get the money to Montana. If he didn't, what would happen to his pa? Crawford had committed to staying three months. If he couldn't help Pa in that time he wouldn't continue on because he'd found he couldn't do anything more after that. Seth had written the man saying he'd been delayed and would be there as soon as possible with the man's wages. Crawford's response had been terse. "I have others interested in my services. Please return immediately." Seth had written again. "Please stay until I get there. I'll be home in a week and I'll pay you extra." But he had no assurances Crawford wouldn't leave and Pa would suffer. Pa was all Seth had left and he meant to get home and take care of him.

He spared a glance at his leg. His buff-colored trouser leg was dark and sticky with blood, which dripped from the heel of his boot. He would need to stop soon and tend to the wound.

And hide his money so those who shot at him wouldn't discover it.

He rode on at the same frantic pace for fifteen minutes then pulled to a stop on a knoll that allowed him a good view of the back trail. After watching a little while he decided he had outrun the shooter. Or shooters. He reined into a grove of trees that provided a bit of cover yet allowed him to keep watch for anyone following him. As he swung off his horse, his leg buckled under him. What kind of damage had the shot done?

Knowing he had to stop the blood flow, he yanked the neckerchief from his neck and tied it around his thigh. He needed something to tighten it so he hobbled toward the nearest tree, biting back a groan at the pain snaking up his leg and wrapping around his entire body. He broke off a finger-thick branch then plopped, as much as sat, on the ground, stuck the length of wood between his leg and the neckerchief and twisted until the blood stopped. Resting his back against a tree trunk, he held the tourniquet tight and considered his plight.

The wad of money was his major concern. Seemed someone had discovered he carried four months' worth of wages in his pocket and decided to lighten his load. He stared at his feet, trying to decide what to do. Hard to hide anything on the horse. He had his saddlebags, but that was the first place a thief would look after searching Seth's person. No hiding a secret pocket in his ruined trousers. He continued to stare at his feet. Hadn't he once heard of a man who hollowed out the heels of his boots to hide something?

He didn't fancy trying to pry a boot off his right leg. Figured it might start bleeding again. For sure, it would increase the pain that even now hammered against the inside of his skull. Ignoring the protest from his injured leg, he used it to pry off his left boot then took his knife from his pocket and set to work. He glanced down the trail every few minutes to make sure he wasn't being pursued.

By the time he'd worked the heel off and dug a hollow in it, his head had grown wobbly. He brushed at his eyes to clear his vision. Then he rolled his money into a tight wad and wedged it into the hole he'd made.

Now to put the heel back on. He found a rock the size of his fist to use as a hammer.

Getting the heel on proved harder than removing it but after ten minutes he decided it would do. Had his foot swollen? Must have because he could hardly pull the boot back on.

His head seemed full of air. He swiped his eyes again. Tired. So tired. He shouldn't have pushed so hard the past two days. Now he was paying for it. He'd rest before he moved on. Just a few minutes.

"Mister, wake up."

Seth squinted against the blare of light assaulting his eyes. Awareness of his surroundings came slowly, reluctantly. First, pain. Then thirst. Then the persistent questions of the man kneeling at his side.

How long had he been lying on the ground? Asleep? Unconscious? Either way, he'd wasted precious time. He tried to sit up but the world spun and he decided against the idea. "Who are you?" he managed to croak.

"Eddie Gardiner. Who are you?"

Gardiner? The name seemed familiar but Seth couldn't place it. "Water," he croaked.

The man held a canteen to Seth's lips and he drank greedily before he gave his name. "Seth Collins."

"Let's get you on your horse. I'll take you

where you can get help for that leg."

Seth wanted to argue. Needed to. He had to get to his pa. But his leg hurt like twelve kinds of torture. A little tending wouldn't go amiss so he let Eddie Gardiner push him onto his horse and lead him away.

He clung to the saddle, which took far more effort than he would normally exert. He managed to tell Eddie about someone shooting him. "Didn't see them."

They approached a ranch. A pretty place with a big house on a hill overlooking the outbuildings. Among the structures below the house were a couple of two-story buildings, a cluster of red shacks all alike, a log cabin and a barn. All laid out nice and neat. A bridge spanned a river on one side, leading to more pens and small buildings beyond.

They approached the big house. "This is where I live," Eddie said. "You'll get help here."

Seth managed to swing himself off his horse but didn't protest when Eddie grabbed his arm and steadied him.

A young woman opened the door.

Seth's vision was clouded with pain but he was alive enough to note the brown eyes that seemed to smile even when her mouth didn't, a thick braid of rich brown hair

27

coiled at the back of her head and a flawless complexion. Peaches and cream, his ma used to say.

"This man is injured. He needs our help."

Someone shoved a chair under him and he sat. Several women clustered around him.

Eddie answered their questions. "His name is Seth Collins. He's been shot. I found him a few miles to the south." He gave a wave in that direction. "He didn't see who did it."

One of the women addressed Seth. "You're welcome here. My name is Mrs. Gardiner. This is my sister-in-law, Jayne Gardiner." She indicated the young woman who had answered the door. Again, the Gardiner name seemed familiar but his brain couldn't find any more information.

"These are her friends, Mercy Newell and Sybil Bannerman."

He noted Mercy had reddish-brown hair and brown eyes. Sybil was a pretty thing with blue eyes and blond curls. He hadn't seen any white women in days and now he was surrounded by them. And him in such a sorry state.

"I wish the circumstances of your visit were different," Mrs. Gardiner said.

The other three women had been whispering together and now Miss Jayne Gardiner cleared her throat. "I think I might have been the one who shot you."

Seth stared at this sweet, young thing. His mind couldn't make sense of her confession. "Why would you shoot me?" How would she know about the money he carried? He pushed aside the remnants of his fatigue. Refused to acknowledge it was pain that clouded his mind. Had someone at the ranch heard he'd collected his wages and ridden south? Were they all in this together?

"It was an accident. I wanted —" she swallowed hard "— I wanted to learn how to shoot a gun so I could protect myself and the ones I care about."

Eddie jammed his fists on his hips. "I warned you about messing around with guns. I told you to leave them alone. Now do you see why?" He glowered at his sister.

Jayne tipped her chin up and faced her brother. "I must learn how to defend myself. I refuse to be a helpless female."

Eddie sputtered but before he could get out a word, his wife intervened. "Let's get this man upstairs so I can look at his wound."

Jayne brought her attention back to Seth. "It's my fault. I'll take care of him."

Mrs. Gardiner made a protesting sound

that ended abruptly. "That would be fine."

Eddie helped Seth regain his feet and steered him up the stairs that swept to the second story. At the top, he turned them right and into the first bedroom. Seth settled himself on the edge of the bed.

For the first time he gave his leg a good, hard study. It throbbed clear to the top of his head. His trousers were blood- and dirt-caked. He didn't anticipate the skin beneath looked any prettier.

Mrs. Gardiner and Jayne had followed into the room.

"Eddie, he'll need to remove those trousers so we can get at the wound," Mrs. Gardiner said.

"Not my pants." Seth's protest sounded weak and he clamped his teeth together. Weakness was not something he cared to reveal.

"We'll wait outside until you're decent," Mrs. Gardiner said as the ladies left the room. He heard them murmur in the hallway, Mrs. Gardiner asking Miss Jayne about the shooting.

Eddie knelt at Seth's feet. "I'll help you with your boots and pants." He tugged at a boot.

Seth would have protested but had to bite

back a groan. Cold sweat beaded his fore-head.

"Can't you simply roll up my pant leg?" Seth asked through his clenched teeth.

"Seems to me you'd welcome a clean outfit. Do you have another pair in your saddlebags?"

He grunted in the affirmative.

"I'll get them later. First, let's get you cleaned up." Eddie helped remove the second boot and the soiled trousers then eased Seth to the bed and covered him with a sheet, but not before Seth saw the dirty, bloody wound.

"I'll send the ladies in to tend that." Eddie piled Seth's boots and pants beside the door. Good. So long as the boots were where he could see them.

Jayne and Mrs. Gardiner again entered the room, Jayne carrying a basin of water.

He closed his eyes knowing he must endure having the wound cleansed. Ironic that it was at the hands of the same woman who had inflicted it.

Mrs. Gardiner eased back the sheet to expose his leg. "This doesn't look good."

Seth nodded. "I saw it."

"It's very dirty." She shifted her gaze to Jayne. "When did you shoot him?"

She swallowed hard. "It was yesterday."

Yesterday? He hadn't realized he'd slept through the night. The urgency of his task struck him. He could not afford this delay. He half sat then fell back. Wouldn't hurt none to have the wound cleaned up before he moved on.

Jayne pressed to Mrs. Gardiner's side. She gasped as she saw the wound. She looked at Seth, her eyes wide as she met his gaze. Whether he saw distress, regret or something else entirely, he couldn't hazard a guess.

"It was unintentional." She sounded so defensive that in spite of his pain and the awkwardness of being flat on his back with two women in the room, he grinned.

"Seems you should have tended it a little sooner," Mrs. Gardiner offered.

"Got someplace to be." Again urgency gripped his innards. The last letter from the caregiver, that one Seth picked up a few days ago at the ranch headquarters, had been dated three weeks ago and gave little information to ease Seth's concern about Pa's well-being. *Expecting you soon with necessary wages. Job here done.*

How could a man give so little assurance in his few words? Seth needed to get to Pa before Crawford left. Might be he was already gone. He'd signed up for three months and no more. If he wasn't there, who would be looking after Pa? The uncertainty burned the inside of Seth's stomach.

Mrs. Gardiner tsked.

"Is he going to be okay?" Jayne asked. Her eyes filled with concern. And well they might. She'd shot him.

"We'll fix you as well as we can," Mrs. Gardiner said. "But you're going to have to be careful you don't get an infection." She turned to Jayne. "You can clean it up." She gave instructions.

He closed his eyes to endure the pain that would surely come from having the wound tended.

At first her touch was tentative then it grew firm, more assured. She was gutsy. He'd give her that.

"Why is it so important for you to learn to shoot?" His voice sounded hoarse. He hoped they'd put it down to some strong virtue, not the pain that seemed to clutch every part of his body.

"I need to be able to defend myself and others if the need ever again arises."

He lifted his eyelids. "Again?" He ignored the pain as he eased up on his elbows to watch her.

"You best lie still." She pressed firm, damp hands to his shoulders. "Moving makes you bleed more." Her face was so close to his he could see the porcelain purity of her skin, the dark streaks of brown in her irises and something more — the determination in her gaze. He was beginning to think she was a headstrong woman who gave little heed to the results of her actions. Just the sort of woman he normally gave a wide berth to. For now, though, he must submit to her ministrations.

He sank back on the pillow. "You've been involved in gunplay before?"

"Only as a spectator. I saw someone shot to death." Her jaw muscles tightened. "And I did nothing to prevent it because I didn't know what to do. Didn't even know how to shoot a gun." Her gaze had shifted to a distant place beyond the walls of this room. "That's when I decided I would never again be a helpless, pampered woman." She gave a decisive nod. "I will learn to shoot a gun and be ready and able to defend myself and those I care about." Her voice rang with determination. "Nothing will stop me."

Seth watched her warily. He knew the folly of insisting on doing foolish acts. Good thing he would be leaving here in a matter of hours. He wouldn't be around to see the result of her decision. But pity poor Eddie Gardiner trying to keep a rein on his sister.

He hoped for both their sakes that the job wasn't too much for the man.

If he had time to spare he might offer to help with the task simply to prevent a worse disaster than having her shoot some innocent passerby in the leg. But thankfully he didn't have time. Because for a man like him who took his responsibilities seriously, this was the sort of woman who spelled a heap of trouble.

CHAPTER TWO

The ragged edges of the wound were covered with dirt and blood. As she cleaned it, fresh blood oozed out and thickened into globs. Jayne swallowed hard, holding back nausea. She'd never taken care of an injured person. Never even entered a sick room. But she would take care of this injured man. It was her responsibility, no matter how tight her lungs grew or how hard her pulse banged behind her eyes.

"Take the wet cloth and sponge away more of the dirt," Linette said.

She dabbed at the dirt and allowed herself a moment of satisfaction. Another step on her journey to move beyond a pampered young lady who couldn't take care of herself or help others.

"You need to scrub a little harder to get the dried stuff," Linette said.

She rinsed the cloth clean and tackled the job again. When she'd finished the area around the wound, she turned to Linette. "What about the blood?"

"Clean right to the edges." Linette leaned past Jayne's shoulder to inspect the job. "Good. You've got it nice and clean. Now we need to use antiseptic on it." Linette handed her a small container marked carbolic acid.

"Won't it hurt?" she whispered to Linette.

"For a moment or two. But it's necessary."

Jayne turned to Seth. Knowing whatever pain he endured was her fault tore at her innards. "I'm going to use antiseptic. Linette says it might sting."

Gritting her teeth at what she must do, she splashed the carbolic in the wound.

His knuckles whitened as he gripped the edge of the bed. His eyes caught and held hers. The dark, pain-filled look brushed a tender spot inside her.

"I'm sorry." Her hands trembled as she set aside the bottle.

Sweat covered his brow.

She grabbed a towel from the stack nearby and dabbed at his forehead, which provided her plenty of opportunity to study him. He was big. She'd noticed that as he'd hobbled up the stairs at Eddie's side. He had a thatch of dark — almost black — hair in need of a good combing. His hazel eyes, although clouded with pain, held her gaze in a steady grip.

She turned from her musing as Linette handed her dressing material. As she placed a pad over his wound and wrapped strips to secure it, she was aware of him watching her and longed for words to assure him she had nothing but his well-being in mind.

"I truly regret that you must suffer for my ineptness."

"You're doing fine." The hoarse words grated on her heart.

She'd meant shooting him, but he'd taken it to mean her ministrations. "I'm doing my best."

"I'll get you a clean shirt," Linette said. "Yours could do with a good scrubbing." She slipped from the room.

Jayne turned to meet Seth's gaze. "I very much regret that I am responsible for your pain."

He studied her for a moment. "Who did you see shot to death?"

His question jolted through her, bringing all the memories of that day forward in a flash. "My fiancé, Oliver." She twisted the towel she held, knotting her fingers into the material.

"I'm sorry for your loss." He lifted his hand and caught her fingers. His hand was large, work-hardened and steadying.

She tore her gaze from their linked hands and stared into his eyes. Her imagination read a dozen things into his gaze — comfort, concern, perhaps even the offer of protection.

She jerked her eyes away and stepped back from the bed to hang the towel over the back of the chair. The last thing she wanted was to be taken care of by anyone. "I'll be fine on my own." Her words were firm, almost as if daring him to think otherwise.

"No doubt you shall." He sounded dismissive. And why not? He had no reason to concern himself with her and she didn't want it.

Linette returned with a clean shirt and helped Seth slip out of his dirty one. "It's a spare. Eddie has gone to tend your horse and get your things," Linette said. "In the meantime rest and allow the bleeding to stop. We'll be back in a bit to see if it has."

Jayne followed Linette down the stairs and into the kitchen. She glanced about and let out a relieved sigh when she saw Sybil and not Eddie. She did not want to face her brother and once more insist she meant to do certain things that he might not consider appropriate for a proper, genteel young lady fresh from England. His concern about her behavior was at such odds with the free rein he gave Linette. He didn't protest her doing all sorts of things Father would have objected to. Perhaps that was the difference. He didn't have to answer to Father for Linette's actions.

She dumped out the red-tinted water. No doubt Father would be shocked that she'd dirtied her hands in such a fashion. But with or without the approval of the men in her family, she meant to be more than a pretty fixture in some fancy house. She'd prove she was capable, though she wondered if anyone would ever believe it. Eddie didn't think she needed to learn to protect herself because someone else would do it. Not many years past, her father didn't think there was any reason for her to continue her studies because once she was married, Oliver would expect her to run his home and provide him with children. Other than that, she'd sit around the house doing needlework and looking content, eager for nothing more than for her husband to return and favor her with a smile.

As for Oliver, well, she'd proven she was of no use to him.

But she'd sailed across the Atlantic Ocean, crossed the hills and rivers and mosquito-ridden land of most of North America for the chance to start over. And to be a person who could take care of herself.

"Is he going to live?" Sybil asked.

Before she could reply, Linette spoke up. "He'll be fine so long as he doesn't get an infection in his wound." She turned to Jayne, squeezing her arm. "This might be the perfect thing for you." Her smile was gentle. "You couldn't help Oliver but you can help this man. You'll need to check his dressing in a couple of hours. If the wound stops bleeding he'll doubtlessly be wanting to leave. But until it does, he needs to keep still."

Jayne nodded. Linette was right. This was her chance to atone not only for what she'd done to Seth but what she'd failed to do for Oliver.

She'd grabbed his soiled trousers and shirt as they left the room. "I'll wash these and mend them." At least she had a certain amount of skill with needle and thread.

"There's a tub and washboard hanging on the side of the house," Linette said. "Scrub out the blood in cold water. I'll heat water so you can give them a good wash."

She went out to the back step, filled the tub with water and plunged the trousers and shirt into it. Though she'd never used a scrub board, she'd seen maids using one.

41

Mimicking their actions, she rubbed the soiled shirt and pants up and down the ridges.

Mercy came around the corner of the house as she worked. "Do you remember the young cowboy named Cal?"

"I met him the first day when Eddie took us around and introduced us." Good. With repeated rubbing across the scrub board, the blood came out, staining the water a muddy brown.

"He says he'll teach me how to ride."

"You already know how to ride."

Mercy made a dismissive noise. "Side saddle. I'm going to learn to ride astride."

Jayne straightened to give Mercy her full attention. "Mercy Newell, have you taken leave of your senses? Your parents will be shocked."

Mercy's merry laugh said enough but she spoke her mind, as well. "Who is going to tell them? Besides, I intend to enjoy every opportunity for adventure this trip offers."

Jayne sighed. It was useless to try and dissuade Mercy. Besides, who was she to say what was safe and proper for anyone? If she were to listen to the voices around her, she would continue to be who she'd always been and she had already decided against that. She returned to scrubbing the clothing.

Mercy studied her for a long, quiet moment. "Why are you washing his clothes? Can't he take them with him and tend to them himself? I understand he'll only be here a few hours." She tipped her head from one side to the other as she studied Jayne. "Does this have something to do with Oliver?"

Jayne didn't bother trying to hide her shudder. "I shot some poor passing cowboy." As she talked, something became clear. "But no, this isn't about Oliver. It's about me."

Mercy wrapped an arm about Jayne's shoulders and drew her close. "You can do it."

Linette brought out hot water and helped Jayne fill the tub. "Here's the soap." At least her sister-in-law understood Jayne's need to exert more control in her life. From what she'd heard, Linette had much the same desire when she came west. She said her first hurdle had been convincing Eddie she could be a pioneer wife. Her second had been making him understand he needed such.

A few minutes later Jayne had the shirt and pants pegged to the clothesline. They would dry quickly in the warm sunshine with a breeze to aid the process.

Seth jerked awake as Jayne entered the room. He hadn't meant to fall asleep. Only to rest for a few minutes. He'd glanced at his dressing earlier. It had grown pink, which meant he was still bleeding. How much blood had he lost? Enough to make him feel weak. Not a state he liked.

Jayne moved to the side of the bed and folded back the sheet covering his leg. Her eyes softened with concern. "I'll have to change the dressing. It's blood soaked."

He nodded. "Fix it up as best you can. I can't afford to lie about."

"What's your big rush? I thought cowboys came and went and did pretty much as they pleased." She folded back the dressing as she talked. Her cool fingers on his skin made it possible to ignore the pain as she uncovered his wound.

He sat up on his elbows to study it. "Is there an exit hole?"

"Yes. Linette checked for it earlier."

He fell back on the pillow. "Well, that's good news. And the bullet missed the bone."

"This would never have happened if Eddie would have given me shooting lessons."

"Why doesn't he? Seems it would be the

wisest thing to do."

A quick smile curved her lips. "He doesn't see it that way. Seems he still sees me as his little sister whom he was taught to protect." She shook her head. "I keep telling him I don't want to be protected anymore." Despite the determined tones of her words, her voice remained calm, the English accent soft and soothing. Like the song of a dove.

"How long have you been here?" Then lest she think he meant this room he added, "At the ranch."

"My friends and I arrived a few days ago. Mercy, Sybil and myself."

Three unmarried young women in the Northwest Territories. They would draw men from every direction within a hundred-mile radius, if not more. Especially Miss Jayne. The light from the window next to the bed settled in her hair like a net. Brown was such a flat word for the richest color of hair he'd ever seen.

"We left England for various reasons," she was saying. "Sybil's parents are both dead and she longed to get away from her memories. Mercy lives for excitement. The whole trip has been one big adventure for her." She eased his leg up so she could wrap strips of cloth about it. "That ought to take care of it for now." She stepped back.

45

Pain pulsed in the wound. He wanted to ask her to press her fingers to the spot. Her touch would ease the hurt. He turned to her, then thought better of his foolishness. "And you came to forget about Oliver."

Her expression hardened. "I will never forget. Nor do I want to." She fluttered a hand. "Not that I wouldn't gladly erase the images from my mind. But I don't want to forget the helpless feeling I had as I stood back not knowing what to do." She curled her hands in a gesture that suggested resolve.

Resolve was good but not when it was combined with stubbornness and refusal to listen to wise counsel. And he had already learned enough about Jayne to know in her case, it was. Despite her brother's warnings she'd gone ahead and shot a gun. Shouldn't the accidental shooting have persuaded her to abandon her idea of learning to shoot without a proper teacher?

She was a dangerous woman to know or be around. The kind that left others to bear the consequences of her choices. In this instance, he was the unfortunate one to pay for her recklessness. His jaw tightened as he thought of the burden her stubbornness placed on others.

He stared up at the ceiling. "What time is it?"

"Almost supper time."

He sighed heavily. "I really need to get on the trail."

"Where are you going in such a hurry?"

"I got a pa who needs me. He's all I have."

Her smile softened her expression and made her eyes dance. "He's expecting you?"

He tried to think how to answer her question. Yes, Pa was expecting him, though not likely with the generous welcome she appeared to imagine.

Taking his silence for denial of her question, her eyebrows rose. "You're planning a surprise? How nice. How long since you've seen each other?"

"Not exactly a surprise, though he isn't likely expecting me. I joined a cattle drive four months ago and haven't seen him since."

Sympathy darkened her eyes. "Well, then of course you're anxious to see him, but will a day or two make any difference? Especially if your leg needs the rest?"

"It's not just my pa." Shoot, he might as well tell the whole story. "My pa had a stroke five months ago. It left him crippled on one side and barely able to speak." As he talked the memory of the situation tightened his throat. "I will never forget finding him alone and helpless."

She patted his shoulder. "I think he wasn't the only one who felt helpless. I think you did, too."

He nodded. Held her gaze. Maybe she understood because of her own helpless feeling of watching her fiancé die. "The doctor said there were new treatments. Some patients had been having good success with manipulation of the paralyzed limbs. I would do anything to help my pa so I arranged to hire one of these people who do that. A man by the name of Crawford would care for my pa for a price, and put him through the exercises. In order to pay for his services, I joined a cattle drive. I paid him what I could up front and promised to deliver the rest at the end of the drive."

"Surely a day or two won't change that."

"I don't know. Our agreement was for three months but our drive ran into trouble crossing the Oldman River. Crawford drove a hard bargain. I sent a letter a few days ago saying I'd be there in a week. I don't expect he'll give me much leeway in my arrival time." He sat up on his elbows and checked for his boots. They were there but his pants and shirt were missing. Never mind them. Eddie would find his clothes in the saddlebags. "I need to get there. I don't want to put my pa's health at risk. But more than that, I want to see for myself how Pa is."

"You said he was all you have left. Your ma is dead?"

He nodded. "She passed away a few years ago." She'd been ill a few days before he'd gone away on a job but she assured him she was fine. "Go on and do what you need to do," she'd said. "I'll be here when you get back." She'd been there sure enough. In a pine box. He shouldn't have left her knowing she'd been ill. Pa said he didn't realize she was so sick. Seth knew even if he had, Pa wouldn't have sought medical help. He didn't think doctors had anything to offer. If Seth had been there he would have taken her to a doctor. She might still be alive.

"I'm sorry about your mother and I respect your anxiety about your father but it seems to me you better let your leg stop bleeding so you can get on your way without fear of dying on the trail." She shuddered. "This is all my fault."

No getting around that fact and yet he wanted to reassure her. But what could he say? "It was an accident." His words offered little comfort to her and certainly didn't provide an excuse in his mind. Accidents were usually the result of foolhardy choices and as such could, with a little common sense, be prevented.

"If I could ride I would deliver your money myself. I'd make sure your pa was cared for in the best possible way. I'd do it myself."

Seth held back a protest. But he wasn't sure she was the kind of person he'd send to care for his pa.

Fire filled her eyes. "See, that's what's wrong with being helpless. I need to learn to ride like a Western woman."

He chuckled. "It's a long ride for anyone not used to the saddle." She'd be off the horse and leading it before she'd gone twenty miles. The idea tickled him clear to his toes.

She smoothed the sheet over him then poured a cup of water and offered it. Her cool fingers brushed his. Such fine, soft fingers. Evidence that she'd led a privileged life. Hardly the sort of woman to shoot a gun, or ride a horse, or do many of the things required of women in the west. Yet she seemed determined. And some things she needed to know, like starting a fire in the stove, or practical things like that, but where was her common sense? Even if she thought she needed to know how to shoot a gun, there was a reasonable way to do it and a bullheaded way. His leg was evidence that she'd chosen the latter, unwilling to bide her time for proper instruction.

He knew the risks of people who didn't listen to common sense. He lived daily with the consequence. He scrubbed at his chin, vaguely aware he needed a shave.

"Linette said if your wound was still bleeding you should continue to rest. You have lost a lot of blood already. I don't know how much a person has to lose." She shuddered. "Seems like a lot."

He wondered if she meant Oliver. Had she watched him bleed to death?

She sucked in air and appeared to dismiss whatever thoughts shivered up and down her spine. "She says she'll provide you a tray so you can eat in bed."

"Eat in bed? No way. Only invalids and weak women take their meals in bed." He was neither.

"That's just your pride speaking. If it means your leg would stop bleeding, shouldn't you be willing to do it so you can resume your journey?" She sounded so reasonable that he felt like a small child having a pout.

"Very well. I'll take supper in bed." He held up his hand to make sure she understood. "But only this once so my leg will stop bleeding."

She patted his shoulder. "One meal in bed won't make you a permanent invalid."

How could he protest when she sounded so reasonable? Pride was a foolish emotion that he had never struggled with before, and now it had reared its ugly head. He didn't like it.

"I'll be back later. Try and rest." She slipped from the room.

He stared at the ceiling. He curled and uncurled his fingers and lay as still as possible, willing the bleeding to stop. Only common sense kept him in this bed. Like Jayne said, he didn't want to die at the side of the trail. That would not help Pa. But being sensible had never before been so hard.

Please make the bleeding stop. Help me get there in time. He didn't know if God had a mind to listen to a prayer from a cowboy with little faith. God sure hadn't listened to any prayer from him in the past, but Ma had often counseled him to "cast all your cares on God." He'd done little of it in the past but he was powerless at the moment to do anything else. Guess he had nothing to lose by casting.

Maybe he should ask for a hedge around Jayne while he was at it. Seems she'd need divine protection, as would everyone around her if she meant to blindly pursue her own plans despite the risks.

Seemed to him people should consider the dangers involved before they blindly followed their own path.

CHAPTER THREE

Jayne paused outside the door to Seth's room to adjust the tray on which she'd placed soup, buttered bread, pudding and tea. It was heavier than she expected and hard to balance as she turned the knob. Never before had she realized how skilled the serving maids were to carry on one hand trays piled high with dishes. How did they do it?

"I brought you tea. Supper," she corrected herself as she then stepped inside the room. She positioned the tray over his legs. She plucked another pillow from the shelf and reached around to tuck it at his back. Their faces were inches apart. His eyes flashed pine green and held her gaze so she couldn't jerk away. Her heartbeat fluttered in her throat like she'd swallowed a tiny butterfly and it was trying to get free. Her cheeks grew warm. Why was she staring into the eyes of a stranger? And why did it cause such an odd reaction?

From somewhere deep inside, her up-bringing exerted itself. She finished adjust-ing the pillows so he could sit up enough to eat and stepped back, her hands folded at her waist.

"Linette is going to check on your wound after you've eaten. She has something that will stop the bleeding. She got it from an Indian woman in the area." She rattled on, not allowing herself a chance to consider her silly behavior.

He tasted the soup. "This is very good. Sure beats the beans and biscuits I've lived on for the last few days."

"I'll tell Linette you like it. I'm learning to cook, too. Linette says it's not difficult. She came out west last fall and had to learn the hard way."

"The hard way?"

"By trial and error." She chuckled as she thought of Linette's stories. At Seth's questioning look, she said, "She didn't know how to bake bread and tried to bury the lump of failed dough in a snowbank but Ed-die found her doing it." Baking bread was another thing to add to her list. "And she didn't know how to cook beans and served them hard. I don't know any of those things, either, but I will learn."

"Far more practical than shooting guns."

"Did your ma know how to shoot?"

He considered her. "Well, now I suppose she did though I don't recall her ever doing so. Why would she when there was Pa and I and —"

She waited for him to finish but he suddenly concentrated on his food. "And?" she prompted.

He shrugged. "And other people. How did you get to the ranch?"

His question, so out of context, caught her by surprise and she answered without thinking. "We crossed the ocean on a ship then took a train, a steamboat and then the stagecoach."

"You and your two companions?"

"An older couple escorted us as far as Fort Benton. Why do you ask?"

"Because you talk like you are helpless yet I think it took a great deal of guts and ability to navigate that trip."

She stared at him. No one — not even she — had acknowledged that it had been a challenge. "I learned a lot."

"And maybe discovered you could do more than you thought you could."

"Maybe." She handed him his tea. His words echoed in her head. Could she do more than she thought she could? She

56

intended to find out on this visit to the ranch. Funny that it had taken a stranger, a victim of her ineptitude, to point out something she'd overlooked.

"Thank you." She ducked her head at the surprised look he shot her way.

"For what?"

"For making me see that I'm not a helpless, pampered woman."

He grinned. "I don't know about pampered. I suspect you are a woman of many privileges but no one has to be helpless unless they choose to be."

"And I choose otherwise. In the past I have been far too compliant."

He put his spoon down and considered her solemnly. She considered him right back. "Miss Gardiner —"

"Please, call me Jayne."

"Jayne, then. There is a vast difference between not being helpless and being foolhardy."

Her breath stalled halfway up her lungs. She forced her words past the catch in her throat. "Are you saying I'm the latter?" Her words were spoken softly but surely he heard the note of warning.

"What do you think?" But he didn't give her a chance to say. "Shooting a gun willynilly without regard for passersby, without knowing proper safety technique sounds just a little foolish to me. Doesn't it to you?"

"It sounds to me," she replied, her tight jaw grinding the words, "like a woman ready and willing to do whatever is required to learn how to take care of herself." She headed for the door. Then she retraced her steps to face him. "I came here intending to do my best to make your evening pleasant. I meant to bring my friends to visit you."

He quirked an eyebrow. "Too big a job for you to do alone?"

"I think I can handle one lame cowboy."

"Just like you can handle a gun."

She pressed her hand to her lips. The man had a way of saying all the wrong things and igniting an irritation that burned away reason. "You know I even thought of reading a book to you so you could rest." She let out a blast of overheated breath. "But now I believe I will leave you to your own devices. After all, you wouldn't want the company of a foolish, useless —" Heaven help her, she couldn't stop her voice from quivering and stopped to get control of her emotions. "Silly woman." She hurried toward the door.

He was just like her father and her brother and, come to think of it, Oliver. None of them saw her as having any useful purpose other than to grace their table, encourage them whether or not she agreed with them and do nothing to upset the status quo.

Well, they could all look for that kind of woman somewhere else. She would no longer be such a person.

She didn't need any of them to help her achieve her goals.

Seth's voice reached her before she made it down three steps. "Miss Gardiner, Jayne, please come back. I didn't mean to upset you."

Ignoring his call, she returned to the kitchen where the others had cleaned up the dishes from the meal.

"How is he?" Linette asked.

"Anxious to be on his way."

"Is his wound still bleeding?"

"I didn't check. I said you would do it."

"Of course." Linette went to the pantry and returned with a small leather pouch. "I'll take this along in case I need it." She headed for the stairs. "Aren't you coming?"

Jayne shook her head. "I don't think he needs two females fussing about him." Especially one he considered foolish. His words continued to sting.

Mercy draped an arm about her shoulders. "What happened?"

Jayne gave a tight smile. "What makes you

think anything did?"

"Because I know that look. Right, Sybil?"

Sybil moved to Jayne's other side. "Was he rude to you? Inappropriate? I knew you shouldn't have gone up there alone."

"He wasn't rude or inappropriate."

"Then what?" Mercy demanded.

"He said I was foolish to want to learn to shoot. Said there were lots of people around to take care of me." He hadn't exactly said that but it was implied. "He seems to think I'm a threat to everyone's safety because of my desire to know how to handle a firearm."

Mercy choked back a chuckle. "I suppose he might have cause to think so."

"I'll be more careful in the future."

Sybil sighed. "I do wish you'd give up this idea but you are far too stubborn to do so."

"I'm not stubborn. I'm — I'm resolved." She liked that word much better. "I am resolved to never again feel helpless in the face of danger. To never again feel useless when something needs doing. Why, I might even learn to ride astride like Mercy plans. Just think of the things I could do." She could offer to ride to Seth's pa with the money. Of course she would never do such a thing. Despite Seth's very harsh opinion of her she understood some things simply weren't safe for a woman, like riding alone

60

across the prairie.

Linette descended the stairs, carrying the tray. "I think that will stop the bleeding so the poor man can get on his way. Jayne, he asked that you keep him company for a few hours. I would do it myself but Grady needs to get ready for bed." Grady was the five-year-old-boy Linette had become guardian of after his mother died on the ship to Canada. Originally she meant to leave him with his father in Montreal but the man said he couldn't take care of a small boy. Jayne's heart went out to Grady. Imagine having your father turn away from you. Why, it had to be every bit as bad as watching a fiancé die from a gunshot wound. At least Grady had Linette and Eddie who loved him and had adopted him.

Jayne's resentment at Seth's comments vanished as she thought of how harsh life could be. Besides, she was responsible for his injury.

"Why don't you two come with me?" she asked her two friends. "I'm sure he'd enjoy your scintillating company." She didn't want to be alone with him, provide him with another opportunity to share his opinion of her.

"Sounds like fun." Mercy steered them down the hall without giving Sybil a chance to voice her opinion.

Seth stared at the blank white ceiling. Not even a crack so he could make childish pictures in his mind. There were days in his past when he'd thought how pleasant it would be to have nothing to do but lay about. He'd changed his mind in the last few hours. Every ten minutes he decided he'd had enough rest and his leg was well enough for him to move on. After all, it wasn't like he didn't have things to do. Important things. But he wasn't foolish enough to risk his life or limb. Mrs. Gardiner had packed the wound with some kind of powder and said she hoped that would stop the bleeding.

She'd given him a smile. "You could do your part, too, by staying still."

He meant to do his best to comply.

He grinned at the ceiling. Jayne had taken exception to his suggestion she might be foolish in pursuing her desire to shoot a gun. He'd been careful to add without someone to teach her.

Jayne's voice came from the stairs and he turned to the door. Another voice answered her. And then a third. He couldn't hear what was said.

Perhaps she wasn't coming to see him.

He lifted his head, watching the door. As the footsteps neared, paused, he held his breath.

The door opened. Jayne stepped in, her two friends behind her.

"We've come to keep you company," Mercy said.

Jayne had said Mercy wanted adventure. The way her eyes danced as if she had a secret she couldn't wait to divulge, he guessed she managed to find her share of excitement wherever she went.

"It's partly my fault Jayne shot you," Mercy said. "You see, I was attempting to teach her to shoot the pistol but she closed her eyes. Completely missed the target."

Sybil shivered. "I tried to warn them it wasn't a good idea."

Seth shifted his gaze to her. Jayne had said Sybil wanted to get away from sad memories. There was a darkness in her eyes that spoke of hard times. He recognized it from seeing it in the mirror if he looked hard enough.

Then he brought his gaze to Jayne who hadn't said anything yet. He wanted to tell her he didn't mean to hurt her. But he didn't know how without retracting his words, and he meant them. Foolish choices caused unbearable consequences. He didn't want her to learn that the hard way.

She shifted her attention to something past his shoulder.

Mercy eased closer. "Tell us about yourself."

"Not much to tell. I'm just a cowboy who's finished a cattle drive. But I expect you all have your stories." Maybe he could get them talking about themselves.

"Tons of them." Mercy appeared to be the spokeswoman. Sybil looked ill at ease and Jayne looked stubborn. Must be a mule somewhere in her heritage.

Compliant, she said? Not a hope.

"I'm going to learn to ride," Mercy said.

"Like a man," Sybil murmured, her voice conveying shock.

"Men are allowed to do all sorts of things that women aren't. It's not fair." Mercy gave another little pout. Then she brightened and gave Seth her attention. "We were talking about you, though."

He shrugged. "I'm sure you're far more interesting than I am." He'd told Jayne about his pa and even his ma. But he didn't intend to reveal any more. There were some things best left buried in the past. "Tell me about your families. I know Eddie is Jayne's brother but nothing more."

"I'm an only child," Sybil said with a

heavy tone.

"It sounds like you regret it."

She nodded. "I suppose I do. With my parents dead I am all alone except for an elderly cousin."

Jayne and Mercy pressed close to her on either side. "You have us."

Sybil smiled and gave a little chuckle. "So I do. One of you set on turning the world upside down." She nudged Mercy. "And the other bound and determined to shoot her way to forgetfulness." She patted Jayne's arm as if to say she meant no harm.

Mercy laughed. "She's got a way with words, doesn't she?"

Jayne shifted her gaze about the room until it came hesitantly, and likely reluctantly, to Seth. The way she squinted dared him to point out he had said something similar to Sybil's words. "It's not like that at all. I only want to be strong and prepared."

Sybil patted her arm again. "Of course. We understand."

Mercy continued to grin at her friend.

Seth jerked his chin slightly hoping she'd understand he had no desire to continue their disagreement.

The look she gave him had the power to start a fire. He tore his gaze from her scowl. "What about your family, Mercy?"

65

She sobered and got a faraway look in her eyes. "I'm the only living child. I had a brother who died when he was eight."

"How old were you?"

"Six."

A lot younger than he had been. Was it any easier at a young age? He couldn't imagine it was.

"He got sick," she added, then shook herself and turned to Jayne. "Jayne here is the one with an abundance of family. Tell him."

"He already knows about Eddie. I also have two younger sisters."

He nodded encouragement and she continued.

"Bess is almost eighteen and Anne is fifteen."

"Do you miss them?"

A smile curved her lips. "More than I thought I would. The things with brothers and sisters is you get used to having them around and don't think about it much then you find yourself turning to speak to them and with a start, you realize they aren't there."

She'd so concisely identified how the loss of a sibling felt. He fixed his attention on the ceiling as a distant pain surfaced. Not as strong as it had once been but still pulsing with life. He'd reconciled that it would never die.

Mercy, the bold spokeswoman, broke the silence. "So where are you headed?"

"Corncrib, Montana."

"Got someone there waiting for you?" She waggled her eyebrows teasingly. "A wife, a girlfriend?"

"Just my pa."

"Oh." She sounded disappointed.

"What? You think I look like a man who has a wife?"

Jayne didn't give Mercy a chance to answer. "His pa is sick."

Sybil edged closer. "I'm sorry. I suppose you're anxious to get there and see him."

He heard her unspoken conclusion that his pa was on the verge of death and set out to correct it. "Pa had a stroke. He's in the care of a very capable man. But it's been four months since I've seen him. I'm anxious to see how he's doing. I'm hoping he's greatly improved."

Jayne patted his shoulder and for the first time since she'd fled his room upset by his comments, the tension in his neck eased. "I'm sure everything will work out. Doesn't God promise us that 'all things work together for good to them that love God'?'"

Her gaze delved deep into his, searching,

challenging.

"I know God's in control of the universe and nature." He spoke slowly, bringing his thoughts into words. "But I think He expects us to take care of the details ourselves." He watched Jayne's expression change as she considered his answer. It went from surprise to denial to confusion.

"I think we have to trust Him even when we don't understand or we don't possess enough faith," she said.

Mercy spoke. "I kind of think Seth is right. I mean, why would God bother with little stuff?"

"Oh, no. It's not like that," Sybil protested. "He cares about everyone. We have to believe that."

"I do believe." Jayne shook her head. "But sometimes it's a struggle to feel it, especially when awful things happen."

"That's when we need to trust even harder."

Silence filled the room for a moment after Sybil's comment. Seth lacked the energy to argue against it.

"We should leave you in peace," Jayne said and the three of them walked toward the door.

The loneliness of the room lay on his chest like a weight, and fleeting memories clawed at his throat. He didn't fancy being alone any more than he had to be. "Wait a minute."

Jayne hung back.

"Do I recall you offering to read to me?" he asked her.

"That was before."

"Before what?" He knew what she meant but pretended otherwise.

She shrugged. "Before now."

The other two hovered at the doorway. Mercy nudged Sybil. "Are they talking about the fact he called her foolish?"

Sybil studied Jayne and then Seth. "I suspect so." Her gaze bored into Seth's. "Be warned, if you hurt one of us you deal with all of us."

He held her look steadily for a moment, pretending to be contemplating her warning. But he couldn't maintain a serious expression as he imagined being pummeled by their girlish punches. He grinned widely. "I'll keep it in mind."

"Good." Sybil took the girls each by an arm. "We'll help Jayne pick out some books," she said as they disappeared out the door.

He settled back, wondering if Jayne would return. He didn't regret being honest with her but hoped she would get over feeling offended.

She returned in a few minutes with four books. "Which would you like me to read?" She gave the titles.

"The Arabian Nights."

"You're familiar with the stories?"

"My father used to read it aloud." He hadn't thought of that for years. At one time, Pa would read aloud every night during the winter. Stories of adventure in a different time and place. When had it stopped?

The answer came readily. After Frank's death.

All day he'd been fighting the memory but could no longer push it aside. He was fourteen, Frank sixteen. Seth's long-time friend, Sarah, had caught Frank's attention and the two of them had been acting silly all afternoon. But when Frank teased Sarah to slide on the thin ice of the river, Seth had begged them to be sensible.

"Life is too short to waste on rules and cautions, little brother," Frank had called as he ran onto the ice and skidded a good distance. "This is fun."

"Sarah, don't go. The ice is too thin," Seth had said, wanting to yank Frank back to safety.

"It's holding Frank okay." Ignoring his warning, she'd raced after Frank.

Seth had hovered on the bank, longing to join them but knowing the dangers.

He'd heard the crackling of the fragile ice and called out a warning but Frank and Sarah only laughed and continued their merriment. Then suddenly Frank had broken through the ice. Sarah, chasing after him, had fallen in, too.

A shudder raced through him as the horror of that day returned to his memories. Oh, how he'd tried to erase it from his mind. He'd succeeded in burying it so deep he thought it would never surface. But today proved how futile his hope for forgetfulness was.

Frank and Sarah had screamed Seth's name. Their panicked voices echoed through his head and he closed his eyes, which did nothing to stop the pictures playing in his head.

He'd grabbed a branch that lay at his feet and raced to where they'd broken through. His feet had moved like lead. His legs had refused to make the speed he wanted. Every yard had seemed an eternity. Sarah had clung to the edge of the ice. He couldn't see Frank and then he'd bobbed up.

"I'll get you. Hang on." He'd flung himself on his belly and wriggled forward, holding out the branch before him. As soon as Sarah could reach it, he'd called out to her to grab it. "Lay as flat as you can. I'll pull you out." The ice dipped toward the hole and water crawled toward him. Would they all drown in the murky water? He'd toed himself more firmly in place.

Inch by inch he'd pulled her to shore and threw his coat over her before he went back for Frank.

But Frank had disappeared. Seth called his name over and over. He'd jabbed at the hole. In desperation he'd yanked off his boots and dove into the cold water. The shock had numbed him clear through. He'd opened his eyes underwater, tried to find his brother but saw nothing. The current tugged at him. He'd surfaced before it sucked him away. So cold he could barely function he'd somehow managed to pull himself out of the hole. He didn't recall getting himself and Sarah to the house. Only the emptiness of returning without Frank. And the shocked look on his parents' faces.

Frank's body was found three days later, caught on a log downstream. The same day that Sarah had died of pneumonia.

The emptiness had stayed, a permanent, unwelcome guest that consumed their home. Consumed Ma and Pa, too, and took residence in Seth's heart.

Never would he forget how he'd failed. He had done all he could but had been unsuccessful in taking care of those he loved.

He realized Jayne was speaking and jerked his thoughts back to the present.

"Eddie read them to me, too, when I was much younger." She adjusted his pillows, straightened his covers. "Are you comfortable?"

He almost caught her arm as it passed over his chest. If he had something to hang on to he might be able to escape the awfulness of his memories. Instead, he pushed them back, deep inside, and slammed a door to keep them at bay. But like wisps of black fog, the remnants of horror lingered. Sooner or later, he knew, they would dissipate. He steadied his voice. "Reasonably so."

"Very well." She drew the chair close and began to read the story of "Ali Baba and the Forty Thieves."

Her voice soothed him, filling him with happy memories of life before Frank had died. He drifted pleasantly on her words. When she finished he couldn't lift his eyelids, even when he heard her whisper, "Good night," before she slipped away.

What a crazy couple of days it had been.

Shot. Rescued. Cared for by the hands that shot him. No one would ever believe that. It was as if God had played a role in orchestrating it.

God! He couldn't imagine that God cared one way or the other what happened to Seth or most of the people he met. The Almighty sure hadn't cared about saving Frank or Sarah from drowning. Or how his death had affected their ma and pa. And even Seth.

But Jayne had suffered a painful loss, too. And she continued to trust God. A smile tugged at his lips. She also fought back, mostly by taking control of life in every possible way — even to shooting a gun, despite the fact no one seemed to care to give her instructions. Except Mercy, and he wondered how valuable her lessons would be. He rubbed at his leg. It didn't seem she was a very good teacher.

For the safety of everyone within shooting distance, someone should give Jayne lessons.

CHAPTER FOUR

Seth wakened as someone stepped into the room. He sat up and stifled a moan at the pain that reminded him why he was in a strange bed in a strange room with a strange man standing at his side. Then his mind cleared and he recognized Eddie.

"Good morning," Eddie said.

"Morning." The word croaked from his dry throat and he reached for the cup of water Jayne had left on the table beside him.

"I brought you your things. I was here last night but you were already asleep. Linette wants to check your leg one last time."

"Thanks."

Linette joined her husband and changed the dressing. "It's not bleeding but I believe a couple more days rest would be in your best interest."

"Thanks. But I have to get going."

"We'll leave you to get dressed, then." Eddie handed him his saddlebags. "I believe your other things are waiting for you down-stairs."

"Please join us for breakfast," Linette added. "Turn right at the bottom of the stairs and the kitchen is at the end of the hall."

"Thanks." He waited until they left the room before he threw back the covers and sat on the edge of the bed. A stark-white dressing covered his wound and would keep it clean until he reached Corncrib. He pulled on his dark gray trousers, and his black-and-white-striped shirt. Putting weight on his leg caused his wound to protest but it wasn't anything he couldn't ignore. He tugged on his boots, pulled a comb from his supplies and ran it through his hair then stood tall. There. He felt like a man again. He slung his saddlebags over his shoulder and left the room.

The stairs were wide and led down to a big door that stood open, allowing a cool breeze to blow through the screen. This was the door he had stumbled through with Eddie's help yesterday. So much had happened since then that it seemed more like a week ago.

He paused at the bottom of the stairs to stare at the view. The house overlooked the neat ranch buildings he'd noticed yesterday.

Several cowboys crossed toward the nearest two-story house. He gave it all a quick study then lifted his gaze. The view of the mountains caught at his breath. They were gleaming with the morning sun. So big and majestic. So powerful. The words of one of Ma's oft-repeated verses entered his mind. "God is our refuge and strength, a very present help in trouble. Therefore will not we fear, though the earth be removed, and though the mountains be carried into the midst of the sea." Ma had been devastated by Frank's death but in spite of it, Seth suddenly realized, she'd remained serene. He hadn't been able to understand. Was it because of her faith?

A faith he shared but to a lesser degree. He wasn't sure God would lend a hand if Seth needed it. He'd called God's name several times when trying to rescue Frank. Where was God then? Or was he blaming God for an individual's own choice? Was not the individual responsible for the outcome? These were oft-repeated questions to which he could never find a satisfactory answer.

He turned to his right and strode down the hall. As he passed a room, he glanced inside at the bookshelves filled with books, a large mahogany desk and an oversize black armchair, plus some very nice paintings. One seemed to be a perfect replica of the mountain scene he'd admired seconds ago.

To his left, he glimpsed a formal-looking dining room that had an empty, unused look. Then he reached the kitchen.

"Good morning," Jayne said, smiling cheerfully as he entered. She was probably eager to see him gone. After all, he was a constant reminder that her shooting had been a failure.

She should be happy he was only slightly injured because of her foolish activity. She might have left a body on the trail. His body. Then who would take care of Pa? Maybe God had been protecting all of them — Jayne, Seth and Pa. He'd study the thought more closely when he had the time.

The room was large, dominated by a big table. To one side were cupboards and a stove, and on the east side, the rising sun shone through the generous windows.

The others greeted him. Linette held a small boy before her. "This is Grady. Grady, say hello to Mr. Collins." The boy held a half-grown gray kitten.

Seth squatted down to the boy's level, ignoring the pain in his leg. "Pleased to meet you, Grady. And what's this fine fellow's name?" He scratched behind the cat's ears earning him a loud purr.

"This is Smokey. He's a good cat. He never fights with the other cats. Not like Snowball. Snowball is always fighting. He's got a torn ear 'cause he fights too much."

"Why, it sounds like Smokey is a very smart cat." The animal pushed against Seth's hand, begging for more attention.

"He is. He can climb a tree faster than anybody and he eats slow, like a gentleman."

"A fine cat, indeed. I expect he's good company for you." He straightened to ease the pain in his leg.

"Yup. But my best friend is Billy. He lives down the hill with Daisy and Pansy and Neil and his new ma and pa, Cassie and Roper. Mr. and Mrs. Jones," he corrected as Linette opened her mouth. No doubt she meant to tell him he shouldn't call adults by their first names.

Seth's eyebrows peaked. "Wow. That sounds like a real good story."

Linette gave her son a gentle shove toward the door. "Put Smokey outside and wash up for breakfast. Seth, have a chair." She indicated one next to Jayne.

He sat. Feeling Mercy and Sybil's gazes on him, he lifted his head to give them each an inquisitive look. "Did you want something?" he asked.

Sybil shook her head.

Mercy leaned forward. "We were wondering how you would explain your —" she tipped her head toward his leg beneath the table "— gunshot wound. Jayne doesn't think you'll admit to your friends that a woman shot you."

He turned toward Jayne.

Her brown eyes flashed a teasing challenge. "They might wonder why you let a woman outshoot you," she said.

He practically choked. "Outshoot? I don't think I'd explain it like that. What I'll say if anyone asks is that I got hit by a stray bullet."

Eddie cleared his throat. "There'll be no more stray bullets. Jayne, I forbid you to continue this foolish endeavor."

She bristled like a cat stroked the wrong way. She ducked her head and stared at her plate but her lips pressed together in protest.

Eddie was right about it being foolish but hearing it from the other man's lips made Seth want to protest. Why didn't he teach his sister what she needed to know? It would surely make it safer for everyone on the ranch. He guessed from Jayne's expression that she had no intention of abandoning her plan, despite her brother's direct order.

"Would you ask the blessing, dear?"

80

Linette said, ending the tension between brother and sister.

Eddie prayed and then food was passed around. Fried pork and eggs, fried potatoes, fresh biscuits and syrup and plenty of milk.

Seth helped himself. "I heard you were a good cook, Mrs. Gardiner. This certainly proves it."

"Thank you. The girls are learning to cook, too. If you were around longer, you would get a chance to evaluate their progress."

He pretended a great deal of shock. "I hope their cooking lessons aren't as deadly as their shooting lessons."

Beside him Jayne choked. He had the pleasure of patting her on the back. At first, he got a bit of satisfaction out of her discomfort but after the second pat, he had an urge to pull her into his arms, rub her back and assure her she would be safe because he would personally see to it. Instead, he dropped his hands to his lap. He didn't need one more person in his life to be responsible for.

After she stopped coughing and wiped her eyes, she turned and gave him a look fit to cure leather. "I could have choked to death."

He felt suddenly remorseful. "I'm sorry. It was a careless remark."

She nodded. "Then consider us even. I didn't mean to hurt you even as you didn't mean to hurt me."

He wondered if she referred to the choking incident or the words he'd spoken the previous day. But it didn't matter which. He was leaving today and would prefer to go with no ill feelings left behind. He nodded. "Agreed."

Conversation around the table turned to more general things — plans for the day, who was going where, what needed to be done.

His nerves tensed when Eddie asked Jayne what her plans were.

"I wanted to explore a bit more."

Seth relaxed. It sounded like a safe activity. He'd be in no mortal danger as he rode away. And may God have mercy on any strangers riding nearby if Jayne meant to continue with her plans.

Again he wondered why Eddie didn't simply give her a few lessons. Surely that would soon satisfy her.

When the meal ended, Eddie pushed from the table. Seth pushed back, too.

"Thank you for your hospitality. I'll be on my way now."

Linette favored him with a sweet smile. "We understand but you're always welcome at Eden Valley Ranch."

That's when he recognized the name Gardiner. Eddie Gardiner and his wife were well spoken of in the western ranches. "I've heard of this place."

"You have?" Linette asked. "I hope it's been good things."

Eddie wrapped his arm about his wife's shoulders. "What else would he hear?"

"It's been good," Seth assured them. "You're known to offer hospitality to all, regardless of race or social status. People say Mrs. Gardiner nurses the sick, helps the poor and Eddie here is considered a man of honor and integrity."

"That's lovely," Sybil said.

"We're honored," Eddie added.

Seth leaned back on his heels and grinned. "I heard a tale about feeding a starving Indian family and outrunning wolves. Is it true?"

Linette and Eddie grinned at each other.

Jayne answered his question. "It's true. My brother refused to hang an Indian who tried to steal a cow to feed his starving family. Instead, he took him meat. On the way back, wolves attacked them and Linette helped beat them off." She jammed her fists on her hips. "I intend to become just as brave and proficient."

Linette reached out and squeezed Jayne's hand. "And you shall."

Eddie opened his mouth but Linette jabbed her elbow into his ribs and he closed it without speaking. Had he been about to reissue his orders to Jayne?

Instead, he said to Seth, "I'll take you to the barn. Your horse is there."

"I'll go with you," Jayne said and no one argued otherwise. Certainly not Seth who looked forward to a private goodbye. "Wait a moment." Jayne turned aside and brought him his shirt and pants, neatly folded as if they'd come from the best Chinese laundry.

"You washed them?"

Mercy didn't wait for Jayne to answer. "She washed them, mended them and ironed them. Your clothes could not be in better hands." Her dark eyes challenged him as if informing him that Jayne had many admirable qualities.

He wasn't about to argue. No doubt she did, but shooting wasn't one of them any more than was being bullheaded about it.

"Thank you. I didn't expect this."

She tipped her head to one side and lifted one shoulder. "I doubt you expected to be shot by a woman, either."

He choked on a startled laugh.

Mercy and Sybil chuckled.

"Jayne, there's to be no more shooting." Eddie sounded like he was used to giving orders and having them obeyed.

As the three of them traipsed down the hill, he heard Jayne whisper beside him, "You can't order me around." No doubt she hadn't meant for anyone to hear her. Seth worried that things might get a little tense between her and her brother if they kept up the way they were.

Grady shouted from the doorway. "Papa, I'm coming, too."

Eddie turned to wait for him. "You two go ahead."

Jayne and Seth continued onward. He shoved the barn door open, and a cowboy nodded a greeting as he saddled a horse.

Seth found his horse in a nearby stall and grabbed his saddle and bridle that hung in the tack room. He noticed they'd been cleaned until they shone. He hadn't expected that kind of service.

The animal, too, had been groomed until his coat shone. Someone certainly knew how to look after things.

As he lifted the saddle into place, his leg spasmed painfully. It was only a gunshot wound, he reminded himself. Not much more than a flesh wound. Nothing to slow him down.

He led the horse through the door, Jayne at his side.

"I hope you arrive in good time, that the man is still tending your pa and that he is much improved."

He smiled down at her. "Thanks. I can't say it's been fun but it's been unusual meeting you."

She chuckled. "I dare say it's the most unusual meeting either of us has had."

He nodded, suddenly reluctant to leave. Like that made any sense. But something about Jayne pulled at his thoughts. Of course she did. The woman needed someone to keep an eye on her and make sure she didn't get herself into more trouble.

He chomped down on his molars. It would have to be someone other than himself because he'd had more than his share of trying to take care of people who didn't bother to take care of themselves.

"You stay out of trouble, hear?" He swung up into the saddle. "Don't go shooting any more cowboys."

A stubborn look crossed her face and then she smiled. "One has proven to be enough trouble. I won't go for two."

He laughed and touched the brim of his hat.

She stepped back and gasped. "Seth, look

at your leg."

He did. His pant leg was blood-soaked.

Eddie had reached them and saw the same thing. "You can't leave like that. It would be foolish."

Seth stared at his leg then shifted his gaze to Jayne's eyes, saw her look go from shock to compassion. "Seth, you have to rest it."

He nodded. He knew he had no choice. "The money . . ."

"Tell Eddie about it."

Knowing the reputation of the Gardiners, he knew he could entrust his money to Eddie. "It's in the heel of my boot. Can you see it goes to Murdo Collins in Corncrib, Montana? I need it to get there as soon as possible."

He swung from the saddle and began to pry his boot off.

Eddie clamped a hand on his shoulder. "Let's go to the house and take care of that. Linette can tend your wound. Looks like you'll be here a few more days." He called to a cowboy barely old enough to call himself a man. "Buster, take care of this man's horse."

"Yes, boss." Buster's chin had likely never met a razor yet. His hair was shaggy as if it had not seen a pair of scissors in a long time. And his too-short trousers were held in place with a braid of rope.

"Kid looks like he's lost," Seth said as they climbed back up the hill.

"He showed up a couple of weeks back asking for a job. Seems he's all alone in the world. But he doesn't take kindly to help. Linette offered to give him a pair of trousers from her supply closet but he refused. Said when he earned them, he'd buy them."

"Guess you can't fault him for that."

"You have to allow a man, however young, to have a certain amount of pride. He's proving to be a good man. He took care of your saddle and groomed your horse."

He was struck by an errant thought. Maybe Jayne also needed to keep her pride intact by being able to use a gun.

Eddie went through to the kitchen with Seth and Jayne behind him. Seth sank to a chair and removed his boot and pried off the heel. He handed the wad of money to Eddie. "Can I write a note to accompany it?"

Jayne disappeared down the hall and ducked into the room with the desk and books. She returned with paper and pencil, handing it to him with a sad smile.

He wrote a note to Pa saying he had been delayed but would be home as soon as possible. To Crawford he wrote, "There is more here than what I owe you. Please keep it in return for staying with Pa until I get home." He folded both pieces of paper and handed them to Eddie.

"I'll see this gets to Edendale right away. We should be able to catch the stage. Petey, the driver, can be trusted to make sure it gets to your pa." He left the house to tend to the task.

Seth tried to relax. The money would make its way to Corncrib as fast as he could take it himself. But what about Pa? Would Crawford stay? Or would his pa be alone, unable to care for himself?

Linette retrieved her little leather pouch of herbs. "I think it's best if you return upstairs." She went down the hall.

Seth rose, preparing to follow.

Jayne reached out and squeezed his arm. "I'm sorry."

He made up his mind. "The money is on its way. That should keep Crawford there for a few more days." No point in worrying about things he couldn't change, especially when this gave him a chance to change one important thing. "My leg will heal fine if I rest it. While I am here you will get shooting lessons from me. That way I can leave with a clear conscience knowing you won't kill someone accidentally and end up in jail." He went down the hall and up the stairs to have Linette pack the wound with the herbs.

"They'll do their work if you give them a chance," Linette said. "I suggest you don't move around much for a day or two."

"I'd sure like to sit in the sun."

She nodded. "That should be okay so long as you don't put any weight on that leg. I'll put a chair by the door." He hopped down the stairs after her and sat beside the big doors. Being idle weighed heavily but at least he could watch people coming and going.

Jayne and her friends passed the barn toward the bridge. They had said they were going exploring.

He hoped the exploring didn't involve a pistol. Surely she would wait for the lessons he'd promised . . . Unless she was too bullheaded to listen to reason.

Jayne pressed her lips together as she joined Mercy and Sybil. Seth was just like Eddie, barking out commands and expecting her to jump. Yes, she wanted to learn to shoot. But she would have liked it better if he'd offered rather than ordered. Like she'd kill anyone! Her eyes narrowed. Was he any different than her father, or Eddie or Oliver?

Did he see her as simply a foolish young woman who needed him to protect her?

She snorted. "I don't need him protecting me." She spoke the words aloud without regard to her friends.

They stopped and waited for her to fall in between them.

"Who?" Mercy demanded.

"Why, Seth, of course," Sybil said. "Jayne, accept it. There is something about you that brings out the chivalry in men."

"I don't want chivalry."

Sybil made a protesting noise. "Who doesn't want a man who is courteous and considerate, honorable and loyal?"

"Put that way, I have to agree but he thinks he can order me around. He acts like he has to take care of me or I'll cause a disaster." She shuddered, remembering how her lack of action had caused a terrible death. "I don't need a man taking care of me, thank you very much."

"What did he say?"

"He said he would give me shooting lessons."

Mercy and Sybil ground to a halt. "Isn't that what you want?"

"Yes. But I'd like to be asked not told." She wondered if her words sounded as petty to her friends as they did to her.

"Either way, seems to me you're getting a gift," Mercy said. "The lessons you want from a man whose eyes darken when he looks at you." She sighed dreamily.

"They do not," Jayne protested. At least Mercy hadn't said Jayne's eyes got all starry when she looked at him. As if they would. Seth was proving to be rather annoying and overbearing. "I don't need that kind of man in my life."

"Oh?" Sybil's voice was sweet. "What kind of man do you need?"

"Right now? None. My heart is locked up tightly. I won't open it again. It's like asking to be hurt."

"You'll change your mind about that one day," Mercy said.

"Nope. Not me. Now let's go follow the river and see where it goes."

Sybil laughed. "It goes to the ocean. Are you planning to go that far?"

She laughed at Sybil's nonsense. "So maybe I'll see where it comes from."

Sybil pointed toward the mountains. "From the snow up there."

"But it's August. Surely the snow is all melted. So where does the water come from that keeps flowing past the ranch?"

Mercy flung her arms wide. "Who cares? It's a lovely day. Let's enjoy it."

Jayne sighed her agreement. The sun glistened off the rugged mountains and dappled the deciduous trees. A gentle zephyr tickled her skin and danced along the grass. Birds rejoiced from every direction. She breathed deep. "It smells so good. Like the air is full of a thousand wild flowers."

They followed the river past the pens and along a grassy slope. A few steps farther and they entered a grove of trees.

"We should have brought a gun," Mercy said. "You could practice your shooting."

"You don't think there are enough injured cowboys already?" Sybil asked.

"We could go for one each."

Jayne knew Mercy was teasing but Sybil gave them both a this-isn't-amusing look.

Mercy pushed past some prickly bushes and led them into an opening. "Look at the little waterfall."

It hardly qualified as such. It was only the river flowing over some big rocks and making a cheery noise.

Sybil perched on a fallen tree. "It's so peaceful."

Mercy and Jayne exchanged looks and silently agreed to let Sybil enjoy a quiet moment. They sat on the grass behind her and waited for Sybil to be ready to move on.

Finally, with a sigh that came from deep inside, she pushed to her feet. "It's very restful to watch the water gurgle past."

They continued onward and spent a pleasant couple of hours wandering along the river.

Jayne glanced at the sky. "We should get back."

As they retraced their steps, the sun shone hotter. They stopped and splashed cool water on their faces before they reached the ranch.

When they stepped into the open and headed for the bridge, Jayne looked toward the house. Seth still sat in the chair beside the door. He must be bored. The joy of the morning faded slightly. She should have offered to keep him company. Perhaps read to him again. How selfish of her.

As quickly as the thought came, she dismissed it. He surely wouldn't want her company. After all, she was but a silly woman who needed him to guide her. Or so he thought.

She sighed. She certainly was acting foolish. She didn't care about his opinion one way or the other and was grateful he'd offered to give her shooting lessons. Never mind how the offer came.

Mercy saw him, too. "Let's ask Seth about

where the river comes from."

As they drew closer, Jayne saw Smokey curled into a ball on Seth's lap. The cat opened one eye as the ladies approached then closed it again and ignored them.

At least Seth had the cat to keep him company.

"To what do I owe this honor?" He glanced about the circle of friends but directed his question to Jayne.

She answered before Mercy could. "We want to know where the water from the river comes from if the snow is all melted."

He blinked then widened his eyes. "That's a strange question."

"Do you have an answer?"

His eyes dipped into a smile. "I could say the water comes from lakes."

Mercy snapped her fingers. "Lakes! I should have thought of that."

"That isn't the whole answer, is it?" Jayne asked, caught by the darkness in his hazel eyes.

"There are glaciers up there and melted water comes off them throughout the summer. I've seen them. Even walked on some of them." He closed his eyes as if thinking of a time when he had done so. "Imagine cold ice on a hot summer day. And it's really cold."

Jayne sighed. "I wish I could see it."

"Before I leave I will take you to the mountains. Maybe not to a glacier but to one of the beautiful lakes. There isn't anything quite like the views." He again closed his eyes and sighed.

"I'd like that," Sybil said.

"Me, too," Mercy added.

Seth opened his eyes and looked directly at Jayne. He lifted one eyebrow. "How do you feel about it?"

She widened her eyes. Did he really care what she thought?

His gaze held hers. His eyes darkened, tinted now like the forest trees. She could almost hear the birds singing.

She blinked, as if to sever the spell they'd cast on her. "I enjoy seeing the country. It's beautiful." Her words came out in a breezy rush. She grabbed the girls and pulled them toward the door. "Let's help Linette."

"Bye," Seth called.

Jayne added her goodbye to that of the others.

"I thought he was anxious to leave the ranch," Mercy murmured as they headed down the hall. "Don't see any evidence of it. You sure you haven't batted your eyes at him a little too much and made him forget everything but your charming company?"

Jayne blew her breath out in a protest. "I've done no such thing." She hoped Seth hadn't overheard Mercy's comment. A hot blush raced up her neck and she prayed the others wouldn't notice and ask about its cause. She'd never admit that a moment ago she'd gone on a flight of imagination all because the color of his eyes reminded her of the forest.

If either of them noticed and commented on it, Jayne would pretend it hadn't happened. He was only a cowboy she'd accidently shot and who high-handedly informed her he meant to teach her to shoot so no other cowboys would be harmed.

He might prevent another injured cowboy but she wasn't so certain that the shooter would be unharmed. Something about the man threatened her firm resolve. No, she informed her brain. There would be no veering from her goals. No opening her heart. No inviting pain and trouble.

CHAPTER FIVE

When Linette called out for him to come for dinner, Seth hobbled down the hall, careful not to use his leg. The herbs she'd put on the wound could only do so much. He had to be responsible enough to rest the leg until it stopped bleeding.

Eddie came in the back door as Seth entered the kitchen from the other side. "Say, I think you need a crutch."

"Sounds like a good idea."

Grady burst through the door behind Eddie. "Billy and me are going to catch bugs after we eat. Daisy said girls don't like bugs." He faced Linette. "Is that right? Do you hate bugs?"

She smiled. "It depends on the kind of bug. Some I like just fine." She lifted generous portions of fried ham from a skillet.

Grady shifted his attention to Mercy who dished a mound of potatoes into a bowl. "You like bugs?"

"Can't say as I do."

Grady moved on to Sybil as she dumped cooked carrots into a bowl. "You like 'em?"

She shuddered. "No. They give me the creeps."

He continued on to Jayne who sliced a large loaf of richly browned bread.

Seth swallowed back a rush of saliva. Been a long time since he'd enjoyed a meal such as this. Oh sure, he got fed fine on the cattle drive but hunkering around a campfire with a bunch of cussing, spitting cowboys was hardly the same as sitting at a table in the company of a family and some pretty ladies while eating home-cooked food.

"You like bugs, Auntie Jayne?"

Jayne pretended to give the question a lot of thought. Then she answered. "I don't mind bugs . . ." She crossed to Eddie, who scrubbed up at the washstand. "Unless a brother is threatening to stick one down my back." She leaned over him. "Like you used to do."

Eddie slowly straightened, saw the knife in her hand and backed away, his arms up as if to protect himself. "Me? I don't recall doing such a thing."

She stalked him. "Funny how clearly I recall it. You were such a tease." The two of them glowered at each other then broke into laughter. She lowered the knife and he draped an arm over her shoulder.

"I was only trying to teach you not to be a sissy."

"Hmm. And yet you continue to treat me like one."

He leaned away to look into her face. "How do I do that?"

"By overprotecting me. By refusing to teach me to shoot." She tossed her head, sending waves of light through her rich brown hair. "But never mind. Seth has decided to give me lessons."

Eddie stared at Seth. "You did?"

Seth shrugged. Would Eddie feel Seth had encouraged Jayne to defy him? "If you have no objections. I figure it will be safer for everyone if she shoots under proper supervision."

Mercy huffed. "It wasn't my fault she shut her eyes."

Eddie rolled his head back and forth. "Are you sure about this? It might be a bigger task than you know."

"Yeah," Mercy said, her tone aggrieved. "How are you going to keep her from closing her eyes?"

"I'm sure she'll do just fine," Linette soothed.

"I don't know why she wants to learn."

Sybil sounded truly puzzled.

Jayne waved her hands. "I'm here, you know. Stop talking about me."

But they all continued to talk, each defending their previous statements and adding to them.

Jayne jammed her fists on her hips and glowered at the lot but they paid her no heed.

Seth watched her frustration mount and he started to grin.

She met his gaze and squinted at him. "What's so funny?"

He tipped his head toward the others. Then he put his fingers between his teeth and gave a whistle that brought every pair of eyes toward him. "Jayne seems to be annoyed that we're all talking about her. She's feeling invisible."

Eddie patted her shoulder as if to soothe her which, as far as Seth could tell, had quite the opposite effect.

He wondered how long it would be before she blew her top.

Linette no doubt wondered the same thing, as she moved to defuse the situation. "Our food is getting cold. Why don't we sit down and eat?"

Eddie waited until everyone was settled then bowed his head and said the blessing.

After the food had been passed, he asked, "Where did you girls go this morning?"

All three spoke at once then by silent consent they let Jayne answer. "We followed the river for a ways. Wondered where the water came from. Lakes, of course, but Seth says there are also glaciers up there."

Eddie nodded. "Indeed, there are. Way up in the mountains."

Seth took note of the fact that Jayne had said nothing about his promise to take them to one of the mountain lakes. Did it mean nothing to her? For some reason her failure to mention it annoyed him. He'd offered her an outing. At great personal sacrifice. It would mean delaying his return yet another day. Of course, her friends were included. But it was Jayne he'd invited.

Come to think of it, she hadn't seemed any more overjoyed at his offer to teach her to shoot.

Was she reluctant to spend time with him or was it simply her independence kicking in? Perhaps she thought she and her friends could go to a glacier on their own and she resented his intrusion.

Seems the young lady would take some watching if she thought she could handle every situation on her own. Not that he meant to volunteer for the job. He couldn't even explain why he'd offered to take her to the mountains let alone give her shooting lessons other than the one big reason.

It hurt to get shot. He'd do his best to see it didn't happen to another unsuspecting person.

After dinner, Jayne and her friends told Linette they'd clean up so she could rest. Grady went to join Billy in their bug hunt. Eddie rode out of the yard with two other cowboys. The crutch seemed to have been forgotten. Seth wondered what to do with himself but seeing as he was mostly immobile, sitting in the sun again seemed the only alternative, though he'd discovered it a lonely occupation.

He parked himself on a chair out in the grass and stared at the ranch buildings. There must be something he could do to pass the time. Maybe he'd ask Eddie for a job that would last a day or two.

After a bit the girls drifted outside and sat down on the grass beside him. Sybil brought a knitting project and Mercy had an atlas. How far did she expect to go adventuring? Jayne had brought a sock and darning material.

He watched as she wove the yarn in and out.

She glanced up, saw he watched her and

lowered the needle. "What?"

"I didn't say anything."

"You didn't have to. You *looked* something."

"Really? How do I *look* something?"

"Like this." She knit her forehead in a fierce look. "Or this." She waggled her eyebrows like mischief waiting to happen. "Or this." She widened her eyes and very clearly communicated surprise.

Her friends giggled.

"Fine. I get your point. But what look was I giving?"

"I'm sure you know." She returned to her work.

"I'm equally sure I don't. Why, I was simply watching you darn a sock, watching you weave the yarn in and out in perfect little —" He flicked his wrist to indicate what he meant.

"I suppose you're surprised to see me doing something useful."

He glanced at the others but they kept their heads down. Fine. He could deal with this on his own. Though for the life of him, he didn't know what she expected him to say. Why should he be surprised that she could darn a sock? Then he recalled what she'd said about needing to feel useful. Or something like that. He honestly couldn't recall her exact words. His mind had been numbed by the pain in his leg and concerned about how it delayed his trip home.

"I think nothing of the sort." He leaned closer and lowered his voice. "If you want the truth, I admire your quickness with the needle and yarn."

She jerked back and stared open-mouthed at him.

"Shut your mouth," Sybil whispered. "Or you'll catch bugs."

Mercy didn't bother to hide her giggle.

Red crept up Jayne's neck and painted round apples on her cheeks.

Seth sat back and resisted an urge to pound his palm on his forehead. He'd only meant to . . . to what? Encourage her? Make her see that she was more than she saw herself as? Instead, he had come across as a flirt. Him? Seth Collins? A flirt? He opened his mouth intending to explain he never flirted but instead clicked his teeth together without saying a thing. Least said, soonest mended, Ma used to say.

"Look," Mercy said. "There are the boys."

Billy and Grady ran around in the tall grass beside one of the buildings, each carrying a Mason jar.

"I wonder how many bugs they've found." Jayne's voice seemed a little gravelly.

"If they come here with jars of bugs, I'm leaving," Sybil said, already pushing to her feet.

Smokey jumped out of the grass and Sybil screamed. "Silly cat. You frightened me." She headed indoors.

Mercy closed her book, stretched and bolted to her feet. "I'm going to explore. Can you take my book in for me?" She handed it to Jayne.

Smokey arched his back and rubbed against Jayne then leaped into Seth's lap.

"Well, make yourself at home." He stroked the cat and earned a very loud purr.

"The cat likes you," Jayne said.

"You needn't sound so surprised."

She shook her head. "I'm not surprised at all."

"Really? So you think I'm a likeable fellow?" He ducked his head and paid Smokey a great deal of attention. What kind of question was that? When had he ever been tempted to beg for attention before? It must be the result of sitting around all day staring at the world creeping by on leaden feet.

She made a humming sound. "Can't really say, can I? I hardly know you."

"Fair enough. But after I've taught you to shoot a gun well enough to trust you with one, you'll know me well enough to give me your opinion."

She squinted at him. "How long do you think these lessons are going to take?"

He lifted a hand. "I guess that depends on how fast you learn."

"I learn fast."

"Good to know."

"Then you can be on your way." As an afterthought, she added, "To your pa."

That reminder brought him up sharply. He had to get to his pa as soon as possible. He would not fail in his responsibility.

His attention was diverted as Grady and his friend climbed the hill.

Jayne introduced Billy, a boy of about six with blue eyes and blond hair. The boys' coloring was so similar, he could have easily passed for Grady's older brother. Seth recalled hearing that Billy and his brother and sisters had a new ma and pa and wondered what had happened.

Billy pointed down the hill. "I live in that house." He indicated a two-story house beyond the other buildings. It looked recently constructed. "Heard you got shot. It hurt much?"

"Only when I breathe," Seth said.

The children giggled.

"Wanna see what I got?" Billy held his jar toward Seth.

Seth took it and examined the bug collection. "Wow. You've been hard at work catching bugs." There were a dozen or so bugs including several furry caterpillars. He offered the jar to Jayne. "You want to see them?"

She held up a hand and wrinkled her nose. "I see them fine from here."

He chuckled at her expression then turned back to admire Grady's collection of bugs. After a bit the boys set their jars aside and chased after each other.

"It's nice they have one another to play with," Jayne said.

He didn't say anything.

"It must be lonely being an only child."

He heard the question in her voice. Knew she was asking how it had been for him. But he hadn't been an only child. He'd had an older brother he adored. The hollowness in his heart cried out. He moaned then realizing he'd done so, rubbed his leg as if it hurt. It did, a little, but not nearly as much as the spot in his heart where he stored Frank's memories.

He quietly, firmly closed the door on that pain. There'd been a resurgence of his memories in the last few hours but he intended for them to stay safely buried in the past.

Thankfully Linette joined them at that moment and saved him from Jayne's curious study.

Jayne wondered at his sudden withdrawal. One moment he teased her and the next his expression had closed off like he'd remembered something he'd left undone. She didn't think it was because he'd delayed his trip to see his pa. Seems he should be able to relax and trust that this Crawford fellow would not abandon his pa. But she had no idea what else could explain it. Not that it mattered. He wasn't part of her plans for her life.

She resumed repairing the sock but couldn't dismiss his statement that he enjoyed watching her, and stole a glance his direction.

His attention was on the boys chasing each other.

That was fine because part of her plans included being free of emotional entanglements and something about Seth threatened those boundaries.

She folded up her mending project and rose. "I'll help with supper preparations," she said and retreated indoors.

The next morning, Seth appeared for breakfast hobbling on a crutch.

Jayne watched his progress. He appeared a little awkward but it would enable him to get around without using his leg.

Linette had checked the wound this morning and said it looked good.

"I see Eddie found you one." She nodded at his crutch and smiled. Her smile made its way to her eyes, warming them in a surprising way.

"Yup. Now I can get around more and not worry about bleeding." He grinned at her.

Mornings would be a cheerful matter if she saw such a happy grin every day. She resisted an urge to thump the heel of her hand on her forehead. The last thing she needed or wanted was to be dependent on a man's facial expressions to set the tone for her day. She turned to Linette. "Is his leg okay?" She already knew the answer but had to bring her thoughts back to sensible. She hoped Seth wouldn't take her words to indicate anything more than concern that he not do further damage to his leg. She didn't want that on her conscience. No reason he should think it anything more.

"So long as he doesn't overdo it."

Seth made a protesting noise. "You could have asked me. I'm right here." He put his fingers between his teeth as if to whistle, a reminder of how he'd silenced the others

110

yesterday. He grinned at her.

She couldn't help but smile back, and despite her resolve, her heart tumbled over itself like the waterfall they'd visited.

After breakfast, he lingered in the kitchen. When she glanced at him, he tipped his head to signal he wished to speak to her.

She followed him down the hall.

"I'm ready to give you a shooting lesson. Let's go."

Her tumbling heart jerked to a halt as she crossed her arms. "I can be ready anytime I want. Just as soon as I'm asked."

"I just asked."

"No, you told me. Just like you told me I would take instructions from you." She planted her hands on her hips as her insides twisted. "You're just like everyone else. I have the right to make a choice. So ask."

He blinked and opened his mouth. No sound came out. He closed it again and turned to stare out the front door. His shoulders rose and fell as he took a deep breath.

Was it so difficult to give her the right to make her choices? If so, he demanded far too much control. More than she would give up.

Slowly he came round to face her. "I don't know why this is so important to you but

111

fine. I can ask. Jayne Gardiner, would you like me to give you shooting lessons?"

She struggled to put an end to her annoyance, her anger and a whole host of emotions that had nothing to do with him. With blinding insight, she realized that her cauldron of emotions had been building for a long time. They were the culmination of having so many decisions taken out of her hands because she wasn't considered worthy of making them. Added to that was how she bore the consequences of the choices others made for her. Father, Oliver and even Eddie chose as they saw best but their decisions weren't always what she cared to live with.

He shifted, and she brought her attention back to the present situation. He'd asked even though he didn't understand. That raised him considerably in her estimation.

"I would like for you to give me lessons." She waited.

He looked confused then understanding flooded his face and he chuckled. "Would today suit you?"

She nodded. "Today suits me just fine."

"When would you like to go?"

"Give me two minutes."

His chuckles followed her across the kitchen and into her bedroom where she scooped up a Western-style hat she deemed necessary for shooting and the red brocade bag containing her pistol. She'd purchased the gun at the Fort. She guessed even before she reached the ranch that Eddie wouldn't be willing to teach her to handle a firearm. There were times he was so much like their father. But she'd bought it, anyway.

She skipped back to the kitchen. Linette, Sybil and Mercy waited for her.

"Are you sure this is what you want to do?" Linette asked.

"Very sure."

Her sister-in-law smiled. "Then I'm behind you all the way. I firmly believe in women learning as much independence as they can."

"Me, too," Mercy said, giving her a little hug.

Sybil sighed. "Just don't go shooting anyone."

She laughed, then assured them she'd be extra careful and went to join Seth who waited outside.

"Where to?" he asked.

She pointed to the back of the house. "That will get us away from the ranch." As they walked, she gave him a studying look.

He had a gun stuck in his belt.

"I have my own gun," she said.

"Figured you did."

The way he said it, full of resignation and despair, brought a burst of laughter to her lips. "So why did you bring a gun?"

"A man should be prepared at all times." He grinned. "Don't you agree?" He stopped, leaning on his crutch to look at her. Their gazes caught and held. A dozen thoughts fluttered through her brain like butterflies. Did he refer to her shooting him and meant to suggest he should have been armed and ready?

The idea so amused her that she tilted her head back and laughed.

"Care to share the joke?"

She tried to stop her laughter but at the bewildered look on his face, she shook her head and waved her hands to indicate she couldn't speak.

He looked heavenward as if seeking divine help in dealing with her — an idea that tickled her so deep inside she couldn't stop laughing despite his pained look.

Finally, she wiped her eyes and took a deep breath. "I wondered if you wished you'd been armed and ready the day I shot you." She pressed her lips together to keep from bursting into laughter again. "Or if you planned to be armed and ready for today." She managed to contain her mirth

114

but her eyes brimmed with the effort.

He shook his head and his mouth drew down at the corners. "If you can't be serious about such a grave matter . . ." He let the sentence trail off as if her failure defied words.

She pulled her mouth into a frown that reflected his expression. "I can be serious. See?"

He lifted his hands in a sign of defeat. "I give up. But how am I to teach you something as grave and deadly as shooting a gun if you only see it as a —" he shook his head "— a mockery."

"You sure you're not mocking me?" She giggled.

"Me? Not a chance."

In a flash of clarity, she realized that he spoke the truth. Likely he took each task with due seriousness. And she didn't find the idea of his seriousness objectionable. It made a man dependable. Not that it mattered to her. She didn't mean to depend on a man in the future.

CHAPTER SIX

They reached a grove of trees. Tall pine, frothy willows and sighing poplar. As they stepped into a clearing, Seth looked around. The area was wide enough to give them room to shoot, and there were no rocks nearby to pose a risk of ricochet. If his bearings were correct, he had been a hundred yards farther on, sitting on a boulder when she shot him.

A stump on the far side of the clearing held a paper target. "Where did you get that?" He wondered why Eddie would have one. He didn't seem the type to be spending time in target practice.

"I got it at the Fort when I got my gun. When I explained to the store owner what I intended to do, he said I'd need a few of these."

Seth stared at her. "You've been planning this a long time."

Her eyes bored into his, full of conviction

and challenge — as if she expected him to oppose her idea. But she wouldn't listen if he did, which was why he intended to give her lessons.

He broke from the intensity of her look and shifted his gaze to the target. "I see it's unmarked."

She laughed. "I haven't come within a mile of it." Her expression sobered. "But I've left a mark on you. You will never know how much I regret that."

Again her gaze found his and held it in a look that burned away every argument he might have imagined to her plan. In fact, if he let it, her look might have broken down walls he'd built around his heart to protect it from the pain of losing Frank and Sarah. That couldn't happen and he jerked his gaze away so sharply it put him momentarily off balance. Only his firm grasp on the crutch kept him on his feet.

He was here for one purpose only — to teach her how to handle a firearm so no one else would be injured. She might have shot herself. He shuddered at the thought.

"First thing is to move the target closer so you have some hope of hitting it." He hopped over and brought it to a stump much closer. "Let's see what sort of gun you have."

She dug in her brocade bag and brought out a .45 Colt Single Action Army revolver. A decent enough gun. She held it gingerly.

"First thing is always consider it loaded. Hold it like it's serious business. That way you aren't in for any surprises."

"Okay." The gun still dangled like a spider.

He gingerly removed it from her hand and walked her through the process of loading, unloading, cocking the hammer, ejecting the spent shell. "Have you got all that?"

She nodded.

"Then let's see you do it."

He walked her through it several times until each move was certain.

"Now for the stance. Your first instinct is to stand with your legs slightly apart facing your target. However, that allows you to sway sideways. Instead — Are you right-handed?"

She nodded again.

"Then you want to put your left foot forward and hold the gun with both hands. Like so." He let the crutch fall to the ground so he could illustrate. "Try it."

She followed his instructions. She clenched her jaw so tightly he wondered if her teeth would survive her first lesson.

"Now take the gun and hold it."

She did so, extending it at shoulder height,

her shoulders hunched practically to her ears. It looked most uncomfortable. If she found the task so offensive, why did she persist with it?

He knew what her answer would be if he asked. Because of her helplessness in the face of Oliver's death. He could tell her that feeling would never leave but didn't see the point. It wouldn't make her change her mind.

Not for the first time, he suspected she was part mule.

"Rock back and forth a bit. Do you feel solid?"

They went through the stance several times then he addressed her grip.

She listened and practiced the steps he gave. "You sure pack a lot more into a lesson than Mercy did."

"Hopefully with better results." He touched his leg.

Her hands wavered. He edged closer. Hesitated. But there was only one way to show her how to hold her arms. He closed the distance between them. "Like this." He reached around her, steadying each arm with his own.

He felt her arms twitch.

An answering jolt raced up his limbs and landed in his heart with the force of lightning. Thunder echoed through his insides. Here was a woman who needed taking care of.

What was he thinking? He had a father he was responsible for and he took his responsibilities seriously. He would go home, hopefully find Pa much improved and take over his care. He would devote the rest of his life, or however long Pa lived, to that job.

He didn't need any complications. Especially from a headstrong woman whose only concern was becoming independent at any cost. However foolish her choices were.

He knew where that led. He was the one who paid the price for Frank and Sarah's foolishness. He certainly wasn't about to venture in that direction again.

It was impossible to say who moved away first. Though he figured it was mutual. He knew she didn't want someone taking care of her any more than he wanted the obligation.

"My arms are getting tired," she said, shaking one then transferring the gun to shake the other.

"Let's take a break." He sat on a nearby log and she sat on another. She couldn't get much more distance between them and remain in the same clearing. The air fractured with unspoken cautions, goals that

120

took them in different directions.

After several tense, silent moments, Jayne sighed. "You're putting a lot into this." She sliced her gaze toward him. "Why?"

Perhaps explaining his reason would ease her tension. "I'm just concerned that if you intend to shoot, you are prepared to use a gun appropriately."

"But why does it matter to you? You'll soon be gone and our paths will likely never cross again."

"I suppose that's so." She didn't have to act so relieved about it, he thought. "But I would still feel responsible. The way I see it, if you see someone doing something foolish, you do your best to stop them. If you can convince them to make better choices, you might save them from disaster." His voice caught but he hoped she wouldn't notice.

She cocked her head. "Are you speaking from firsthand experience?"

"Yes, I am. I lost two people very close to me because they wouldn't heed a warning."

"How close?"

He shrugged. "Does it matter? The point is, I will always do what I can to keep people from making disastrous choices."

She turned away and seemed greatly interested in something at the far side of the clearing. "How disastrous?"

"They died." The words tore out of his chest and scratched the length of his throat and they vibrated in the air.

"Oh, Seth. I'm sorry. An accident?"

He nodded, trying to push every remembrance of that day from his thoughts.

"Did you —" She hesitated.

He looked at her. She scrubbed her lips together and seemed to struggle with her emotions. No doubt she was remembering watching her fiancé die.

He hobbled over to her side and sat down. "I should have never started this conversation. It reminds you of a painful event."

She shuddered and his instincts to protect her took over. He slipped his arm across her shoulders and offered his strength. "I'm sorry."

Another shudder raced through her then she turned to look into his face. Her eyes were wide and so dark he thought the pain must be searing them. Ah. How could he have been so thoughtless?

"Did you see them die?" Her words were barely a whisper.

He nodded. "I wish I hadn't."

She squeezed his hand. "Me, too."

He understood her to mean her fiancé. "The pictures fade with time."

"Do they?" She shook her head. "How do you ever forget watching someone die?"

"You don't. But you learn how to live with it and how to keep it in the past."

She clung to his gaze, probing his soul for truth.

He couldn't hide it from her. He let her glimpse the pain, the despair, the guilt — and hopefully the determination that carried him through every day until it became second nature.

"Seth, who died?"

Her question jerked him to his feet. It was one thing to talk in anonymous terms. It was quite another to talk about Frank and Sarah. "Let's run through the whole thing again. If we're both comfortable that you're ready, I'll let you shoot a real bullet."

She rose slowly. "Seth, there are some things you can't control. Like death, as you've already learned. And people. Guess you didn't learn that quite so well because you're trying to control me and I won't give you that right." She stalked to where she had practiced her stance. "I will never give anyone that right again." She shifted her left leg forward, gripped the gun in her right hand and steadied it with her left, just as he'd shown her. She held the stance firmly for several seconds than flung him a hot look. "I think I'm ready for a bullet."

It took every ounce of Jayne's strength to hold the gun steady before she turned to Seth. He'd lost friends. Knowing the pain and shock and despair of watching someone you cared for die, she sympathized with that. She even understood his need to be in control. It was how she'd reacted.

But she only meant to be in control of her life, her choices and her boundaries.

While he, foolish man, thought he could be in control of everything and everyone. It surely must put him in opposition with numerous people.

"I'm ready," she repeated.

He picked up his crutch and hobbled to her side. "One more thing. You must practice squeezing the trigger." He cupped his hand over hers. "Hold the gun like you don't want to lose it." He tightened his fingers to illustrate, crushing her flesh into the cold steel. "This way you always have control."

Earlier, he'd wrapped his arms about her to steady her arm. She'd felt safe in his solid grasp. So safe, it sent alarm skidding along her nerves. She didn't need anyone holding her or keeping her safe. She meant to be independent.

Now the way his fingers closed on hers, she felt again his strength. It raced up her arm and into her heart like a promise of protection. She gritted her teeth. If she gave the slightest encouragement she suspected he would gladly play that role. He'd become her protector, her defender, her knight in shining armor for as long as he chose to stay around. And then he'd leave and she would be the weaker, the more uncertain for having allowed him that role.

She would not do it. She would not give him control.

She nodded. "I've got it. Let me show you."

He dropped his hand from hers and stepped back. "Show me."

She held the stance he'd taught her, gripped the gun in her hand, held it steady and she crushed her fingers around the gun.

"Squeeze the trigger slowly, keeping your grasp tight all the while. That way your other fingers can't spasm when you squeeze and you won't get the same amount of recoil."

She obeyed his every instruction. In this matter, at least, she welcomed his lessons so she allowed him the right to tell her what to do. He showed her how to line up the sights on the target and made her practice until

125

she could steady the gun on the bull's-eye.

"Good," he said when he was finally confident she had the whole procedure down. "Now for a bullet."

"Finally. I was beginning to think I might have to do this for hours, even days, before it led to the real thing."

The look he gave her said plenty but that didn't keep him from saying what he thought, as well. "Need I remind you that I am living — thankfully — evidence of you shooting live ammunition when you didn't know proper technique?"

"I haven't forgotten." She spoke meekly.

He put one bullet in the chamber, stepped behind her then lifted the gun in front of her. "Forget there is a bullet in it. Simply do everything I've taught you." Slowly, quietly, he repeated the steps as she followed them.

A frisson of fear raced through her as she cocked the hammer. Last time she'd pulled the trigger she'd shot someone.

She knew the damage a bullet could do. Thank God that in Seth's situation, it hadn't been worse. She tried to swallow but her throat was constricted. What if she had been forced to live with two deaths on her conscience?

He brought his arm around her and steadied her hand. Her fears subsided, settled back to the dark spot behind her heart.

"Good grip. Now squeeze."

She did. The explosion of the bullet battered her eardrums.

She opened her eyes and squinted at the target. "There's a hole right through the center."

He dropped her arm and backed away.

She turned to face him, laughing.

"No thanks to you. You closed your eyes."

"I did?" Her shoulders fell as did her sense of victory. "I did."

"Guess I missed one very important step in your lesson." He leaned closer and narrowed his eyes. "Keep your eyes on the target." His eyes flashed shades of green. "Keep them open so you aim true."

"You're angry."

His breath whooshed out, and his expression softened. "Not angry."

"Do you expect me to believe that?" She put more distance between them.

He leaned back on his heels, struggling with his emotions. Suddenly he barked out a laugh. "Like Mercy said, how am I going to persuade you to keep your eyes open?"

"They're open now." In fact, they felt too large for her face as she stared at the man who had gone from anger to roaring with laughter. He sure knew how to laugh with abandon. The sound rumbled up and down her chest and tickled behind her ribs. She began to laugh, as well, though she had no idea what they were laughing at. Only that it was pure enjoyment to do so.

He shook his head and pointed at her. "Maybe I should use matchsticks."

She understood he meant to hold her eyes open. The idea tickled her and she laughed harder. Her knees weakened and she sat on the nearby log.

Seth joined her and they both sobered as they sat side by side. She stretched out her legs as did he. His went on several inches beyond hers. He was a big man, as she'd already noted. A solid man. A steady man.

Good thing he was leaving soon because she was finding it harder and harder to remember why she didn't need the care and protection of such a man.

One glance at the gun she still held brought her reason back. She drew her legs in. "I'd like to try again."

He sighed. "I don't have any matchsticks with me."

"You won't need them." She marched over to the spot where she faced the target. She could do this. All she had to do was focus on the target and keep her eyes open.

He chambered another bullet and edged in behind her. She could feel the warmth of his body, the shelter it provided from the slight breeze . . . the shelter from life's storms. His breath caressed her cheek as he lined up the sights over her shoulder.

Confusing emotions raced through her. Determination that she found hard to cling to when his arms were about her, dismay at what her ineptitude had cost Oliver . . . and herself. Fear of firearms and an emptiness that she wouldn't allow herself to investigate. Her arms quivered ever so slightly but enough that he noticed. Again he brought his hand up to steady her. "Line it up. Keep your eyes open and squeeze."

She curled her trigger finger, held her breath as she anticipated the explosion. It was so loud.

"You closed your eyes again." He held his head in his hands as if it hurt him to even think about it.

"I can't help it. It's so loud." She refused to look at him.

"Jayne, it's a gun. Guns are loud and heavy and cold and dangerous."

"I know that." He didn't have to treat her like an idiot.

"Why are you shooting one if you're so all-fired scared of it?"

She flung him a defensive glance. "Because I refuse to let fear control me."

He lowered his hands and studied her, his eyes wide as if he couldn't believe what he'd heard.

"Yes, I am afraid of guns. I admit it. But my fear held me immobile when Oliver was shot. I won't allow it to make me useless ever again."

"What happened?" His gentle voice melted her resolve. That, and knowing he had a similar experience.

She moved to the log and sat down, folded her hands in her lap. Seth sat beside her and she told him the story. "I met Oliver when I was fifteen and he eighteen. His family is old friends of my family but they'd been abroad and had only just returned." She tried to think what had attracted her to him. Strangely she couldn't remember anything specific. He didn't tease her, didn't make her laugh . . . at least not on purpose. He didn't give her looks that made her want to laugh and cry at the same time. Nor had his arms about her ever made her feel like she'd found a secure shelter.

She shifted to meet Seth's hazel eyes, saw the gold showing in his irises. She clung to his gaze wanting him to understand how she could have been attracted to Oliver, even though she wasn't sure she understood it herself. "He seemed so wise. So sure of himself." At first, she'd liked that but soon discovered it meant he didn't need her. Not like she needed him and wanted to be needed. "I thought him so grown-up. He did things and took me places I'd never been." Places her father would have forbidden. "Oliver liked to gamble. Claimed he was good at it. If the amount of money he spent indicated anything then he must have been. But money didn't impress me. My father is rich and could provide my every want. After a while, when he either didn't invite me on his exploits or I refused to go because I didn't care for the type of company I met, I found myself more and more alone. Gambling was his mistress and I couldn't compete." She hadn't meant to say the words aloud. Hadn't meant to spill all the detail but Seth didn't indicate shock or disinterest. He cupped his hand over hers on the log.

It gave her the courage to continue. "One day he offered to take me shopping. I didn't need anything but I was thrilled he wanted to spend time with me." She groaned. "That makes me sound needy and immature. Perhaps I was. But not anymore." She drew in a refreshing breath and continued.

"Someone came out of the alley demanding money and a key. Oliver gave him all his money but had no key." She gave the rest of the details. How a gun had been within her grasp but she couldn't bring herself to touch it. How Oliver had been shot. "There was so much blood." She shuddered.

He squeezed her shoulder. "What a horrible, senseless crime. You should never have witnessed it."

No words came to her mind. Her head was filled with regrets and wishes. "I will learn to shoot. I will overcome my fear of guns."

"Of course you will. Just as soon as you keep your eyes open and on the target."

She nodded.

"Did they catch the killer?"

"No. He escaped."

"He's still on the loose?" He grabbed his crutch and hurried to his feet. He limped to the far side of the clearing and stared out into the trees. He turned and faced her.

"Then I think it's very important that you learn to shoot a gun and shoot it well."

Tension skidded up her spine and grabbed the base of her head at the harsh tone of his voice. "You think he's after me?"

"You are a witness to him murdering Oliver, aren't you?"

She wrapped her arms about her. "Thanks for scaring me." She rose and took a deep breath. "But he'd never follow me to Canada. Even if he did, how would he ever find me? Canada is a very big place."

He scrubbed at his eyes. "Yes, of course. I'm sorry. I was being foolish. Forgive me?"

She nodded absently. Was it possible Oliver's murderer would try and track her down? "It's not like I'm in London and can identify him. It's to his advantage that I've left the country. I'd say he should feel like he got away with murder. Literally."

He gave a mirthless laugh. "You are right."

His assurances did not alleviate the tension in her muscles. "I think I'm done with shooting lessons for today." She secured the gun back in her bag.

She waited for him to fall in at her side, and they slowly began their way back to the ranch. "I said far too much. I'm sorry." She should never have opened the floodgates on her experience.

"It is I who should apologize for expressing concerns that have no basis. I guess I'm turning into a worrier. Always seeing and expecting something bad to happen."

Sympathy and understanding erased her tension. "You witnessed the death of two close friends. That's reason enough for your caution."

"It's generous of you to give me that excuse."

She drew up and faced him. "For goodness' sake. Are we going to apologize and wallow for the rest of the day or can we be done with this?"

He burst out laughing. "Oh, Jayne, how refreshing you are. Yes, I'm ready to be done." He laughed again.

"Good. Now can we plan another shooting lesson tomorrow?"

He rolled his eyes. "The one thing you need to learn I can't teach you."

She planted her hand over his on the crutch. "I'll keep my eyes open. I promise."

He leaned closer as if examining her eyes.

She forced herself to meet his look without blinking.

He stared at her so long her eyes began to water. Still she would not blink first. She concentrated on the way the clouds reflected in his eyes, how his irises darkened to forest green, how the shards of gold were revealed when the clouds moved aside and allowed sunlight to hit his face.

Finally he nodded and straightened. "Good. Let's see you do that tomorrow."

She sucked in air to relieve the sudden dizziness. The man had the most intriguing eyes with the power to make her forget every rational thought — which was not a good thing. Being weak and vulnerable was not part of her plan.

He moved onward and she hurried along. The weight of the gun in her bag reminded her of what really mattered. Learning to take care of herself. Being prepared to take action, especially with a gun. Still, she prayed she would never have call to do so.

CHAPTER SEVEN

Seth had accepted Eddie's invitation to continue using the bed in the upstairs room though he could have likely found a bunk with the cowboys in the bunkhouse. Somehow, especially after Jayne's story, he felt the need to be close at hand.

She was right. Her fiancé's killer would likely stay in England where he could move about scot-free. Seth pressed the heel of his hand to his forehead as if he could force wisdom inside. What had he been thinking to voice his fears about the murderer? He regretted it the moment he saw his worries reflected in her eyes. He'd wanted to yank the words back. Wanted to pull her close and promise to protect her.

How could he even hope to promise such a thing? He didn't have the right and didn't want it.

But still there was a concern. The killer had wanted something from Oliver that he didn't get. Would he come after Jayne for it? *God, I'm not much of a one to ask anything of You but this isn't for me. It's for Jayne. Keep her safe.* He wished he could feel some assurance that God would hear and answer his request. He had never understood how Ma continued to believe after Frank and Sarah's deaths.

For the moment he didn't regret his injured leg. It forced him to stay at the ranch for a few days. As long as he was there he could guard her. But he couldn't stay. Besides, Eddie would take care of his sister.

But making sure she could protect herself, should the need arise, took on a greater importance. She must learn how to shoot a gun and hit her intended target.

If only he could figure out a way to make her keep her eyes open.

The next morning he rose with fresh determination. He planned to start lessons again as soon as breakfast ended. As usual, the food was excellent and the talk about the table friendly.

Grady eased forward, anxious to share some news.

"What is it, son?" Eddie asked, giving the child permission to speak.

"Billy's mama and papa are dead. Right?"

"Yes." Eddie sent a questioning look in

Linette's direction. She shook her head to indicate she had no idea where the question was going.

"So Cassie and Roper adopted them."

"That's right."

"Because they had no mama and papa?"

"Yes. Why do you ask?"

The boy practically bounced off his chair. "If I find a puppy who has no mama or papa can I adopt him?"

Eddie stared at his son.

Seth ducked his head to hide a grin. The little guy certainly knew how to present an infallible argument.

Jayne nudged his elbow and they secretly grinned at each other.

Eddie and Linette silently consulted each other.

Eddie nodded and turned back to Grady. "I couldn't say without meeting such a puppy. Why do you ask?"

"Billy's new pa said someone left a puppy at the store in Edendale. I guess he needs a good home, wouldn't you say?"

"I expect there are lots of people wanting a dog. What makes you think he'll still be there?"

Grady slouched forward. "I was only hoping. That's all."

"Well, son, I can't say if this puppy still

needs a home but I'll check, and I'll leave word at the store that we might be in the market for a new dog. How about that?"

Grady bounced again. "That's good."

Seth stole a look at Jayne and saw a reflection of his own pleasure. Eddie was a good pa.

The meal ended and Seth turned to Jayne but she didn't give him a chance to suggest another shooting lesson.

"You need to meet Cookie. She knows you're here and has likely seen you outside. She likes to meet everyone. Besides, she makes the best cinnamon rolls." She headed for the door and signaled he should follow her. "She always has coffee and some kind of goodies ready."

At first he didn't make any move to join her.

She grabbed his crutch and handed it to him. "Are you coming?"

"Would it do any good to say I'm not?"

"Not a bit." She grinned. "Believe me, you won't regret it."

He gave an exaggerated sigh. "I guess I don't have a choice." He gave slight emphasis to the last word.

Her eyes narrowed and he knew she remembered how she insisted she deserved to be given a choice. She smiled. "You're right, of course. Seth, would you care to meet Cookie? I'm sure she's anxious to meet you."

His grin widened. "It seems like a fine idea." He tromped down the hall. "Shall we?"

As they descended, she told him about the ranch. "Eddie came out two years ago with instructions to build a replica of the Gardiner estate back in England. However, he found the circumstances were so different that he had to adjust the plans Father had given him. At first, Father opposed him but I'm proud to say Eddie stuck to his convictions and Father came around."

She waved at Eddie who mounted up in front of the barn.

"Father especially objected to his marriage to Linette. He said her family wasn't suitable. And Linette's notions of helping people regardless of race or social position especially upset him."

"Seems to me Eddie and Linette make a fine couple."

Jayne slowed her steps. "I agree. And Father has come round."

"So this stubborn, independent streak runs in the family?" He kept his tone light and teasing because, although it was true, he had almost convinced himself it didn't

140

matter to him. He would leave. Continue on with his plans. What Jayne did was not his responsibility. His conscience would be clear if he did his best to teach her to shoot.

"I prefer to think of us as people with principles and resolve."

The airy, dismissive way she said it made him chuckle.

She didn't give him a chance to say anything more on the subject as she went back to her discussion about the Eden Valley Ranch. "The ranch is like a small town. Over there are supply buildings. Eddie lined one with tin to keep the rodents out." She beamed with pride in her brother.

Seth turned away. He'd had the same pride in Frank. Had thought his older brother could do nothing wrong. Then he'd gotten all goofy about Sarah and did something so stupid it cost him his life.

Jayne drew his attention back to the present as she pointed to the new house where Billy had said he lived. "Roper and Cassie live in a new house, which is large enough to accommodate them and the four children they'd adopted. You met Billy. Besides him, there's Daisy. She's thirteen and very pretty. She obviously adores her younger siblings as well as her new parents. Neil is a year younger than Daisy and imitates Roper right down to the rolling swagger. There's Billy who's six then little Pansy who's two. As the baby of the ranch she gets lots of attention."

"Four children is a lot to take on."

Jayne nodded. "Cassie and Roper handle it like old hands. I suppose it isn't hard when you all love each other."

"Still, it's got to be challenging." Love was not enough sometimes. It didn't conquer pain or make people responsible.

"See that little cabin?" Jayne indicated a log cabin next to the trail. "That's where Linette and Eddie lived the first year she was out here." She chuckled. "I don't suppose you heard their story." She drew closer to the cabin and slowed her steps. "Linette came out expecting a marriage of convenience but Eddie was still working on the big house and expected his former fiancée. He said Linette's arrival was a mistake and he'd send her back come spring." She grinned at Seth. "By spring he was head over heels in love with her."

Love again. As if it would fix everything. He knew it wasn't enough. He'd loved Frank. He'd loved Sarah in a boyish way. He'd loved Ma. It hadn't fixed or prevented anything.

Jayne turned toward the other two-story

building. "That's the cookhouse. Cookie and Bertie — her husband — run it." She drew in a deep breath. "I better warn you about Cookie."

He gave her a hard look. "Warn me? Why?"

She shrugged. "It's nothing, really." But her eyes sparkled like she had a secret joke.

"Jayne Gardiner, what are you not telling me?"

She did not manage to control the twitch of a smile. "I wouldn't say anything except I'd hate to see your leg hurt."

He stiffened. "What do you think she'll do? Beat me with a broom? Fly at me with a skillet?"

She laughed hard enough for tears to fill her eyes. "Can't say as I've ever heard tell of her doing so." She sobered with a great deal of effort. "But she does like to hug her guests."

"Hug?" He stared at the cookhouse. "I need to think about this." Hopefully she thought he was teasing. When was the last time he'd been hugged? Ma had been affectionate before Frank died. After that she had grown cautious and sparse with her hugs, though she used to pat his arm or touch the back of his neck.

He realized his hand had gone to that spot

of its own accord.

Jayne studied him, her face wrinkled in curiosity. "Do you have something against hugging?" Her voice was low, as if she tried to keep from revealing any opinion.

" 'Course not." How else could he answer?

She patted his hand. "You'll like it. I know you will."

The smile gleaming from her eyes made him want to be hugged just to please her. He curled his fingers into his palms. When had he ever been so addlebrained?

"I just want you to be prepared so she doesn't catch you off balance."

"Okay. Fine."

She climbed the steps and opened the door. He swung up after her, keeping a firm grip on his crutch.

A mountain of a woman steamed toward them.

"About time. I thought Jayne meant to keep you to herself." The big woman bore down on him with the speed of a freight train.

He braced himself.

She engulfed him in a hug that threatened to shatter bones but filled his nostrils with cinnamon and yeast and a thousand pleasant memories.

She clapped his back twice and released him.

Jayne nudged him. "Was it so bad?"

He shook his head, unwilling to meet her eyes as something hungry and lonesome tugged at his heart and it wasn't hunger for food.

"Come. Sit. Tell me everything about yourself." Cookie herded them toward the table and put forth steaming cups of coffee and a plate of the rolls Jayne claimed were famous.

Cookie waited until he'd savored a bite of one.

"Mmm. Jayne was right. These are the best I've ever tasted."

She beamed at him. "Pshaw, they're nothing. I make them by the dozens every day."

"And the cowboys eat them by the dozens," Jayne said, earning her a beaming smile from Cookie.

"They certainly do." Seeing he'd finished the first roll, Cookie offered him another.

"Thanks. Don't mind if I do."

She let him enjoy the roll then leaned forward. "You from these parts?"

"My pa lives in Corncrib, Montana."

"I do believe someone mentioned that. Didn't Eddie arrange to have something delivered there?"

"I guess he did." Her reminder put his thoughts back on track. He had responsibilities. He must teach Jayne how to shoot so he could get to his pa. He gulped the rest of his food. "Thank you for the coffee and delicious rolls. 'Preciate them. Now, if you'll excuse me, I need to teach Jayne how to shoot a gun."

"My goodness. You've taken on quite a job from what Mercy says." Cookie turned to Jayne. "No offense but she says you're not the best shot she's ever seen."

Jayne made a protesting noise. "I'm learning."

Seth hobbled to the door. The warmth of Cookie's welcome and the homey atmosphere reminded him of a time when he belonged in a happy family. A time that had come crashing to an end all because Frank cared more about a little fun with Sarah than he did about his own safety. Or Sarah's. It had left Seth with regrets and guilt that chewed at his insides at the most inopportune times. It had also left him with the task of keeping Ma and Pa safe. He'd failed on Ma's behalf but he wouldn't fail his pa. He must get back to Corncrib and make sure Pa was safe.

Jayne jumped to her feet to follow Seth. He

seemed in an awful hurry. Guess he was anxious to see her learn to shoot so he could leave. "Thank you, Cookie."

"Come again. Anytime."

Outside, she saw Seth at the corral fence beside the barn. Grady talked to him and waved his arms in animated conversation.

Seth nodded and Grady turned toward the barn. He called, "Kitty, kitty."

Within seconds, four cats raced out and tangled around Seth's legs.

Grady picked up one of Smokey's littermates and said something to Seth.

Seth nodded, backed up to the fence, rested his crutch at his side and took the kitten Grady offered. When he glanced up and saw her standing there, he smiled.

She caught up her skirts and trotted across the yard to his side. When she reached out a hand to stroke the purring cat he held, their hands brushed and warmth jolted up her arms, zapped through her heart. What was there about this man that made her forget her hard-learned lessons? Made her aware of emotions she'd never before experienced?

His hand grew still. Distractedly, she realized hers had, too.

Grady offered her a cat. "This is Smokey's sister, Sandy."

She gratefully took the cat, glad of something to divert her foolish thoughts. "Sandy? But she's gray."

"She likes to dig in the dirt. Billy said we couldn't call her Dirt so we decided on Sandy."

"I see." She glanced at Seth, saw a reflection of shared humor. As her heart clattered against her ribs, she ducked her head. Something about his strong hands softly cradling a half-grown cat threatened the barriers in her heart.

Grady patted the cat in Seth's arms. "Her name is Mouse."

"Mouse?" Jayne laughed. "Odd name for a cat, don't you think?"

Seth chuckled. "I expect they had a good reason for their choice."

"When she gets a mouse she won't let anyone near her," Grady said.

Billy came toward them. "You coming to play, Grady?"

Grady called a hasty "Goodbye" and ran to join his friend.

As Jayne and Seth studied each other her heart ticked an uncertain beat. He had strong hands. A gentle heart. He was a man worthy of trust.

He lowered the cat to the ground and slowly brought his gaze to her. But after a second it shifted past her. He scrubbed at the back of his neck, tilting his hat so it concealed his eyes.

Had he done it on purpose? Had the moment burgeoned with possibility for him as well as her? What was she thinking? There was no place for possibilities between them. She clung to the cat in her arms. Thankfully, it didn't appear to mind her tight grasp.

"Are you ready for another lesson?" he asked.

It took two seconds to realize he meant shooting lessons. If she needed anything to pull her back to rational thinking, this was it. His only interest in her was teaching her to shoot correctly so he could leave. After all, he had a father that needed and deserved his attention.

"I need to get my gun."

"I'll go with you." Side by side they climbed the hill.

She purposely slowed her steps so he didn't have to hurry on his crutch. Back at the house, she rushed to her room and got the bag containing her gun and joined him outdoors. They returned to the clearing where they'd been the day before.

"I think you need to practice shooting without bullets until you can keep your eyes open." He sat on a nearby log as she assumed her stance. "Walk me through each step so I know you remember."

She did. He obviously didn't plan to steady her arm or offer any assistance today. Fine. She needed to do this on her own.

"Now aim and fire."

She did, determined to keep her eyes open. It shouldn't be difficult. After all, there was no bullet in the gun.

She squeezed the trigger. It clicked into place.

And even though there was no explosion, she blinked.

He sighed. "You need to keep your eyes open."

"I know." And not just to shoot a gun. She needed to keep them open to the dangers of a man like Seth. A strong, protective man who tempted her to abandon her quest for independence. A gentle man who made her long for the kind of protection he would provide.

Yes, she had to keep her eyes wide open in that regard. She did not want or need protection. Besides, he had no intention of staying around to provide it.

Determination firmly in place, she lifted the gun and repeated the procedure.

She would keep her eyes open.

Widening her eyes in preparation, she

pulled the trigger. *Click.* "Did I do it?"

He sighed. "Almost."

CHAPTER EIGHT

Jayne glanced at the position of the sun. It was growing late and they'd need to return to the ranch.

She'd practiced shooting a number of times but failed to keep her eyes open a single time. Oh, she'd tried. She'd widened her eyes until they felt like they might pop from her head. When that didn't work, she'd narrowed them to slits. She'd even tried closing one and then the other.

"I give up." Jayne let out a long sigh, letting her arm fall to her side, the gun still clamped in her hand.

"Really?" Did he have to sound so relieved? Though it surely wasn't his intention, his tone merely served to renew her resolve.

"No. I won't give up."

"Kind of figured that." His resignation scratched along her nerves.

"You don't have to feel obligated to teach

me." No doubt, he was getting annoyed at her failure.

"I never accept defeat."

She snorted. "I guess there is always a first time." She stowed her gun away. "It's dinnertime. We should get back to the house."

He picked up his crutch and stood. But he didn't move.

She grew aware of his waiting and glanced in his direction.

He smiled. The lift of the corners of his mouth had the power to lift her heart. "Jayne, you can do it. I believe it's important for you to do this. So I will continue to help you until we're both satisfied."

She lowered her gaze in order to keep her thoughts clear. "Why does it matter to you, anyway?" Against her will, she stole a look at him to see his reaction.

He shrugged. "Maybe because I don't like to see people fail."

No longer concerned about her silly reaction, she wondered at the meaning behind his words and looked straight into his face. She studied him a full thirty seconds. Watched a chain of emotions flash through his eyes. Determination, kindness, concern and something so deep and heart-filled it made her lose her breath.

He brushed his knuckles across her jaw.

"This is a wild, untamed land. You should know how to defend yourself should the occasion arise." Then, as if realizing what he'd done, he shifted away and started toward the ranch.

His touch had sucked the air from her lungs. Left her struggling to think straight.

She realized he'd moved on and hurried to catch up. As they returned to the ranch, Jayne had little to say.

She said little all throughout the meal, as well, content to listen to the others. Her thoughts went round and round. She had only one thing in mind in her dealings with Seth — learn to use a gun. And yet . . .

And yet. Those two words encapsulated her problem. Despite her resolve, despite understanding Seth only cared because of his sense of responsibility, despite everything, there was something about him that left her confused and dizzy.

She joined the others in cleaning the kitchen after the meal. Whatever she said to add to the flow of conversation must have made sense because no one commented.

"I'll show you how to do that pattern," Sybil said to Linette when the dishes were done. She was showing Linette how to knit a sweater for the expected baby.

"What can Mercy and I do to help?" Jayne

154

needed something to keep her hands and her mind busy.

"Yes, what can we do?" Mercy gave her a look ripe with curiosity.

It wasn't like they didn't help out around the place. But Mercy must have wondered at Jayne's haste to get a job.

Linette suggested they could wash the windows and Jayne hastened to start the task, though there wasn't any need for her sense of urgency.

Not until Seth hobbled down the hall and out the front door did her actions slow to normal. Hopefully he would find Eddie or Roper or one of the other cowboys and amuse himself the rest of the afternoon. Jayne did not want another shooting lesson today.

As soon as the last window was done and the rags they'd used were hung to dry, Jayne grabbed Mercy's arm and hustled her out the door.

"Where are we going?" Mercy asked.

"Walking. Exploring." She didn't care where they went or what they did so long as it wasn't with Seth. All morning she had struggled to remember she didn't need or want anyone to take care of her.

"Okay." Mercy trotted along at her side. "Any place in particular?"

"Just out." She tucked her arm through Mercy's. "What have you been doing with yourself?"

"Would you believe Cookie has been teaching me how to make cinnamon rolls?"

"Really? Maybe I should come along and learn, too. Are they difficult?"

"Not with Cookie supervising. But aren't you pretty busy with Seth?"

"He'll be on his way soon." The reminder brought her thoughts back to their proper place. They both had plans and goals that did not include each other.

He'd leave to take care of his pa and she'd be in a position to take care of herself. Shouldn't the idea make her feel better?

"How are your shooting lessons coming?" Mercy asked as they walked.

Jayne admitted she struggled to keep her eyes open and Mercy laughed.

The two of them spent a pleasant two hours wandering along the road that led to Edendale then returned in time to help Linette with the evening meal.

And Jayne succeeded in paying no more attention to Seth than she would to any visiting cowboy.

The next day was Sunday. Sybil came to Jayne's room as she prepared for church, and sat down on the edge of the bed.

Sybil had already put on her golden dress and brushed her hair into a tidy roll about her head.

Jayne eyed her up and down. "You look ready to walk into the finest church in London."

"I'm ready to go to church here." Without hesitation she added, "You're spending a lot of time with Seth, aren't you?"

"He thinks he needs to teach me to shoot properly so I don't hurt another unsuspecting cowboy."

"It's more than that, I think." Sybil took the hairbrush from Jayne and indicated she should sit on the stool.

Sybil began to brush Jayne's hair.

"That feels good." Jayne welcomed a chance to change the direction of conversation Sybil had started.

"We did this for each other every day on the boat trip. I miss it."

Jayne closed her eyes and let the brushing soothe her. "I miss it, too."

"I don't want to see you hurt."

"Is it that badly tangled?" She knew that wasn't what Sybil meant. Had she seen how Jayne reacted to Seth even when she vowed she wouldn't notice his presence? But Sybil didn't need to worry. Jayne understood the boundaries of her time with Seth. He would teach her to shoot then move on. And she would stand tall, strong and confident in her ability to take care of herself.

Why just this morning at breakfast, hadn't she sat at his side, cool and detached, her determination to remember that Seth was only a temporary visitor firmly in place? But when their arms brushed as they reached for something, she had almost jumped off her chair.

Maybe the church service would arm her with strength.

Sybil stopped brushing and scooted around to look straight into Jayne's eyes. "He's just a cowboy. He isn't the sort of man you need." She pressed her palms to Jayne's shoulders to stop her protest. "He won't give you what you want."

"How do you know what I want?"

"You're a city girl. You couldn't fit into a cowboy's way of life." Sybil resumed brushing Jayne's hair as if the matter was settled.

Sybil was right. She'd never be the strong adventurous type who welcomed the challenge of ranch life. Or whatever a cowboy like Seth did. The connection she imagined between them was simply that — imagination. And, she realized with blinding clarity, the hungry cry of a needy heart. She would not be needy any longer. Strength and resolve returned. Jayne Gardiner meant to be independent, self-sufficient, armed and ready to face any and every challenge life tossed in her path.

Seth had done his best to stay as far away from Jayne as possible yesterday. He'd sat and watched her struggle to handle the gun when every instinct told him to give her a hand.

But he'd found giving her a hand brought out a whole bunch of feelings he wasn't prepared to deal with. Besides, she didn't need or want his protection.

He must remember that in a few more days he would be on his way to his pa. Jayne would then be on her own — exactly what she wanted. Surely he would be able to avoid her easily enough today, it being Sunday.

Eddie had informed him they held church services in the cookhouse and invited him to attend. It would be rude to refuse. Not that he didn't want to go. But he suspected it would be hard to ignore Jayne for the entire service.

Seth waited until the others left to descend the stairs and follow. Unfortunately it gave him plenty of opportunity to study those ahead of him.

Linette clung to Eddie's arm as Grady raced ahead. Jayne, Mercy and Sybil walked arm in arm. The trio was such good friends.

Mercy's hair had been tamed to a coil at the back of her neck and further subdued by her bonnet. She wore a muted green dress. Sybil, her hair tidy, wore a gray bonnet. She was like a flash of evening sun in her dark gold dress. They walked on either side of Jayne.

Jayne. He could no longer keep his gaze off her.

Like the others, she'd pulled her hair into a demure coil at the back of her head and wore a navy bonnet. A faint rustling sound reached him as her navy skirt swung with every step. A blue-striped shirtwaist completed her outfit.

Her full-throated laugh rang out as Mercy said something.

He slowed his steps and leaned heavily on his crutch. He'd considered not using it anymore but Linette had checked his wound and suggested one more day. Just to be on the safe side.

The others reached the cookhouse and stepped inside except for Jayne. She dropped her friends' arms and waited for Seth.

So much for keeping his distance from her

160

but he couldn't find a hint of disappointment in his thoughts.

"You'll want to meet the others," she said as he reached her side.

He told himself that was a good enough reason to accompany her despite his decision to confine their time together to the shooting lessons. They stepped in.

The benches had been arranged to face the table. Cookie sat behind it with a smaller man at her side. "Come in, come in," she called.

Seth and Jayne moved toward Cookie.

"Seth, this is Bertie, Cookie's husband."

Bertie held out a hand and they shook. Seth liked the friendly welcome in the man's face.

Jayne led him toward a young couple. "This is Ward and Grace Walker and little Belle." The woman had flaming-red hair. The little girl bounced on the bench with what he could only interpret as a zest for life. Ward beamed as if so proud of his wife and child he could hardly restrain himself from pointing out their virtues.

He must love them a lot.

Seth envied the man, though he didn't want the responsibility of love for himself.

Next he met Cassie and Roper and the other children. Then three cowboys. Eddie had said there were a dozen cowboys about but most of them were with the cattle. He met Cal, who kept glancing at Mercy, and Slim, a tall, quiet man. He'd already met Buster.

Introductions over, Jayne and Seth sat down side by side, in the only available place. Their elbows brushed, flooding his brain with sweetness. He told himself he had enough responsibilities and didn't want any more. Even if he somehow convinced himself he'd like to add Jayne to that list, could he even succeed? Or would he fail to protect her? He couldn't live with failure of that magnitude.

Thankfully, Cookie stood before his thoughts rambled further astray. She led them in singing three hymns. It was a rowdy choir but full of enthusiasm. Beside him, Jayne's voice was clear and sweet. He mumbled the words of the song in a sort of daze as the spot where her arm touched his grew warmer.

Then Bertie stood up to speak. "I want to warn the ladies from England that I ain't a preacher. No siree. But I know my God. I've known Him for more years than I care to tell. And there's one thing I'm certain of. He is as good as His word and you couldn't ask for more. He says in Matthew six, verse twenty six, that He watches the fowls of the air and not one of them falls to the ground without His notice. Imagine, He watches the little sparrows. I guess one of us is worth a whole lot more than a sparrow. Why they ain't even good for a pie."

Everyone chuckled.

"But His eye is on the sparrow so I know it's on me for my good. It's on every one of you, too, for your good."

When the short service ended, Seth didn't immediately move. Bertie's words filled his heart. God watched over sparrows? So why did some fall to the ground and die? He couldn't believe as simply as Bertie did.

People shifted about and Cookie served tea, coffee and cinnamon rolls. And the whole crew sat around and visited.

Cal edged closer to Seth. "Heard you got shot." His gaze slid toward Jayne and he grinned.

Seth kept his expression bland but bristled inside. "It was an accident." His soft words gave away nothing. The man would never know that Seth resented the way the cowboy wanted to make an issue of it.

"Sure glad I wasn't in the line of fire." Cal laughed.

Beside Seth, Jayne stiffened. Then she relaxed and chuckled. "I'm glad you

163

weren't, too. Wouldn't it be awful if I injured two cowboys? But just think of all the attention you would garner." She grinned at him.

Cal's gaze went to Mercy and lingered. When he looked at them again, he looked thoughtful. "Might be worth it. When are you going shooting again?"

Jayne laughed. "I won't be shooting anyone accidentally again. Seth is making sure that doesn't happen." She turned to him, favoring him with a smile full of gratitude that slipped into his heart like a silent intruder . . . though not an unwelcome one, he realized. His resolve seemed to have no lasting effect on his thoughts. Or his heart. And at the moment it didn't matter.

He smiled into Jayne's eyes, letting his heart speak for him, telling her he was glad to be able to help her. Glad to spend a few days with her.

Apparently Sundays included going up the hill for Sunday dinner for, at Linette's invitation, Cassie, Roper and their children, Ward, Grace and Belle joined the guests of the house in climbing the hill toward the big house.

Eddie took the men into the front room while the women and children went to the kitchen to prepare the meal.

Seth sat back in one of the easy chairs,

content to listen to the conversation among the other men and the laughter and chatting from the kitchen. But it was not to be. The men wanted to know where he'd been, what he'd seen and any news he could pass on.

The hour or two as the women worked in the kitchen passed pleasantly enough as he told about the cattle drive, the number of animals that had successfully arrived at the ranch northwest of the Eden Valley Ranch. He described the owners and every other specific he could recall until Linette announced the meal was ready.

Extra chairs crowded the table that had been extended to its full length. Seth tried to position himself for a place away from Jayne but Linette waved him to her side.

And to be honest, he truly didn't mind. He held bowls and platters for her as she served portions for herself. He snagged a dish of butter for her when she looked about for it. He asked her advice when Linette asked him to choose between raisin or pumpkin pie.

"I recommend the raisin," she said. Her smile was both sweet and teasing, filling him with sweetness.

He chose the raisin and wasn't disappointed.

After the meal ended, men, women and children helped clean up the dishes and put away the extra chairs then they again retired to the front room.

Linette settled in the green armchair before the window. Her gaze went outside and she sighed then faced the others. "Eddie says the lumber for the new church should arrive any day. I can hardly wait, though I will miss the coziness of meeting in the cookhouse."

Seth studied the gathering as the conversation circled about him. Across from him, Jayne held out her arms to little Pansy and lifted her to her lap. The child pressed her head to Jayne's shoulder and closed her eyes.

Jayne's gaze crashed into Seth's and he saw the longing and a hefty dose of hopelessness. No doubt she had dreamed of babies with Oliver. His heart twisted at her pain and loss. If they had been alone, he might have ignored his intention of not getting involved and taken her in his arms and comforted her.

Her look went on and on, delving deep into his soul, seeking something he couldn't offer her. Assurances he couldn't give. Promises he couldn't keep. Not that he wasn't tempted to give it a try.

Pansy shifted and drew Jayne's attention away.

Seth glanced at the other children playing quietly with Grady's toys. His eyes lit on Cassie. Four children was a lot of responsibility. They could get hurt, sick, have an accident, so many things. That had to be a heavy weight for Roper, too.

As if the cowboy read his mind, he took a seat next to Seth and began to talk.

"I could never have guessed how much joy the children would bring to our lives. Bertie's talk about God watching over the sparrows really encouraged me, reminding me, as it did, that these children aren't solely my responsibility. They are, above all, God's children. He saw fit to bring them into my life and Cassie's. Then He saw fit to enable us to keep them. For sure, I can trust God with the rest. Their future, their health, their happiness." The man let out a satisfied sigh.

His words startled Seth. Was it possible to accept responsibilities and expect God to take care of them?

CHAPTER NINE

The next morning, Jayne and Seth left the house in the direction of the clearing for another lesson. The sun was warm in a cloudless sky. A breeze promised modest relief from the heat that would build throughout the day.

Seth walked without a crutch, limping slightly.

"How is your leg?" she asked.

"It's okay. No lasting damage."

"I'm relieved to know it." She watched him from the corner of her eye. Yesterday he had seemed a little distant, as if he regretted his offer to stay long enough to teach her to shoot well. If that was the case, she needed to make sure the lessons were satisfactorily concluded as soon as possible.

"I am determined to keep my eyes open today."

He chuckled. "Weren't you determined the other days?"

"Yes, but this time I am really determined." They reached the clearing and she took out her pistol, got into position and spoke his instructions aloud so he would know she remembered and followed them. She set her sights on the target, gritted her teeth — *eyes open, eyes open* — and squeezed the trigger. *Click.* The gun wasn't loaded so there was no explosion to startle her.

She stared at the target. She'd seen it the whole time.

Lowering the gun, she turned to Seth. "I did it. I did it." She jumped up and down and ran to his side to grab his arm and shake it. "I kept my eyes open."

He covered her hand with his, anchoring her to the spot. What was there about him that reached out to her, making her want to stay connected to him?

She withdrew her hand and backed away. "Isn't it time for a real bullet?"

"I don't think you should rush. Let's see if you can keep your eyes open more than once."

She tipped her head and studied him. "I thought you would be anxious to be on your way now that your leg is ready."

His gaze watchful, guarded even, his mouth flat, he revealed nothing. He nodded. "Not so anxious to leave before you can shoot a gun with reasonable accuracy and with your eyes open." His eyes narrowed. "I do not want to live wondering if I'm in any way responsible for someone being injured or dead."

She hurried back to the place where she must stand. So it was for his conscience. For unknown people. Didn't he care at all to stay for her sake, because he was concerned about her, or even because he might be enjoying her company a tiny bit?

She jerked the gun into position, and eyed the sights. She gripped it tight and focused and then —

Something brushed her skirts. Her heart crashed against her ribs and she screamed and bolted to the side.

"Smokey." The cat plopped down where Jayne had been standing and started to groom herself.

Seth scooped the cat into his arms. "What are you doing here?"

Jayne pressed a hand to her chest and willed her heartbeat back to a normal pace. "She about scared me to death."

Seth chuckled. "You did jump rather high."

Her breath whooshed out. "Good thing I didn't have the gun loaded or I might have shot her." Seeing the shock on Seth's face, she hurriedly added, "Not on purpose."

"How many accidents are you planning?" The way he cocked his head and studied her without revealing his thoughts left her floundering, especially as he petted the cat and received grateful purrs.

"I hardly think you plan accidents." Her fright continued to make her edgy.

He looked out into the distance as if considering her words. "A lot of accidents could be avoided if people planned not to have them."

The sorrow in his words made her think he wasn't talking about her. "You're referring to the death of your friends." He'd said so little about something that had such an obvious impact on him. She wanted to learn more. "Were they shot?" She shuddered.

"No." His answer was abrupt.

She waited, giving him plenty of opportunity to say more. When he didn't, she pretended she wasn't disappointed and returned to her place before the target.

One by one, deliberate enough to satisfy the most critical teacher, she went through the steps and — *click* — kept her eyes open.

But when she turned for his approval he still stared into the distance, his hand mindlessly stroking the cat.

Smokey was satisfied with his distracted attention.

Jayne wasn't. Yet she couldn't demand more. She didn't have the right. But her heart went out to him. He looked lost.

Smokey jumped down, jerking Seth back from wherever he had gone. He sighed and when he turned toward her, he blinked as he saw she was watching him.

Had he forgotten her presence? Was she that unimportant? She squared her shoulders. Perhaps she needed this reminder that she must depend on no one.

"Let's see if you can keep your eyes open again." His smile, likely meant to be encouraging, seemed rather forced.

But she turned and went through the steps again, keeping her eyes open at the click.

"Good."

She told herself she wasn't disappointed at his lack of enthusiasm. Why would she be? But she failed to convince herself. And it made her angry. She was doing this so she could be independent and unafraid. She had no intention of substituting one weakness and dependency for another.

"I'll do it again." And again and again, until she was the best, most confident shot in the whole of western Canada. She lined up the sights and squeezed the trigger. This time she didn't even flinch at the sound.

Without waiting for him to tell her to do it again, she did it over and over, six more times then faced him.

The grin he wore erased all her annoyance. "I think you're ready."

"I'm more than ready." She let him load the shell and as she lifted the gun, she almost did it without giving in to a little quiver of fear.

He stepped close behind her. "This time counts. I'll make sure the bullet doesn't go astray." He cupped his hand over hers on the gun and steadied it.

Heavens but it was tempting to lean back and feel the strength of his chest, the comfort of his arms.

Instead she stiffened and squinted down the sights. *Eyes open. Eyes open.* She widened her eyes and squeezed.

Crack!

She shuddered at the sound but she kept her eyes open.

He patted her shoulder. "You did it."

Her hands shook clear to her shoulders. Her breath came in sharp gasps. "I need to sit down."

He'd left Smokey sunning by a log and she collapsed near the cat and stroked it, finding comfort in the motion and in the gentle rumble in the cat's chest. "I hate guns," she muttered.

"Is it really necessary to learn to shoot?"

"We've had this discussion already and yes, it is. My fear will not control me. I don't know if I'll ever hear a gunshot up close and not have my mind fill with pictures of Oliver's death." She shuddered again. "Death is not pretty."

"No, it's not."

She realized she clung to his hand or did he cling to hers? It didn't matter who had reached first. Nor did it matter that she meant to be strong. At the moment she was a quivering mass of nerves.

"Jayne." His voice was soft. "You might learn to shoot just fine but that doesn't mean you'd ever be able to use the gun against a living soul."

Misery wrapped about her like a wet blanket. "I know it won't be easy." She sat up straight and gave him a look full of despair and determination. "But I will if I have to. It's got to be easier than standing idly by while someone you care about is gunned down."

Her misery was reflected in his eyes. "I hope you never have to face such a situation."

"Me, too." She thought about the sermon

Bertie had given. "The Bible says God watches the sparrows. If God watches us for our good why do bad things happen? I don't understand."

"What's to understand? It isn't like God said he prevents the sparrow from falling. Only that He takes note."

"That makes it sound like God stands back and observes without any concern for what happens. I can't believe that."

"Why not? Like you said, bad things happen."

"But —" She struggled to think of an argument. "He has promised to never leave us or forsake us. I don't think I could survive without the sure knowledge that God will help me."

He studied her. "You have firsthand experience with this aspect of God?"

"After I watched Oliver die I thought I didn't deserve to live. I was nothing but a useless, foolish woman." She raised her eyebrows. "Just as you said."

"I wasn't referring to something like that. I only meant if you were insistent on doing something without being properly prepared you put yourself and others at risk and that would be foolish."

She drew in a deep, sustaining breath and

released it slowly, willing tension to leave with it.

He dropped a hand to her shoulder. "Jayne, I think you are very brave to learn to shoot a gun when it brings back such dreadful memories. It doesn't hurt to be prepared."

She nodded, clinging to him with her gaze.

He didn't shift away, didn't blink. He simply met her look for look.

The moments ticked by as she floundered in fear and uncertainty.

He continued to offer silent support and encouragement.

She swam in the depths of his gaze until she found solid ground. Out of sheer gratitude and relief, she touched his cheek. "Thank you." His skin was warm, rough with the day's whiskers.

He smiled beneath her hand. "You're welcome."

She should move away but she liked the feel of his cheek . . . how it crinkled with his smile.

He reached up and caught her hand, held it to his face for a heartbeat then drew it down and curled his fingers around hers. "Jayne." His voice was a hoarse whisper. "I will never forget you."

She lost herself in his eyes, so full of power

and strength and purpose.

Purpose. The word seemed to ground her, to bring her back to reality. Her purpose was to be independent. His was to teach her to shoot and then move on.

She touched his injured leg. "I expect you'll remember me every time you look at the scar your leg will have."

He blinked. His eyes went from forest green to hazel, all full of golden flecks, and he burst out laughing. "I'll always have that, won't I?"

They grinned at each other. The tension-filled moment had ended and they had settled back into a relaxed friendliness.

"Do you want to try another bullet today?"

"Not really, but I will."

He again came along to steady her arm. "I don't want to take any chances that you'll close your eyes and have the shot go amiss."

She gave an exaggerated shudder. "Nor do I." Nor could she object to his steadying arm about her.

Because it was only temporary and she could allow herself a few hours, or even days, of something that would soon be gone.

Seth had been up and down a wide range of emotions. Her question about how Frank and Sarah died punched him in the middle of his chest with the force of a hammer blow. He never talked about them. His folks had never talked about them. No friends had ever asked about them. Yet he felt he could tell Jayne and she would understand the pain, the shock, the helplessness, the anger and finally the determination to make sure something like that never happened again. She'd been through a similar experience. He almost opened the door to his memories and told her how they had died.

But once open, would he ever be able to close the doors again? And if he couldn't, would the memories and regrets and pain consume him?

It wasn't worth the risk.

Then she'd wondered if God cared about sparrows. What she really asked was did God care about people even when bad things happen? It wasn't a question he could answer.

He had reluctantly released her to shoot again at the target when he would have preferred to hold her close and tell her to forget about the gun. Guns were dangerous.

She fired one more shot. She kept her eyes open but the bullet splintered a stump to the right. Her shoulders sank. "That's enough for today. Who knew learning to shoot could be so exhausting."

Likely it was the memories and emotions that the sound of a gunshot brought to mind that left her shaking.

He took the gun from her hand and wiped it clean then dropped it into her bag. He draped an arm about her shoulders, felt her quivering and pulled her close. For a heartbeat, he considered pulling her into his arms and crushing her to his heart. He'd hold her fears at bay. But she didn't want that. She wanted to prove she didn't need anyone.

And he had other plans, as well. A pa to take care of. A heart to guard against risk.

They returned to the house and joined the others for dinner.

As they ate, Linette announced, "There are peas ready to pick."

"I'll help," Jayne said. Mercy and Sybil echoed her offer.

"Thank you. I warn you, it will take all afternoon."

"That's fine." The three girls nodded. "We don't mind."

No one suggested Seth should help. He got the feeling the garden was the women's domain so he didn't offer. Which left him the entire afternoon to amuse himself. He would check on his horse. Maybe exercise him.

As the meal ended and people dispersed, he headed down the hill to the barn. His saddle was in the tack room and he went to inspect it. Buster had done a good job of cleaning it.

A bunch of leather hung on the wall ready to be used to repair harnesses and saddles. Pa had been a leather worker, a tanner, saddle maker and repairer so Seth examined the leather with a knowledgeable eye. And he had an idea. If Eddie approved, he would make Buster a real belt.

As he selected the leather he would choose for the project, the voices of children reached him.

"Billy, that knife is sharp. Put it down."

Seth guessed Billy's older brother, Neil, was the speaker.

"I'm just looking."

"You're also touching and that's not safe."

"Aww, I won't hurt myself."

"Billy, put it back." Neil's voice was firm.

"I'm being careful."

Seth's scalp prickled. Seems Billy was set on getting into trouble. Trouble with a sharp knife could be disastrous. Seth headed for the tack room door, ready to intervene and prevent an accident.

"No, Billy. You could get hurt. Put it back."

Seth heard something thunk and he paused before he reentered the barn, out of sight.

Neil spoke again. "That's better."

"Why's it matter to you, anyways?" Billy groused.

"Because you're my brother. Remember how our mama made us promise to be responsible for each other?"

"Before she died?" The resentment level in Billy's voice lowered.

"Yes."

"That was when we come looking for Pa, right?"

"That's right."

"He was already dead, too, huh?" Billy sounded confused about the events.

" 'Fraid so. Good thing our new pa found us."

"Neil, what does 'sponsible mean?"

The boys scuffed along the barn floor as they moved about.

"It means we watch out for each other. I make sure you're safe. You watch out for me and make sure I'm safe. We do the same for Pansy and Daisy."

" 'Specially Pansy 'cause she's still little."

"That's right. Now let's take water to the

chickens like Ma said."

They trotted from the barn. Buckets banged the side of the water trough and water sloshed. Then their voices faded into the distance.

Seth stepped into the barn and picked up the knife Billy had wanted to examine. He stuck it in the slot of wood where it belonged and where it would be safe from little fingers.

He and Frank had watched out for each other. Many a time, Frank had pulled him back from falling through the hole in the loft of the barn, or helped him get down from a tree that he'd climbed too high. And although younger, he'd helped Frank, too. One time he'd helped him hold a colt Frank had roped and found too much to hold. Then there was the time Frank got into a fist fight with several town boys. He was outnumbered but when Seth stepped in, they'd been able to defend themselves and chase away the tormentors. He could think of many other times he and Frank had helped each other.

But you couldn't take care of someone set on doing something foolhardy.

He walked the length of the barn, glanced out the back door then wheeled around and returned to the front. He stared at the busy ranch scene. A cowboy he didn't recognize rode past the far pens. Women's voices reached him from the garden.

He had to find something to do or he would drown in memories.

Eddie stepped into view toward Roper's house and Seth trotted in that direction.

"I find myself at loose ends this afternoon and idleness bores me. Could you give me a job?"

Eddie stopped and rubbed his chin. "You good with hammer and nails?"

"Good enough, I think."

"Fine. A bull damaged the wall of the oat bin." He indicated a building near the barn. "You'll find supplies in the barn if you care to fix it."

"I sure would." He trotted back to the barn, limping on his sore leg. He fetched hammer and nails then went to the bin. Someone had placed new pieces of wood nearby so he was set.

Pounding nails to fix the damaged wall did little to make him forget how foolhardy Frank had been. Reckless. Irresponsible. *Bang, bang, bang.* Every hammer blow echoed in his head.

He fixed one side and moved around the corner. His position gave him a view of the garden and the women bent over plucking peas from the vines. The sun shone hot and furious, something he hadn't noticed until he saw Jayne and her friends out in the open with nothing but broad-brimmed hats for protection. The blue sky held only one frothy cloud in the distance. A reluctant breeze barely stirred the grass. They must be sweltering in the sun.

Shouldn't he warn them not to get overheated?

Jayne's laughter drifted to him. Seems she wasn't bothered by the heat. Or did she think she was impervious? Perhaps she gave no thought to consequences.

Was she foolhardy? Or strong and brave? Could she be both?

He grabbed a nail and drove it in with one vicious blow.

It didn't matter who or what Jayne was, only that he did what he could to prevent any more accidents. Then he would be on his way.

CHAPTER TEN

"Are you ready for another shooting lesson?" Seth asked Jayne the next morning.

She resisted an urge to rub the pain in her neck and swallowed back a moan. Who knew picking peas was backbreaking work? Or that the sun could be so demanding? "Linette needs help shelling peas. We're all going down to the cookhouse to help."

"Well, have fun."

Did he sound disappointed? Because she would be busy all morning or because it delayed him leaving? "I might be free later." She had no idea how long the job would take.

"I'll maybe see you then." With a touch to the brim of his hat, he left the house and went down the hill. What did he plan to do for the day?

"Are you ready?" Linette asked her, laden with several large bowls.

Jayne, along with Mercy and Sybil, joined

her in the trek down the hill. They gathered in the shade of the cookhouse where Cassie already awaited, along with Grace, who had come to the ranch with Ward and their daughter. As they approached, Cookie came outside, bringing with her the scent of cinnamon and yeast.

They set out blankets, but since Cookie claimed she'd never get up if she sat on the ground, Cassie brought out a chair.

Daisy supervised the children playing. Their laughter filled the air like music.

Linette showed the English girls how to snap the pea pod open, scrape the tender green peas into a bowl then toss the pod into a bucket. Jayne settled into a routine at the mindless task and listened as Cassie asked Grace how she liked living in the west. It was pleasant to sit here and forget everything. Except one thought intruded. What lay ahead for her?

She didn't know but wasn't about to let the thought mar a perfect morning.

"Will your cowboy be leaving soon?" Cookie asked Jayne.

Jayne pretended she had to think who Cookie meant. "Seth? I expect so."

Mercy snorted. "Could have fooled me." She batted her eyes and tipped her head, doing her best to look coy.

186

Jayne waved a hand in a way she hoped said Mercy's opinion was of no matter. "Don't pay attention to her. She's prone to be dramatic." She'd never let any of them know there was something about Seth that tugged at her heart and occupied her thoughts in a way that confused her.

Mercy grinned. "I'm not making it up."

"Leave her be," Sybil said gently. "She only wants to learn to shoot a gun." She shivered. "Though I still think it's a bad idea."

Grace studied her fingers curled in her lap. "There was a time I wished I had a gun. A big gun. And had the nerve to use it."

Jayne had heard how Ward had rescued Grace from a man who made her dance in a saloon by holding little Belle captive.

Cassie squeezed Grace's hands. "Thankfully, God sent Ward along to help you."

"If God watches us for our good why do bad things happen?" The words came from Jayne's mouth before she could think to stop them. At the way each of the other women grew serious, Jayne almost wished she hadn't asked the question but she ached to know, to understand.

Cookie planted her feet more firmly on the ground and shifted so she faced Jayne. "Maybe we only see the dark side. The pain, the sorrow, the loss. But we would never see a rainbow without the rain."

Sybil's hands twisted into a knot as she considered Cookie's words. "Is the rainbow worth it?"

"I would go through what I did again if it was what brought me and Ward together." Grace's face flooded with joy and serenity.

Jayne stared at her. Would she ever look back at what happened to Oliver and say something so wonderful had happened because of it that she thought it was worthwhile?

Grace spoke again. "But I would avoid it altogether if I could and still meet Ward."

The women murmured agreement. All of them had endured their share of loss and pain except perhaps Mercy. She never confessed to anything but joy and excitement.

"Maybe," Mercy said, "it takes something tragic to push some people off their comfortable log into the adventure that lies ahead of them."

Sybil chuckled. "Like Jayne learning to shoot. What an adventure she started. Poor Seth, though. He didn't ask to be part of your adventure."

The others laughed. Several of them commented that the challenges of their lives had indeed led them to go places, or to try things they wouldn't have without the impetus.

"Look at you," Mercy said to Jayne. "Not only are you learning to shoot a gun but you would have never left cozy old England if you'd married Oliver." She squeezed both Jayne's and Sybil's hands. "And we all get to share your adventure. I, for one, am grateful for the opportunity."

Jayne couldn't argue with Mercy's rationale. Oliver's death had pushed her to explore new horizons. She'd never be grateful for it but she had to move forward and this was a good place to do it. She looked about the ranch but didn't see Seth. She would forever be thankful that he played a part in helping her achieve her goals.

She meant the thought to be reassuring. It wasn't. Instead, it quivered restlessly in the pit of her stomach. She popped some fresh green peas into her mouth to still the sensation. "Mmm, good."

The others also ate a few and nodded agreement.

The conversation shifted to other things until Cookie lumbered to her feet. "Time to cook up some grub for hungry cowboys."

"You'll eat with us," Cassie said to Grace and they scrambled up to prepare food for their hungry men and children.

Linette checked around the circle. "The peas are done. Thank you all. Many hands make light work."

Jayne and her friends climbed the hill with Linette and helped her prepare a quick dinner for everyone who ate at the house.

When it was time to eat, Grady entered at Eddie's side.

But where was Seth?

She caught her breath and waited.

He entered the back door and her breath eased out. She couldn't take her eyes from him.

He'd rolled his sleeves up to his elbows, exposing strong forearms. He took his hat off and hung it on one of the many hooks.

He turned, and their eyes met. She felt a strange tightening in her throat as he smiled.

Slowly, his gaze lingering, he shifted, and turned to wash.

She jerked back to helping Linette.

Mercy nudged her. "I see you don't even have to bat your eyes."

Jayne made a protesting sound and took the bowl of fresh peas to the table.

Throughout the meal, she forced herself to think about the food. The peas and potatoes tasted better than anything she'd ever had before.

But all the while, her nerves vibrated at Seth's nearness and the hope of him asking her to go to the clearing.

"Are you helping Linette this afternoon?" he asked, sending a frisson of excitement through her.

"I don't need everyone," Linette said. "Sybil wants to help me. That's all I need."

"Then I guess I'm free for more shooting lessons." Jayne emphasized *shooting* just enough to inform Mercy it was the reason for the two of them spending the afternoon together.

A little later, Seth and Jayne returned to the clearing.

She prepared her gun. "I believe I'm ready for real ammunition today."

"Try it once without and convince me you haven't forgotten anything." He grinned, teasing lights flashing from his eyes. "Like keeping your eyes open."

She wrinkled her nose at him.

He stood with his hands on his hips and his legs wide as if preparing for a long afternoon of fun.

Her cheeks grew warm. He only wanted to see her succeed in this so he could leave, she reminded herself. She had pinned her own silly desires on the poor unsuspecting man. She jerked her attention back to the reason for being there, lined up the target through her sights and squeezed the trigger. *Click.* Her eyes had remained open. She turned and curled her fingers to indicate he should give her a bullet.

He handed her one, supervised as she slipped it into the chamber then stood very close as she took the stance he'd taught her. He steadied her hand then eased back.

She swallowed hard. She was on her own. She squeezed the trigger, squinting to keep from closing her eyes at the explosion.

She lowered the gun and studied the target. "Did I hit it?"

"Almost. You have to keep your hand steady all the while you squeeze the trigger. Grip the gun so your fingers can't move."

He dug another bullet out of his pocket but before he could hand it to her, Smokey appeared and meowed around his feet. "Go away, cat. It's not safe for you to be here."

Smokey took a step away then stopped and meowed over her shoulder.

"Go home, silly cat."

Smokey meowed louder. She returned to Seth and meowed up at him then took two steps. Again she meowed.

Jayne stared at the cat. "Is she trying to get you to follow her?"

"Nah. She's just a cat."

But Smokey continued to call at them.

"Maybe we should see what she wants." Jayne put the gun on the log and stepped toward the cat. "Where do you want us to go?"

Seth scooped up her gun, tucked it into his belt and followed them.

Smokey headed for the trees to the right, turning often to make sure they followed.

Then Jayne saw what the cat wanted and drew to a halt. She pressed her hand to her throat. "Seth," she whispered. "Look."

He was at her side. "I see it."

Under the trees lay a fawn, curled up, its wide eyes watching them.

Smokey licked the animal's face.

"Seems Smokey has made a friend."

Jayne tiptoed closer.

The fawn bleated and tried to get to its feet.

Seth grabbed her arm to stop her. "Stay back. It's frightened."

Jayne saw blood on its back leg. "It's hurt." A dreadful thought grabbed her throat. "Did I shoot it?" Her legs buckled and she would have folded to the ground except Seth held her up.

"I don't think it's a gunshot wound."

Her legs got their strength back and she

straightened. "Are you sure? How can you tell?"

"It looks more like a tear." He pulled them back to let the frightened animal relax. Smokey rubbed against the fawn and purred loudly.

Seth eyed the trees around them. "I wonder where the doe is. Let's have a look." He took her by the hand and led her into the trees. They moved as quietly as possible.

They passed through into the open. It was the same place she'd found evidence of Seth's blood and she groaned.

"There." He pointed into the shadows.

All she saw was a brown rock. Then it moved. "That's the mother deer?"

"Looks like it's injured. Wait here while I see."

But she grabbed his hand and followed. They crossed the grassy clearing. The doe didn't lift its head but its sides heaved with frightened breaths.

Bright red blood covered the animal's front quarters. More oozed from a hole high in the chest.

Horror as dark as the blackest pit choked Jayne. How could she think she could shoot a gun and not hurt someone? "Is it a gun-shot wound?"

He knelt over the animal. "No. This is the

work of a wolf or maybe a mountain lion." He straightened, his expression hard. "Go back to the clearing where your stuff is."

"Aren't you coming?"

"I'll be along straightaway."

She rocked her head back and forth. Why would he order her to leave? "I'll wait for you. I don't fancy meeting a wild animal that will claw me to bits."

"I'm sure the gunshots you fired will have scared them away. Now go. I'll be right behind you."

She stared at him, wanting to argue but something in his eyes, the brittleness of them, the darkness behind them made her obey. She lifted her skirt and headed back. She'd barely entered the trees that circled the practice area when a bang came from where she'd left Seth.

She could think of only one reason for him to shoot. The doe. He'd killed her.

Her heart pounding, she raced to the log that served as a seat and sank down. She pressed her elbows to her stomach and her chin to her fists. Puffs of air raced in and out of her lungs without providing any relief. Her head grew dizzy.

Seth stepped into the clearing and crossed to her side. He sat close and rubbed her back.

"I had to do it. She was suffering."

"You shot her."

"I'm sorry."

The pressure of his hand on her back, the little circles that he made, eased her lungs. She sucked in air.

"Was there —" She swallowed hard. "Was there a lot of blood?"

He didn't answer.

She didn't want him to. She wished she could erase all memory of blood from her mind but the pictures were as vivid as the day they came. A sob threatened to strangle her.

Seth pulled her into his arms. She grabbed his shirtfront and buried her face against his shoulder. Only one sob escaped. When his arms tightened about her, the horror faded and she felt safe.

She stayed there until her heartbeat calmed.

"The fawn!" She sat up. "We have to help it." She jumped up and raced toward where they'd left the little animal.

Seth caught up to her and grabbed her hand. "It's wild and afraid."

She pulled away. "Nevertheless, it needs help." She continued onward, tiptoeing now so as to not frighten the fawn.

Seth followed though his expression informed her he did so reluctantly.

She paused before the fawn, far enough away so it didn't lurch to its feet. "I mean you no harm. I just want to help you." She slowly narrowed the distance and squatted down.

The fawn's eyes widened and it tried to escape.

Smokey meowed a protest and rubbed against the fawn's legs.

Jayne pressed her hand to the wild animal's shoulder and held it down. "You need someone to take care of you." She needed help and sent Seth a pleading look.

"Jayne, what do you think you can do?"

"It seems pretty obvious. We'll take it back to the farm. Fix the wound and feed it."

"We? I haven't agreed." He scrubbed at the back of his neck, tipping his hat forward over his eyes.

"Why ever not? I don't understand. I thought you'd feel a responsibility to take care of this helpless little thing."

He squatted beside her. "You take on a job like this, you better think about the consequences."

"Like what?"

"He'll be frightened of the horses, the cows and the curious children. Chances are the poor thing will pine for its freedom, refuse to eat and die before your eyes."

"Nice picture you've drawn but we have to at least try."

His expression remained stubborn.

Anger exploded in her, boiling over into her words. "You're afraid of risks. Afraid you might fail. Well, I would sooner fail trying than fail to try."

"What are you going to feed it? How are you going to keep it safe from predators? You'll end up regretting this when you have to watch him die."

She gave him a look that ought to make his insides burn with shame. "I am not so foolish as to think I can guarantee he'll live but I intend to give him a chance. Are you going to help me or not?"

He studied her then sighed. His expression full of regret, he wrapped his arms under the fawn and lifted it to his chest, murmuring calming sounds when the creature struggled.

She didn't care if he helped willingly or not. She meant to help the little creature.

Smokey trotted at their heels as they retraced their steps. Jayne scooped up her bag as they passed through the clearing and walked at Seth's side.

Seth held the fawn's legs so it couldn't kick. They rushed past the house and down the hill to the barn.

"Whatcha' got?" Billy called as he saw them.

At the sound of a voice, the fawn struggled.

"I told ya," Seth mumbled to her. "Curious children."

Jayne turned aside and went to Billy. "We have an injured fawn that is very frightened. Would you make sure none of the children come to the barn until we have it settled down?"

The boy's chest expanded. "I sure can." Then he grew curious again. "Then we can see him?"

"If the fawn is feeling well enough," she replied. Seth went into the barn and she hurried after him.

He was in the far pen. He'd put the fawn in a bed of sweet hay. Smokey curled up beside the animal.

Seth knelt at the fawn's side. "Eddie has dressings in a box in the tack room. Can you bring it here?"

Tack room? She wasn't sure what he meant but she raced down the alley. A little room held saddles, harnesses and an assortment of horse items. She opened a cupboard on the wall and saw a box of bandages and a tin of something. Likely an ointment Eddie used on his horses. She scooped up the box and raced back to Seth's side.

"Hold his front legs while I look at this cut."

She folded the fawn's leg back as Seth showed her and watched his big hands gently examine the fawn's back leg.

"It doesn't look too bad." He cleaned it, applied smelly ointment from the tin then wrapped a dressing around it.

"Let him go."

She did and the fawn struggled to its feet. It ran into the corner and tried to hide but all it could do was press its nose into the boards.

Smokey followed and purred around the tiny legs. The fawn seemed to forget Seth and Jayne were there and turned its attention to the cat.

Seth leaned close to whisper in Jayne's ear. "Smokey has found a new best friend."

She nodded. Tears were too close to the surface for her to speak. They couldn't save the doe. She understood that. But somehow, being able to help the fawn made her feel as if life sometimes made sense.

"What are you going to feed it?" Seth asked.

She faced him. "Why, I have no idea. What do you suggest?"

His expression was soft as if he, too, had found some healing in helping the fawn. "I suppose we could try bottle feeding it. Or maybe it's big enough for grass and oats." He eased to his feet, slowly backed from the pen so as not to frighten the fawn. "I'll go get some and see."

She followed him and helped pull grass. He trotted to the oat bin and scooped out a handful of oats. He paused to fill a bucket with water. They returned to the pen and put the feed down. The fawn wouldn't move with them there so they backed out, closed the gate and tiptoed away then turned to watch. The fawn nosed at the grass. Ate a few mouthfuls. Ducked his nose into the water.

"Maybe he's not hungry," Jayne said.

"I think you'll have to bottle feed him."

"But —"

"It's not that hard. Though I'm not sure who would have a baby bottle."

"I'll ask Linette." She trotted up the hill and explained her need to Linette.

"I think there is a bottle in the things the Arnesons left." She'd heard the story of the family who sought shelter with Linette and Eddie as they fought a fever. They died under Linette's care. Her admiration for her sister-in-law grew as she realized how difficult it would be to watch people die.

Linette took her to a room upstairs and found a bottle complete with a nipple. She gave Jayne milk from the supply in the house and warmed it for her. Along with a warning that wild things often didn't take to being helped.

"Seth said the same but like I told him, I have to try." Calling out her thanks, she hurried back to the barn where Seth watched the fawn and cat in the stall. Smokey licked the fawn, which seemed to calm it.

"I've got an idea," she said as they entered the stall and the fawn bolted to its feet. She handed the bottle to Seth and scooped up Smokey then sat against the wall. She crossed her legs and put Smokey in her lap. "Bring the fawn."

He picked up the fawn and knelt in front of Jayne. He positioned the fawn so it sat with its head almost touching Smokey then offered the bottle.

At the first taste of milk, the fawn jerked back and fought. Seth let it struggle a moment then again stuck the nipple in its mouth. This time it swallowed a mouthful.

Smokey stretched up and rubbed her head against the fawn's head. She smelled the milk and licked the fawn's muzzle to capture the drips. The fawn calmed. After a few false starts the little thing managed to figure out how to take milk from the bottle.

Jayne beamed at Seth. "We might be able to save this little one."

His eyes were soft green and full of hope. "Maybe."

Maybe the fawn would be a source of healing for both of them. She could save something instead of standing helplessly by without taking any action. He could accept that some risks were worth taking.

Was this what the women meant when they said bad things had a place in life, bringing blessings in their wake?

"This morning I asked the women how they explained God's love when bad things happen. They all said good often came from bad. Or at least they can be used for our good."

He considered her words. "We can use bad things for our good. I like that. But is it something we do, or God does?"

Jayne contemplated his question. She liked how he pushed her to think about serious things. "I'd have to say I think it's both. God can use it but we have to cooperate."

"I like that, too." He smiled. "Like getting shot. That's a bad thing. But it's allowed me to meet you and a very smart cat." Smokey meowed.

His eyes darkened to deep green as he smiled at her.

She couldn't tear herself from his gaze. Couldn't think of a rational thing to say as her heart leapt within her chest. Something shifted inside her. A thought sang through her head, echoing what Grace had said. *I'd go through it again if it brought us together.* She realized how foolish were her thoughts. How far from reality . . . even possibility.

She jerked her eyes free and stared down at the fawn, who had stopped struggling, and drew in a deep, steadying breath. Seth was only the cowboy she'd shot. He was here only because he felt a responsibility to make sure she didn't shoot someone else. He couldn't wait to leave.

And yet he'd said he was glad to have met her. Maybe he only meant because it gave him a chance to give her shooting lessons. Seems his biggest concern was to avoid another accident.

She stared at his hands cradling a tiny fawn and feeding it milk from a bottle. No, he hadn't exactly said he was glad. Simply that his being shot had allowed him to meet her.

So what did he mean?

She stole a glimpse from under the protection of her eyelashes. His expression gave no clue. She sighed. She was simply a responsibility to him.

The fawn tossed its head. Seth released it to run to the corner and Smokey meandered over to join it.

Jayne scrambled to her feet.

She didn't want to be a responsibility. She wanted —

She didn't know what she wanted. Fresh air and sunshine would do at the moment and she rushed out of the barn and stared into the cornflower-blue sky.

Would anyone ever view her as capable? A person to be valued?

And protected? asked a little voice.

Was it possible to have both?

She didn't know and her inner turmoil left her restless.

Chapter Eleven

Seth tidied the little pen where he'd put the fawn. He hadn't had a chance to ask Eddie if he minded. If he objected, Seth would find another place for him. Now that he'd started caring for the fawn, he meant to do his best to see the animal survived.

He put away the vet supplies Jayne had brought him. Why had he said that meeting her was a good thing? The words had come to his mouth without forethought. But now that they were spoken, he had to consider them.

Was meeting her a good thing?

He tried to think how it wasn't and smiled when he couldn't come up with one reason.

Except the one he'd started with. His responsibility was to care for his pa. No doubt most people would think he could do that and pursue a friendship — or more — with Jayne.

Not that he didn't consider the possibility.

If she would let him, he would offer her protection. But she didn't want that.

Jayne was headstrong. Determined. Seeking independence.

Seth had had his share of dealing with headstrong people who left him to carry on in their wake.

He had nothing to offer her but some shooting lessons.

He left the barn and returned to the oat bin. He'd finished repairing the wall but now circled it, putting in a nail here and there, tightening the hinges on the door, looking for things to fix.

He was a fixer. A protector. He took his responsibilities more seriously than most. A long time ago he had promised himself he would not take on more unless they helped him with his current responsibilities.

He saw no reason to change that decision. Jayne was right. He was reluctant to take risks. Best he could do was make sure Jayne could handle a gun well enough to not be a threat to others and also be able to take care of herself should the need arise.

He would have avoided her the rest of the day but she assumed he would help her care for the fawn, so after supper he accompanied her back to the barn. Eddie had assured them he had no objection to the fawn in the barn.

"I asked around," Jayne said. "The consensus is he needs a good bottle feeding twice a day."

He'd pulled a carrot from the garden and broke it into pieces. "Let's see if he can eat some of this." He dropped a bite into the fawn's mouth and it chewed it. "That's good."

They fed the fawn another bottle.

Jayne practically glowed. "I believe he's going to make it. What are we going to call him?"

Seth's insides tightened. Naming the fawn only made it more painful should anything happen to it. But he couldn't quelch Jayne's joy. "How about Deer?"

When she laughed, the skin around her eyes crinkling like rays of sunshine, his insides turned to warm honey.

"You're too funny. No, we need something strong and bold."

"You mean like Thor, the god of thunder." He meant to be amusing but saw a flash in her eyes and guessed she liked the idea.

"Thor. Suits him, don't you think?"

He pretended to give the tiny critter closer study then shook his head. "I really can't picture him throwing bolts of lightning across the sky. Nope. Doesn't look like a

Thor to me."

"It's only figurative." She gave him a playful punch on the shoulder. "Gives him something to live up to."

He grabbed his shoulder and groaned. "First, you shoot me and now you beat me."

She giggled. "As if that hurt."

No, it wasn't pain he felt but the feeling that gripped his heart had the same kind of power to drive all other thoughts from his mind.

A few moments later he realized the fawn had finished eating and Jayne had scrambled to her feet.

His thoughts righted and he landed back in his sensible place.

They left the barn.

Seth wasn't eager to put an end to the evening nor did she appear to be in a hurry to return to the house. By mutual consent they wandered along the roadway between the buildings.

"It's such a lovely evening," she murmured, plucking a blade of grass. "This country is so different from England."

"How so?" He'd never been anywhere but the west.

"It's big. So sunny and bright. And the mountains. Have you seen anything like them?"

"I've seen them all my life but have to say I never tire of them."

She stared to the west where the sun leaned toward the mountain peaks, filling the valleys with sharp shadows. "Linette says she could never get tired of them, either. Have you noticed her paintings?"

"Can't say I have."

"The paintings in the living room are hers."

He had seen the stunning pictures. "I didn't realize she'd done them."

"Linette has painted many pictures but my favorite is in the library. It hangs over Eddie's mahogany desk. A winter scene with snow-covered mountains and snow-draped evergreens." Her voice had grown dreamy as if she had slipped away to another place.

He'd noticed the painting and thought it beautiful.

"It's full of strength. When I look at it I think of a Bible verse I learned as a child. 'Seek the Lord and his strength.' " She shifted her gaze from the mountains to Seth.

"If God made the mountains and holds the world in place by His power, He can surely carry me through the trials of my life even when I don't understand what's going on." She shook her head. "And I so often struggle to understand life."

Her eyes widened and she pressed her fingers to her chin. "Why, of course. It's like the mountains. Even when storm clouds obscure them they are still there. Still solid."

The peace flooding her face made Seth wish he could as easily find the assurance she had. But a rock of disbelief had settled into his heart after Frank's death and over the years had grown more solid. More fixed. He figured it would take four teams of strong oxen to budge it now.

Jayne curled her hand around his elbow. "Let's walk. It's too pleasant an evening to waste."

They crossed the bridge, went past the pens, paused to watch the pigs for a moment then climbed the hill beyond and stopped under a tree that provided a view to the west.

Jayne sighed and leaned toward him. Or did he only imagine it as a queer mingling of hope and yearning filled him? But a dark shadow hovered, an accumulation of fear and caution. His arms ached to pull her close and hold her next to his heart and let his skin absorb her calm assurance. But his head told him he could never give her what she needed — protection, security, safety. He feared failure.

"The sky is alive with fire," she murmured.

The sun dipped behind the mountain peaks, fracturing light into a hundred bright ribbons of color.

"It makes me wish I could paint like Linette."

If she hadn't been leaning close he would not have noticed her stiffen.

"I wish I could do anything useful and practical." She tipped her chin up in a gesture of determination. "And I will learn how."

He longed to be able to say something that would encourage her, make her see her strengths and abilities. Slowly, the words coming haltingly, he spoke. "Jayne, don't sell yourself short. What counts is what's inside you, not what your hands can do. That, you can learn. After all, no one was born knowing how to rope or ride or bake bread."

She turned her face up to him. The deep hunger in her eyes squeezed his heart.

"What if what's inside is fear and cowardice?"

He touched her chin and smiled into her eyes, lost in their chocolate depths. "No coward would cross the North American continent nor pick up a gun and learn to shoot it after seeing the death and destruction it can cause." He trailed his finger along her jawline, marveling at the softness of her porcelain skin. "Fear is a good thing. It protects us from danger. Assessing fear and confronting it takes courage. You, Jayne Gardiner, have shown that kind of courage over and over."

She cupped his hand, stilling his fingers against her cheek. Her eyes filled with warmth and appreciation and drew him into her thoughts.

He swallowed hard. Tried to assess what was happening. Where would this go? But he couldn't think past the feel of flesh on flesh, his hand on her cheek. He couldn't reason beyond the look in her eyes.

"Seth Collins, you are a very kind and generous man. No one has ever said anything like that to me. It makes me feel . . ." She gave a tiny shrug with one shoulder. "It makes me feel strong and . . ." She swallowed hard and her eyes grew wide. "Never mind."

She didn't move but he felt her withdrawal as thoroughly as if she'd shouted it in his ear.

He slipped his hand to his side.

She put the space of a foot-long ruler between them.

Yet neither made any motion toward returning to the ranch. Instead, they continued to watch nature painting the sky in bright colors.

Distant sounds reminded him of a world beyond this place. A horse neighed. In the trees behind them, birds cooed. A noisy crow cawed as it flapped by. If he really listened, he could even hear the rippling of the river.

A breeze caught a strand of Jayne's hair and blew it across her cheek. He lifted his hand, thinking to tuck it into place, but she caught it herself.

She didn't need him. She had Eddie and back in England, her father. Moreover, she meant to become independent.

And he did not welcome more responsibilities. It should have been all the reason he needed to end this time with her. Yet he didn't move. Didn't say anything. He wasn't ready to return to the narrow life he'd built for himself and so he remained motionless and silent, drinking in the view as his eyes swept the ranch.

Beside him, Jayne seemed almost worshipful as she observed the sunset.

Then she let out a breath that seemed to come from the very soles of her feet. She turned and smiled at him. "Wasn't that wonderful? I feel renewed, refreshed." Her eyes blessed him and he knew a soul-satisfying sense that he'd had a part in making the evening special.

They turned and made their way back to the ranch, though she didn't seem in any more of a rush to end the evening than he.

They reached the bridge and she stopped to lean her arms on the side rails.

He hesitated, having no fondness for rivers. But he couldn't resist Jayne's company and joined her, elbow to elbow.

Evening shadows filled the water. Dark. Murky. Unlocking his forbidden memories. Giving them life.

"I had a brother. Frank. He was two years older than me. We were very close. Always watching out for each other." His voice caught and he couldn't go on.

She pressed her hand to his arm. "What happened to Frank?"

"We had a friend, Sarah. She lived across the road and spent a lot of time with our family." Memories came in a flood. "We almost grew up together. Mostly she was my friend and Frank put up with her. Then one day —"

She slipped her hand down his arm and tucked it into his curled fingers. He held on to the lifeline she offered.

"It was early winter. The ice had started to form on the river. The sun was so bright it hurt the eyes. One of those days when a person can hardly contain their enthusiasm and you begin to think there's nothing you can't do."

She squeezed his hand.

"Frank seemed to notice Sarah for the first time and it made him silly. Foolhardy. He dared us to slide on the ice. He knew as well as I that it wasn't thick enough but Sarah laughed and he couldn't be stopped. He went first. Sarah followed. I refused to go. I wanted them to come back. Stay away from danger." He sucked in air that didn't reach his lungs. Instead, it went to his head and made him dizzy.

Jayne gave an almost inaudible gasp. "No." The word came on breathless air.

He nodded. "They broke through the ice. I grabbed a branch and wriggled out to pull them from the icy water. I managed to get Sarah to shore and went back for Frank but I couldn't find him." His voice scraped from his throat. "They found his body three days later. Sarah died the same day he was found. I did everything I could." His jaw ached. "But it wasn't enough."

"Oh, Seth." She shifted, wrapped her arms about his waist and held him tight.

He enclosed her in his arms and pressed his cheek to her hair, breathing in the scent of sunshine and hay.

"Seth, I'm so sorry. I know how much it hurts. How helpless you must feel. But you said it yourself. You did everything you could. You have to stop blaming yourself for their choices."

He knew her words were right. In his head. His heart said otherwise. His heart blamed him. Said he should have stopped them. Should have saved them. *You were taught to look out for each other.* Pa's words reverberated through his head.

"Why did they insist on acting so foolishly?" he said.

"We all make mistakes. I guess it simply proves they were human. Like us all."

"Where was God?" He choked the words out. "Why didn't He stop them from dying?"

Her arms tightened around him and she shuddered.

"Oh, Jayne. Here I am bemoaning something that happened years ago while you deal with something a lot fresher. Forgive me for being so selfish."

"No. Don't apologize. Your pain is as real as my pain. I think —" She tipped her head back to look into his face. "It makes me feel like you can understand how I feel and why I do the things I do. It makes me feel close to you."

They looked at each other in the lengthening shadows. At that moment something healing and eternal occurred. He knew he would never be the same. Not, he silently warned himself, that his circumstances had changed.

His heart swelled with gratitude for her understanding and he lowered his head and caught her lips in a gentle kiss.

Her hands splayed across his back. She appeared to welcome the kiss and return it with answering pressure.

His heart swelled to near bursting with joy. It beat hard with exuberance three times before his lifelong habit of caution took over and he reasoned his way out of accepting what this situation offered — though he couldn't say exactly what it was, maybe a new beginning.

He broke away from her embrace. "I shouldn't have done that. I had no right."

She gave a deep-throated chuckle. "I don't think you noticed me protesting in any way."

When she would have tucked her hand about his elbow, he pretended to stop and listen for something, putting enough distance between them that she dropped her arm.

It wasn't that he didn't welcome her

touch, even yearn for it. But nothing had changed. He was still Seth Collins who lived a life of caution. Who saw responsibilities as all consuming. Who didn't know how to trust God. Who had a pa who needed him and in order to prove he wasn't a failure in the responsibility department, he meant to prove he could look after Pa.

Jayne did not deserve the affections of a flawed man like him.

Jayne felt him pull back. Part of her understood it was his fear kicking in. Now that he'd shared the story about his brother and their friend, she understood why he wanted to control things so much, why he thought people shouldn't take risks and why he kept his heart locked up. But she'd also seen his tenderness and vulnerability.

He'd given her such encouragement by saying she wasn't a coward. She wanted to give him something in return. She recalled his words. *Where was God? Why didn't He stop them from dying?*

She stopped walking and turned to face him.

He looked beyond her, avoiding eye contact.

It pinched her heart to see his withdrawal. "Seth, God was there. Why He didn't stop the accident, I can't say. I don't presume to understand His ways. But more and more each day I understand that His love is unchanging. His arms are outstretched to comfort us. I think life is meant to press us closer to Him. But so often we — and I mean me — let circumstances come between us and then wonder where God is. He doesn't move. He doesn't change." As she spoke, her convictions grew stronger. "I flounder from time to time but joy comes when I return to His side."

His gaze darted to her for a heartbeat then away again. "I'm glad you have found solace in His presence." His words were distant as if pulled from the mountain tops.

"I would wish the same for you, my friend."

He jerked his full attention to her. "Friend?"

"We are, aren't we?"

The seconds ticked by as he stared into her eyes. "Friends?" The word rounded with surprise.

She nodded, hoping he would allow it to be so.

A slow smile curled his lips. "I like that."

"Me, too."

They turned back to the trail.

After a moment he stopped. "You know, I

haven't had a friend since . . ." His voice trailed off.

"Since Sarah?"

"I was going to say since Frank."

She reached for his arm, gratified when he didn't pull away. "Then I'm doubly honored to be your friend." A sense of wholeness, such as she couldn't recall ever before experiencing, warmed her insides.

The next morning she dressed hurriedly and rushed to the kitchen to get milk for Thor. She glanced around, hoping Seth would be there and offer to help. Yes, caring for the fawn had been her idea but she'd never done anything of the sort before. Seth seemed to know what to do.

But he wasn't about. Her heart squeezed out a disappointed beat. She longed to see him again, bask in his smile, revel in their friendship.

Never mind, she could feed the fawn herself.

She gathered together her supplies and trotted to the barn where she went to the enclosure where Thor rested. The pen was empty. An overwhelming sense of fear and dread took hold of her. Had the fawn died and one of the cowboys removed his body?

Her knees weakened. "Thor," she cried. "Thor."

Footsteps thudded. She'd ask where they'd taken him and see he got a proper farewell. She turned, tears welling up in her eyes. "Seth." He'd understand why it mattered so much. "Thor is gone."

"He's okay. Come and see." He held the gate open.

His words barely registered in her brain. She had to force a deep breath into her lungs as she followed him.

He stepped back and pointed to a wire pen with a little wooden shelter. There Thor and Smokey chased each other around the perimeter.

She laughed shakily. "He's okay."

Seth jerked his attention to her. "You thought something had happened to him?"

She nodded, unable to push a word past the conflagration of emotions.

He moved closer and touched her cheek. "I'm sorry. I didn't mean to frighten you."

She nodded, clinging to his gentle look.

He dropped his hand, turned back to watch the pair in the pen.

Her world righted. Came back to sanity and reality. "You built this?"

"He needs space to run and play. He can play here during the day but for his safety, he'll need to be shut in the barn at night."

"I brought a bottle." She clutched it still.

Together they entered the pen. Thor backed into the far corner but after a short struggle to get him started, he took the bottle readily enough.

Once Thor was sucking well, Seth backed away, leaving Jayne to feed the fawn on her own.

She appreciated his vote of confidence but felt he'd put distance between them for another reason. He was cautious about their friendship.

"Are you ready for another lesson today?" he asked.

Relieved that he didn't mean to abandon the lessons, she gave him a teasing grin. "A shooting lesson?" She hoped to remind him of the evening before when, for a moment, she had felt so close to him. Maybe he'd realize she wasn't opposed to courting lessons.

" 'Fraid I can't teach you how to preserve peas," he said. Her eyes twinkled and she understood he only pretended not to know what she meant.

Thor finished and trotted away, jerking her attention back to the animal.

"After breakfast?" he asked.

"Sounds good." She looked forward to it

more than usual. Last night had made her realize how much she had grown to enjoy his company.

They left Thor in his pen and stood outside watching him play with Smokey for a few minutes then they returned to the house.

After breakfast she would have stayed to help clean up but Linette shoved her toward the door. "Don't keep Seth waiting."

Jayne did not need any more urging and went to join Seth. They went to the clearing.

"I think you're ready to go on your own," he said.

A thrill of both victory and fear coursed through her veins. "You're sure?"

He tipped his head and studied her, his eyes soft, his expression gentle. "Don't you think you are?"

She considered the question. His instruction had been thorough. She knew each step. It was time to put aside her fear and move on boldly. "I'm ready."

"Then let's see you do it." He stood at her side, observing as she loaded and aimed. "Good."

He didn't move to her back to steady her hand but remained close by. He really meant to leave her to do this herself. She considered letting her hand waver so he would put his arm around her and hold her hand. But no. She would learn how to shoot. She would do this.

She squinted down the sights and squeezed the trigger. A shudder raced through her at the explosion but she had not flinched.

Seth squinted toward the target. He said nothing.

"I missed, didn't I?"

"Try again."

She shot again. Missed again. But on the third try she hit the target. Only the outer edge but she cheered.

He gave a nod of approval. "You're doing just fine. From now on you have to practice keeping your eye on the target. As you get better, move the target farther away."

He talked like this was the end. She didn't want it to be. Yes, she wanted to be strong and independent. But something deep inside her cried out for more. More than she'd had as a child protected by her father. More than she'd had as Oliver's fiancée, never sure of his devotion. More than she had here as a woman allowed to do things she'd never have been allowed in England.

The trouble was, she simply didn't understand what the *more* was.

She put the gun on a nearby stump and sat on the adjacent log. If only she could find the words to explain what she felt. But how could she when she didn't know them herself?

"You look disappointed." He stood a few feet away, his arms crossed, one foot tipped over the other.

She rolled her head back and forth. "Not disappointed, exactly." He waited for an explanation. "I don't know. It's like now I can shoot. So what? How is that going to change anything? It won't make me feel less like I failed to help Oliver when I could have. It won't . . ." Her voice grew hoarse. "It won't make me any more sure that he loved me. Or that I loved him." The words had come uncensored to her mouth and she clamped a hand to her lips. "I didn't mean to say that." Her eyes felt way too wide.

He sat beside her. "Jayne, you can't change the past. But didn't you say you can use it?"

She tried to recall when she had said that. "I said life is meant to press us closer to God. Is that what you're referring to?"

He nodded.

"Have I let my experience with Oliver press me closer?" She thought for a moment. "It's certainly changed me. Made me want to be strong. Able to take care of myself and protect others. It's also made me see that what Oliver and I had wasn't what I want now. It was enough back then but now I want to be more than a convenient addition to a man's life. I want to be more than a worthy match." She grew firmer, more impassioned as she spoke. "I want —" She clamped back the words. *I want a love that is not only ready to die for me, but to live life to the fullest with me.*

Seth waited and she scrambled for words to finish her sentence.

"I want to be fearless." It was but a fraction of the truth.

He chuckled. "Jayne, I think you are closer to that every day."

His words had the power to ease her worries and she smiled. "I guess I am. Thanks to your help."

He choked back his amusement. "I don't think I can take credit for doing anything but walking beside you."

Walking beside her. What a wonderful thought. That's exactly what she wanted. A man who would walk beside her. Honor her strengths and gently help her through her weaknesses. Why had she picked a man like Oliver who offered neither? And now she'd met one who offered both but for a limited time. She would ask him when he meant to leave but didn't want him to think she thought it was time.

"I told Linette I would get back to help pick beans." They retraced their steps toward the ranch. "I never realized how much work was involved in growing and gathering food and preparing enough for the winter."

The sun was warm overhead. A gopher stood on tiptoe beside a mound of dirt and whistled before it ducked down his hole in the ground.

Jayne chuckled. "Cheeky little thing." She breathed deeply. "Do I smell roses?"

"Over there." He pointed toward a bush with late-season wild roses.

She'd seen them before and loved them. Single petaled in varying colors of pink from palest skin tones to fullest red. She bent over the bush and inhaled the scent. She would pick one and take it home but had learned how fragile the blossoms were. The petals would fall even as she picked the flower.

A flash of blue in the grass caught her eye and she scurried to the spot. Little bluebells hung their clustered heads. Such rare beauty.

Seth waited nearby as she enjoyed the flowers.

She sat back on her heels and let her gaze sweep the blanket of blossoms. Her eyes were drawn to something on the horizon.

A man sat on a horse watching them.

She rose slowly and backed to Seth's side. An English gentleman. Nothing unusual about that. He would have fit in back in London but looked out of place here with his bowler hat and buttoned-up suit. Would she ever see a man thusly dressed and not be reminded of Oliver's killer?

As the man shifted in his saddle, Jayne caught a glimpse of his face. She gasped and grabbed Seth's arm, dragging him behind a bunch of poplar trees.

Seth stared at her. "What is wrong?" He ducked his head to look into her eyes. "You look like you've seen a ghost."

Jayne struggled to suck in air. "It's him." Her voice shook.

Seth looked about. "Who is him?"

"That man." Jayne pointed a trembling finger. "It's him. He's the man who shot Oliver."

Seth moved to where he could see where she pointed. "Are you sure?"

"I . . ." She tried to collect her thoughts, sort out the flashes of memory from that day. "I don't know. Maybe it's only because he's dressed like that man was."

"He's leaving. I wonder what he wanted."

Jayne bent over her knees, forcing air in and out of her wooden lungs. "What if it's really him?" She straightened and stared to where the man had been. "What if he followed me? What if he wants to get rid of the only witness?" She shuddered.

Seth pulled her into his arms and patted her back. "I regret ever suggesting such a thing."

Bile burned the back of her throat, but she focused her entire being on the comforting movement of his hand on her back, and the murmur of his words, though she didn't listen to their meaning. Slowly, her nerves calmed and she relaxed into his embrace, feeling safe and sheltered.

It was a luxury she couldn't allow herself. She must depend on no one to keep her safe. No one but herself and her skills. Thankfully she could now use a gun if she must, though she might not be any threat unless she could actually hit a target.

But she enjoyed several more moments of resting in his care then, exerting every bit of inner strength she possessed, she straightened and escaped his arms.

"If that's him, he is here for only one reason." She squared her shoulders. She

would not cower in the corner if he threatened anyone again.

CHAPTER TWELVE

Seth let her step away, although everything in him wanted to keep her right there in his arms where he could protect her. If he hadn't been so busy watching her enjoy the flowers, he would have seen the man before he turned away. He would have memorized his face and then gone hunting him.

He couldn't leave Jayne now. Not even for Pa's sake. He hadn't been able to protect Sarah and Frank from the cold waters, but he would keep Jayne safe at any cost.

"Let's get back to the ranch." He wouldn't frighten her any more than she already was. Back at the ranch there was hope of keeping her under constant surveillance. He pulled her to his side, kept her tucked safely under his arm as they rushed back to the house.

Jayne hurried into the kitchen and collapsed on a chair.

Linette rushed to her side. "What's

232

wrong?"

She shuddered then said in a deadly calm voice, "I think I saw Oliver's murderer." She explained about seeing the rider.

Linette lifted her gaze to Seth. He saw the same horrible knowledge in her eyes. The Englishman would be in the same vicinity as Jayne for only one reason.

"Where's Eddie?" he asked.

She nodded, relief filling her eyes as if assured her husband would know what to do. "He went to the supply sheds to check on what we need."

"I'll get him."

Linette followed him to the far door.

"Keep Jayne here," he said.

"I will."

Seth found Eddie at the first supply shed. Roper was with him as they discussed a trip to town for supplies.

He told them both about the Englishman.

Eddie's jaw tightened. "Could she have been mistaken?"

"I don't know. Best you talk to her."

Eddie handed his list to Roper. "Tell the boys to keep a lookout for a fancy-dressed Englishman and to bring him in if they see him."

Back at the house they went to the kitchen where Jayne held a cup of tea. Linette sat across from her with a cup held tightly between her palms.

Eddie sat beside Linette. "Tell me everything."

Seth sat at Jayne's side, resisting a protective urge to put his arm about her.

Jayne nodded. "There was something about him. And as soon as he turned to give me a view of his face, I knew it was him."

"You're certain."

"I suppose I could be mistaken but I don't think so. I don't think I will ever forget the look on that man's face when he demanded Oliver turn out his pockets."

It was more than enough for Seth. If Eddie didn't do something, he would. He'd find the tracks on the hillside and follow the man to the ends of the earth.

"I'll send for the Mountie," Eddie said. "Until he gets here I think you better stay in the house."

"I have to take care of Thor."

At the blank look on Eddie's face, Seth added, "The fawn."

"Fine, but stay close to the buildings."

Seth figured it indicated how frightened she was that she didn't object to her brother ordering her about.

Mercy and Sybil clattered into the room.

"We heard. Did you really see the murderer?"

Eddie left the house as the pair hovered about Jayne. Mercy pushed Seth aside to sit next to her. He glanced after Eddie then decided he would stay right there until they knew for sure if the man was a threat or not. Until the man could be confronted face-to-face.

Jayne explained yet again what she'd seen while Mercy and Sybil made appropriate comforting sounds.

Linette offered them all tea and cookies.

Seth took both gratefully, but he couldn't remain at the table. He carried his cup and cookie to the window and looked out. A rider kicked up dust as he rode off the ranch. Probably the man Eddie sent to find the Mountie.

He stayed at the window long after the dust disappeared.

Grady ran past his line of vision and crashed through the door. Billy came in on his heels.

"You got a baby deer?" His voice was filled with awe. "Billy says we can't see it without permission. Can we see it now? Please?"

Seth turned back to Jayne, saw the stress creasing her forehead. It might do her good to leave the house and forget the Englishman but forgetting the danger lurking out there would be foolish.

She sent him a desperate look.

He made up his mind and left his post and headed to her side feeling Mercy's measuring watchfulness. "I'll take the boys to see the fawn, if you like."

She bolted to her feet. "I'll go with you. I need to check on him, anyway."

"We'll come, too," Sybil said and she and Mercy fell in at their heels and the lot of them went down the hill.

The boys were soon joined by Daisy, carrying Pansy.

They went round the barn to the small pen.

"His name is Thor," Jayne said as they crowded up to the fence. The fawn curled up on the ground, Smokey between his paws.

Although Thor's eyes grew wide, he didn't move.

Jayne chuckled. "It looks like he doesn't want to disturb Smokey."

"Thor!" Sybil laughed softly. "Strange name for a little fawn."

Seth checked their surroundings, seeing nothing, then he turned to the ladies. "I said he didn't look much like a Thor but she didn't believe me."

"What does it mean?" Daisy asked.

"In mythology, Thor is a god of thunder and lightning. He carries a big hammer and smashes things. His job is to protect humans." Sybil gave the details.

Jayne grinned at her friends. "In this case, the humans are protecting Thor." Her gaze captured Seth's. He returned it with silent promise that he would protect her as well as Thor.

"Can we touch him?" Grady asked.

"Seth, what do you think?" Jayne asked. "Is it too soon?" She turned to explain to the children. "He's a wild creature and people frighten him."

"Look," Seth whispered and they all turned toward little Pansy. She had edged around the fence to where she could reach her fingers through the wire. Thor licked her fingers then bounced to his feet and pressed his nose close to hers.

"There's one human he isn't afraid of." Seth spoke so softly he wondered if the others heard but they all stayed where they were and watched the two little ones acknowledge each other.

Daisy edged closer to make sure her little sister wasn't in any danger.

Thor skipped away then turned and tiptoed back to Pansy. She giggled as his nose touched her fingers.

"Can we touch him, too?" Grady asked.

"Why don't you let him make friends with you?" Seth said. "Stand at the fence and wait for him to come to you."

Mercy and Sybil sat with their backs to the barn to watch. After a moment, Jayne joined them.

Seth couldn't relax, not that he worried about the fawn. His concern was Jayne and the threat of a fancy-dressed Englishman. He guided the children but all the while he watched the trails leading to the ranch and kept a lookout at the trees nearby where a man could hide in the shadows.

How long would it take for the Mountie to receive Eddie's message and get here?

The boys stayed until the fawn finally came up to explore their fingers. A little after that they trotted off in search of bigger adventures. Daisy gathered up her little sister and headed back. "I'm going to help Ma pick beans."

Jayne bolted to her feet. "I plumb forgot. Come on, girls. We need to help Linette." They raced away to the garden where Linette and Cassie were already at work.

"Jayne," Seth called. But she didn't hear him.

He rubbed at his neck. Shouldn't she

return to the house and stay out of sight? He followed slowly, not headed for the garden but for a spot behind the cookhouse that allowed him a nice view of the entire yard and most of the surrounding area. He hunkered down, alert to the tiniest movement.

He scanned the landscape constantly but his gaze continued to return to the garden where Jayne worked alongside the others, filling tubs with green beans. He repeatedly assured himself no one would ride into the ranch and attack her. Eddie had posted a watch at either end of the trail leading to the ranch.

A shifting shadow beyond the garden drew his attention. Every nerve in his body fired into action. He strained to make out any shape, could see nothing. But he knew something or someone had moved there. He edged his way toward the barn, saddled his horse and left as if making his way to town. Once down the road and around the corner, he cut to his left in a direction that would bring him into line with anyone leaving the spot he'd been watching. He rode as fast as he figured was safe, hoping he wouldn't draw attention to himself, but there was no way to muffle his horse's thudding steps.

He reached the area without encountering anyone. He left his horse at the edge of the trees and went to examine the place where he'd seen something. The first thing he noted was the good view of the garden it provided. He stood there a moment, watching Jayne. He heard his breath whoosh in and out. A man with a good rifle could get rid of her before anyone could do a thing about it. And he could disappear before a man on horseback could overtake him.

His heart hammered a protest against his rib. She was a sitting target. She should be indoors.

Before he told her so, he examined the ground. Footprints. And not those of a cowboy boot. A sliver of wood caught his attention and he picked it up gingerly. One of those fancy new toothpicks. Definitely a city man. No cowboy in his right mind would use such a silly thing. A sharpened piece of wood served the purpose just fine. Or a length of oat straw. Even a stem of grass.

A city man who killed without remorse and tracked witnesses across the world.

Not a man to be trifled with.

He returned to his horse and rode down the hill in a straight line to the ranch. He rode directly to the garden.

Every woman turned to him, knowing his visit had a purpose.

"Jayne, I don't think it's safe for you out here."

She blinked. "Why not? Eddie put two cowboys on the trails and another to watch the place." She pointed toward Slim who leaned in the barn doorway. "And Eddie is within calling distance." He was across the river tending to some chores. "No one is coming in here without being met by a gun-toting man." She sat back on her heels as unconcerned as the cat grooming itself in the sunny patch of grass.

"Yes, ma'am. That's so. But —" He hesitated to speak his fears aloud. He turned to Linette. "Ma'am, I saw something up the hill." He pointed to the place and five women rose and shielded their eyes with their hands to look in the direction he indicated. "Someone was there but I didn't catch him. But I regret to say that from there Jayne is an easy target for anyone with a rifle."

The women turned to confront Jayne.

"Jayne, you aren't safe out here," Sybil said.

Mercy grabbed the beans still in Jayne's hands. "You shouldn't be here."

Linette nodded. "I can't bear to think of

you being a target."

"That's a terribly frightening thought," Cassie added.

Jayne looked confused, frightened and then stubbornness hardened her expression. "You think I should run and hide?" Her flashing eyes informed Seth the question was meant for him.

All the women said, "Yes."

"But the beans." Jayne indicated the rows left to pick.

"We'll take the full tub to the house," Linette said, "and you can begin stringing them."

As soon as he saw Jayne meant to follow her sister-in-law, Seth hurried to the barn to unsaddle his horse. The chore seemed to take longer than usual. As soon as he finished, he trotted up the hill, ignoring the sharp reminder in his leg of his recent injury.

Linette and Jayne worked in the kitchen.

"I can manage this on my own," Jayne said.

"Very well. And thank you. I appreciate it." As she left the house, Linette murmured to Seth, "Keep an eye on her."

"I mean to."

He circled the room, glancing out the windows. It was hot enough to require the door to stand open, which allowed him a view through the screen. Still, he felt as if a man could sneak up on him without warning.

"Do you really think he'd venture close to the ranch when it is swarming with people?" Jayne asked him. "There's no way he'd get in and out again without getting stopped."

"Likely that is true." It was the time between getting in and out again that worried him. "Now would be a good time for you to ask God to take care of you."

"Why me? Or rather, why just me? You could ask, as well."

"I'm not sure I believe He would answer."

Her hands grew still. "You won't know if you don't ask."

"I'll let you do the asking."

"Fine. I will." She bowed her head a moment. Then lifted it again and gave him a direct look that burned through his caution straight to an unguarded corner of his heart. He needed to get away from this place soon or he'd forget the promise he'd made to himself to never take on more responsibility and never put anyone ahead of his pa.

"I said a prayer for you, too," she said, her voice both sweet and daring.

"Save your breath."

"I asked God to show you that He hears and answers your prayers."

He let out a gusty laugh. "You believe that quite firmly."

"That's right." She went back to stringing beans as confident as if it were already done.

He circled the room again, checking out each window and staring out the door a long time. "He's out there. I practically saw him."

"I did see him."

He didn't need the reminder. It was time to stop dwelling on it. He was here to protect her. He'd keep her safe.

He continued pacing the room, stopping at a painting of mountains in full summer array. The grass shone emerald, and the deciduous trees made a light green contrast to the pine and spruce. Flowers dotted the field in the foreground, where off to the right sat a mounted cowboy. He leaned closer. "Looks like Eddie."

"It is. That's one of Linette's paintings. It's good, isn't it?"

"I'm no judge of artwork but I like this. I can almost smell the fresh air and the flowers."

"Exactly. It feels alive."

He studied it a few more minutes than circled the room again, checking out the windows and doors.

"Seth, will you sit down. You're making

me nervous."

"You *should* be nervous."

"Fine. I am nervous enough without you pacing around like a caged animal."

Even as he sat, his muscles twitched. He couldn't shake the feeling that someone was watching . . . that the murdering English-man was very close.

He shifted his chair so his back was to a wall and he faced the door. "Hand me some of those beans. I might as well keep busy."

She moved her chair next to his and placed the tub of beans close by. He'd never pictured himself sitting in a kitchen preparing beans to be bottled, but it wasn't half-bad. Jayne sat beside him where he could protect her. She hummed under her breath as she worked. The scent of flowers and garden soil came to him from her direction. Flies buzzed against the window glass but apart from that sound they might have been alone in their own little world.

If only it could be so. Instead, danger hovered on their doorstep.

Jayne couldn't get a thought straight. She simply continued to pull strings from beans and cut them the size Linette wanted. The mindless task failed to divert her thoughts.

Seth had seen the murderer watching again.

She shivered. When she felt Seth's glance touch her, she raised her eyes, knowing they begged for reassurance. She didn't care.

He smiled but his eyes reflected her concern.

She touched his arm. "At least you're here to protect me." She wanted to say she would be fine without protection but her brave talk about being independent and looking after herself meant nothing in the face of real danger.

He nodded, his eyes forest green and bottomless.

She let herself sink into his gaze, let herself find strength and safety. She drew in a trembling breath as she found what she sought. He would take care of her. With God's help.

Oh, Lord, I press close to You. Protect us all.

She jerked her attention back to the beans and continued to prepare them as the clock on the wall ticked off the minutes.

Every tick echoed like the click of a gun. Oh, why had she allowed that word into her mind?

Her breath escaped in a groan.

Seth took her hand and squeezed. "Don't

be afraid. There are plenty of people here to protect you."

She nodded, again clinging to the promise in his eyes. "I know." A teasing imp prompted her to add, "Besides, I asked God to protect us all."

His smile didn't reach his eyes. "There now. What more do you need?"

"Nothing except for that man to be arrested and sent back to England to hang."

He nodded.

That evening, after supper, she gathered up supplies to feed Thor.

Seth stopped her. "I'll do it." He reached for the bottle of milk.

She hesitated, fighting an inner battle. Part of her wanted to hide in a closet somewhere. But she'd had enough of running. "I will not give in to my fear."

He took her arm and pulled her around to face him. "Listening to fear is not a bad thing. It can prevent people from taking foolish risks."

She studied him. Saw the concern and the pain in his eyes. She pressed her palm to his cheek. "Seth, I am not going to be foolish. I am not skating on thin ice."

The darkness in his eyes informed her he understood her reference.

"We'll take Thor into the barn to feed him. How's that?"

He considered her suggestion for a moment then nodded. "If you stay in the barn while I get him."

"I will. I don't have a death wish, you know."

Their gazes clung for another second.

"And stay close to me on the way to the barn."

She had no objection to being tucked under his arm, pressed to his side as they marched down the hill. From there she felt as if no harm could ever come to her.

The words were contrary to the goals she had set for herself but provided comfort at the moment.

After this crisis ended she would return to learning to be strong and independent.

CHAPTER THIRTEEN

The next day Seth again insisted on being her human shield as they went to feed the fawn. Thor, shut in the barn for the night, raced toward them as soon as he saw the bottle.

She laughed. "Look at that. He knows where the food comes from."

They didn't have to urge him to take the nipple. He grabbed it and pulled eagerly.

She held the bottle, discovering satisfaction and peace in feeding the little animal and in seeing how it had lost its fear of her. Fear. The word covered so many things. She wanted to put her thoughts into words if she could. "I know that fear is a good thing in that it keeps us from danger. But fear can harm, too."

He quirked an eyebrow questioningly.

"Like Thor's fear of us. If he didn't get over it he might have starved to death."

Seth's gaze went slowly to Thor as if he

needed to consider her statement.

"I think our experience with fear has been at opposite ends of the spectrum," she said.

He again brought his gaze to her, full of dark intensity that brushed a tender spot within. She ached to be able to help him leave his fears behind.

She went on to answer his unspoken question. "You lost Frank and Sarah because they didn't heed the fear of thin ice. But I stood by helpless and useless because my fear crippled me."

He nodded. "That's true. But I hope we are together, united with fear about this Englishman who has followed you."

She couldn't look away from his gaze. Couldn't escape his silent demand. *United.* The word pulled at her heart strings, threatening to undo her resolve. She must not allow his concern and her fear to drive her back to the person she'd been when Oliver was shot.

She nodded. "I will never again let fear control me, though."

He narrowed his eyes. "I was hoping for more cooperation than that."

She gave a little shrug. "I will only promise not to ignore danger signs."

"I guess that will have to be good enough."

She didn't bother to ask what else he

wanted. She didn't object to him being her self-appointed bodyguard but she would not become a whimpering, simpering female afraid to stand up and protect herself should the need arise.

Grady raced into the barn. "Did he eat already?"

"He just finished." Jayne showed him the empty bottle. "He's a greedy little thing."

"Aww. I hoped you'd let me help feed him."

Seth ruffled his hair. "Maybe next time. Thor seems to be comfortable enough with people now."

As if to prove it, Thor bumped his head into Grady's hand then watched, his legs splayed awkwardly. When Grady reached out to pat his head the fawn bounced away a few feet and paused to wait for Grady.

Grady trotted after him but Thor bounced away.

"I think he wants to play tag," Seth said.

The pair chased up and down the alleyway. Grady paused at the door. "Can we go outside and play?"

Jayne waited, wondering what Seth would say.

"I don't think you should right now. Let's make sure Thor knows where home is first. We wouldn't want him to get lost."

Grady nodded. "Sure wouldn't." He continued playing with the fawn as Seth and Jayne watched.

Jayne liked Seth's answer. It was wise and thoughtful. And not based on fear.

They returned to the house for breakfast. Afterward, Linette turned to Jayne. "Would you be able to help me preserve the beans today?"

Jayne recognized it as Linette's way of making sure she stayed indoors and hid a smile at the way Seth sighed.

"Sure, I'd love to assist you."

Two hours later she realized how much work was involved. They packed beans into jars, added salt and water and put them in a boiler.

"Now they boil for three hours," Linette said. "Which gives us time to get another lot ready to go."

"How did you learn all this?" It was Linette's first summer on the ranch.

"Cookie taught me. When I came west it was with the idea of being a pioneer wife. I was determined to do all the practical things I thought a woman should do. Eddie would pay a housekeeper if I wanted one but I don't."

The heat from the stove, combined with the growing heat from the August sun made the kitchen like an oven. Jayne wiped her forehead with a corner of the big apron Linette had lent her. How could Linette work so hard despite the heat and her growing belly?

Jayne glanced out the window. Seth sat on horseback, on a hill overlooking the house.

Linette joined her. "He's concerned about that Englishman." She gave Jayne a sideways hug. "And you."

Jayne didn't answer. She could hardly deny it when Seth made it obvious but she wasn't sure what it meant. In a secret place behind her heart she wished it meant he cared about her, and not just because he had an overwhelming sense of responsibility to prevent bad things from happening.

Burying a sigh, she returned to the large tub of beans. "This will take all day." Sweat dripped down her back.

Linette chuckled. "I expect it will but we'll really appreciate it when winter comes. Let's be grateful that Cookie is doing half of them."

Jayne stole another glance out the window. Seth had moved. Her heart slammed against her ribs. Where was he? Who watched to make sure the Englishman didn't come near the ranch?

She crossed the kitchen and stepped out

the door to scan the surrounding area. There he was. Seth and horse stood in the shadow of the trees near where he and Jayne had spent many hours on shooting lessons. Her breath eased out smooth and warm. She should have known he wouldn't forget about her.

Why did the knowledge feel so good and right when it was not what either of them wanted?

Did he watch her? It was impossible to tell at this distance but somehow she knew he would have seen her step outside. She ducked back into the kitchen before he could ride down and order her to stay indoors.

She hummed a little as she turned back to preparing beans. The Englishman posed no threat so long as Seth stood guard.

Not until dinnertime did she see Seth except at a distance. He came in at Eddie's side, pausing at the door to take a look across the yard.

The men protested the heat in the kitchen.

Mercy entered and gasped. "How can you bear this?" She fanned herself.

Sybil did likewise.

"Would you like to take your food outside to the shade?" Linette said.

One glance at Linette's flushed, damp face

and Jayne thought it would be wise. The heat bothered her though she'd never once complained.

"I'd like to," she replied.

Seth pulled her back when she started for the door. "It's not safe."

"Linette is about to perish in this heat. She needs a break." She kept her voice low.

"Let her go outside. But you need to stay here."

The others took their plates outside.

Jayne looked into Seth's eyes, saw stubbornness and caution. Or was it fear? He'd deny it and likely be offended if she suggested so. Was his fear good or not? Was it making him too cautious? How should she respond?

"How likely is it that he'd try and harm me with half a dozen people around?" The question was rhetorical.

"You can never be too safe."

"But you can worry too much." She filled her plate. "Come on. I'm sure I can sit somewhere that is safe enough."

He grabbed a plate, flung food on it and tromped after her. He waited until she sat with her back to the wall then sat facing her, his bent knees almost touching hers.

She pursed her lips. Did he have to be so obvious that he thought her in danger?

Certainly made it difficult to relax and enjoy her meal. Every time she bent her head over her plate she felt exposed and spent most of the meal scanning the trees and hills around the house, hoping and praying she wouldn't see that man.

Seth bolted to his feet and stared down the road. "Rider coming."

Eddie had also risen.

Jayne's heart clattered up her throat and clung to her teeth.

Seth pulled her to her feet and unceremoniously rushed her inside.

She would have protested except his breathing was harsh, his concern obviously genuine. A fact that caused her heart to hammer even more rapidly until her head spun.

The others entered more slowly.

"Whoever it may be, he is riding directly to the house." Eddie moved through to the front door. "Doesn't look like an Englishman to me."

Seth practically glued himself to Jayne's side. She clung to his arm. When he draped his arm across her shoulder and pulled her close she relaxed marginally. She couldn't be much safer.

"It's Constable Allen," Eddie called and he went through to the front door.

Everyone in the room let out a gust of air. None louder than Jayne, unless it was Seth.

"Come on in." Eddie led the man to the kitchen. Beside him stood a Mountie with a yellow stripe on his midnight-blue breeches. Rather than the red serge jacket she'd seen the Mounties at Fort Macleod wearing, he wore a brown canvas tunic. He pulled off his broad-brimmed felt hat and tucked it under his arm.

Eddie made introductions. "You've come about the murderer we saw?"

"Suspected murderer. And yes, I have. Who is the witness?"

"My sister, Jayne."

She had eased away from Seth's side at the announcement of the Mountie's arrival and now stepped forward. "Me."

"I need to ask you some questions. Can we . . ." He looked about at the crowd.

At least Grady had run to play so he didn't see and hear this.

"You're welcome to use the front room," Linette offered, pointing down the hall.

"That would be fine. Thank you."

Eddie led the way. Jayne followed, the Mountie on her heels. Not until she reached the other room did she see with relief that Seth had also followed.

The Mountie waited for Jayne to be seated

then pulled out a little notebook. "Now tell me exactly what happened."

She swallowed hard, gripped her hands together and wished Seth sat at her side instead of across the room beside Eddie.

"I don't know how much you know . . ."

"Pretend I know nothing. Start at the beginning."

Where was the beginning? When Oliver had gambled so often? When he'd found his gambling more interesting than her company? She gave herself a mental shake. The Mountie meant the shooting.

"I was with my fiancé, Oliver Spencer, walking down a street in London, when this man came from an alley." She went on to describe the scene, leaving nothing out, not even her own fear and shame, nor the horrendous amount of blood.

"What can you tell me about the man who shot your fiancé?"

"He was just an ordinary businessman. Suit, bowler hat, white shirt."

"His hair color?"

She shook her head. "I can't remember."

"Think of the scene. Search every detail. Did his hair show under his hat or not?"

She closed her eyes. "It showed. Kind of dirty blond."

"Good. Eye color? Take your time."

She closed her eyes and brought up the scene she had tried so hard to erase from her memory. "Hard. Beady. Blue, I think."

"How tall? Picture him with your fiancé. Was he taller, shorter?"

"Shorter, and Oliver wasn't a tall man."

"Build?"

They went through a number of details.

"Now can you think of anything odd, unusual? A scar. A limp. A birthmark, say on his face or hands. A ring."

"He had a ring. On his right hand."

"What did it look like?"

"A lion's head with emerald eyes."

"Very good. I think I have enough to find this man and send him back to England to face his crime." The Mountie closed his notebook and stuffed it back in the breast pocket of his vest and stood. "I'll check back in a few days with news."

Jayne's eyes widened in surprise. The man certainly seemed to think he'd capture the murderer in no time. He didn't appear to entertain a shadow of doubt.

Eddie showed the Mountie to the door.

"I suppose he means he'll be back with good news." Her voice felt weak as if she'd spent all her energy and she certainly felt that way. "He sounds mighty sure of himself."

"The Mounties always get their man," Seth said with assurance.

A burst of nervous energy jolted her to her feet. "I have to get out of here." Avoiding Seth's outstretched arm, she raced for her room, grabbed the brocade bag where she carried her gun and headed for the door.

Seth blocked her path. "What are you doing?"

"I can't stand being cooped up. I'm going to practice shooting."

He crossed his arms and refused to let her pass. "It's not safe."

"I've got a gun."

"That doesn't insure safety."

"And isn't the Mountie out there looking for the man?"

He shook his head. "It's a big country."

Linette drew to her side. "I think you should listen to him."

She felt the others watching her and tossed her hands in a gesture of defeat. "You all expect me to stay inside forever?"

"Yes," they chorused.

Except Seth. "Only until the Mountie gets his man." He gave a slow, lazy grin that melted right through her annoyance and restlessness.

She sighed and gave in. "Very well. But I warn you. I expect to be entertained." She glanced around at the group. Mercy looked away. Sybil was suddenly very interested in washing a pot. Linette indicated the shrinking mound of beans.

"There's always canning to do."

Jayne brought her gaze back to Seth's. He looked amused as he leaned against the door frame.

"You," she said as she leaned close. "You will keep me company seeing as you insisted I stay indoors."

He shrugged but his eyes smiled, full of promise. "I can handle it."

Mercy chortled but when Jayne scowled at her, she only gave an unrepentant grin.

Jayne tried to remain upset but she couldn't and laughed. "I want you all to realize that you are so controlling."

"Yes," Seth said, taking her elbow and leading her to the table. "But it's for your own good." He sat across from her and helped finish the beans.

The last batch of jars went in the boiler midafternoon. Linette splashed cold water over her face and neck. "Do you mind watching the boiler while I have a little nap?"

"Of course not," Jayne said. "Take as long as you like."

"There's really nothing to do. It's three

hours before it's done."

"Go." She gave her sister-in-law a little shove toward the stairs.

Mercy and Sybil had left an hour ago. Only Seth and Jayne remained. She gave him a long, considering look.

"What?" He seemed oblivious.

"This is where you're supposed to ask me what I'd like to do."

"Nope. I don't think so. You'll probably suggest things you shouldn't do."

"Like what?" She was curious what he thought she'd suggest.

"Like maybe going shooting. Or walking up the hill."

Her cheeks warmed as she remembered their previous walk up the hill. How she'd kissed him eagerly, only to have him apologize. Nope, she didn't care to repeat that. Though perhaps if they changed the ending . . .

"Shucks. You might even suggest a trip to town."

She tapped her finger on her chin. "All very good ideas. I suggest you keep them in mind. But I already agreed I would stay indoors until the Mountie catches the man — supposing he does."

His eyes followed the movement of her finger. She purposely drew it along her jaw-

262

line and back to her chin to watch his eyes move along with her finger.

What was wrong with her? Her life was in mortal danger and she played silly games.

She jerked her hand to her waist and cleared her throat. "Actually, what I had in mind was a game of checkers."

"Sure." Did he sound relieved? Had he been entertaining thoughts similar to hers?

Not likely. She put her unusual response down to nervousness at the threat of the Englishman. Her thoughts settled. She pulled the checkers game from the cupboard and put the board on a side table in the front room. The spot allowed them both a view from the window. She knew he wouldn't be happy unless he could see out.

He scanned the scene beyond the glass as she set up the game pieces.

"Ladies first."

She moved. "Eddie and I played checkers and chess by the hour when we were younger." She sat back and mused. "So much has happened that it seems like a long time ago."

Her entire life had been slashed into two segments — life before Oliver's murder and life after.

Although there were enjoyable parts to the first half — like games with Eddie, tea parties with sisters Bess and Anne and certainly, the lessons under a good tutor — she would never return to who she was at that time.

Aware that Seth waited for her to take her turn at the game, she pulled her attention back to the here and now.

There might be present dangers that frightened her but she would never let them control her as she had when Oliver was shot.

Seth tapped the back of her hand. "What are you thinking?"

"About the past."

"All of it?" He sounded amazed.

"And the present," she added, bringing her gaze to him, silent and challenging. Did she want him to have a place in her present?

Only if he acknowledged her growing strength. Not that she minded him providing an extra pair of eyes while Oliver's murderer lurked about, but he had to understand that she wanted to prove she could take care of herself.

CHAPTER FOURTEEN

For two days Seth rode the perimeter of the ranch looking for evidence of the Englishman, dividing his time between that and keeping Jayne company, mostly doing his best to make sure she didn't leave the house.

The only exception was when she fed Thor, and he stuck to her side like a burr. Thor had quickly become a pet. He raced to the fence when they approached with a bottle. He welcomed the children to play with him. So far, they had restricted the fawn to the barn or his pen but soon he would need more space.

Letting him run about the ranch posed many risks, mostly predators. "You'll have to be responsible to see that he's shut up at night," he warned Jayne that afternoon as they discussed the fawn.

"Me?"

He hadn't meant to make it so plain that

he wouldn't be here. But she already knew that.

A curtain fell behind her eyes. "I'll take care of him."

The same way he would take care of her.

The next day was Sunday and there'd be so many people coming and going. Eddie and Linette invited everyone in the county to visit and attend church. But the Englishman would not be welcome nor would he likely show his face. Instead, he would lurk in the shadows, hoping for a careless moment.

Seth rubbed at the tightness in his neck.

Jayne didn't mean to be careless about exposing herself to someone who might have her in his sights several yards away, but she was so determined not to let fear rule her that she often stood in clear view from any number of spots around the ranch.

He knew she would never consent to remaining in the house for the day so the next morning he put on his best shirt — a buff-colored cotton with pearly buttons — and a clean pair of trousers. He glanced down his leg. He'd worn this pair of trousers when he was shot and he'd figured they would go in the trash, but Jayne had scrubbed them clean and mended them so neatly he could hardly tell they'd been ripped. She certainly knew how to use a needle and thread. But despite her fine job, his trousers were about worn out.

He badly needed to buy some new duds. His boots were in particularly bad shape since he'd pried off the heel. It had taken two hours the night before to get them polished up as good as he could. He studied them. They still looked like they belonged on the range, not at a church gathering. Good thing this was a ranch church where the men were cowboys.

The others left as he waited at the bottom of the stairs for Jayne.

She came down the hall. "I'm ready." She patted her head.

His eyes followed her hand. She'd scooped her shiny brown hair into some kind of curly thing at the back of her neck. Her skin glowed with summer color. A gray bonnet dangled from her hands. She wore a shiny dress in black and white stripes with a pretty collar that framed her face.

His mouth dried. She was a beautiful woman with a brave heart.

She smoothed the skirt of her dress. The fabric rustled with the touch. A very beautiful woman used to fine dresses, luxuries and servants. Used to being sheltered and protected.

The reminder burned through his thoughts.

Could he ever take care of her the way she deserved?

He knew the answer. Had known it from the beginning. No. He had a record of failure in protecting those close to him.

She should meet one of the rich land owners from the nearby ranches. Or a colonel from Fort Macleod. She deserved the very best in life.

He kept her close as they went to the cookhouse and once inside, sat between her and the windows.

She gave him a long, steady look, then shook her head as if to suggest he worried too much.

If they'd been alone, he would have said it wasn't possible, considering the danger out there. Instead, he gave a smile that didn't touch anything but his mouth and turned to the others.

Besides those who lived at the ranch, Ward, Grace and little Belle were in attendance. And two cowboys from the OK Ranch, Buck and Matt.

Bertie's talk was simple and straightforward.

"God loves us and listens to our prayers. He will never fail to fulfill His promises."

Bertie went on to tell of times when God had shown His faithfulness.

Seth believed God loved him in a distant sort of way. After all, if God made him, He must feel some sort of responsibility for him. He just wasn't sure God cared enough to answer his pleas. His doubts had started at Frank's death and simply become a habit. He never gave them much thought. And didn't intend to start doing so now.

As was the custom, after the service the guests enjoyed coffee and cinnamon buns served by Cookie.

Eddie questioned Matt and Buck. "Have you seen any strangers around? Like an Englishman." He described the man.

Matt shook his head. "Ain't seen much but the back end of cows for three weeks."

"Me, too," Buck added. Then he snapped his fingers. "We did see a campfire over toward Dead Man's Coulee. Didn't think much of it. You know how people ride through and stop only to spend the night? Figured it was only that. You think it might have been this here man you're asking about?"

Eddie shrugged. "No way of telling but if you see this man, either apprehend him or come tell me or Constable Allen."

They agreed they would.

Linette rose. "You're welcome to join us for dinner," she said to the pair.

Buck ducked his head. Matt cleared his throat. "Thanks but we thought of riding into town."

Seth grinned.

Beside him, Cal chortled. "Someone new in town? Someone I should know about?"

Matt scowled so hard it should have been enough to dry Cal's mouth to a prune. But Cal only grinned wider.

"There are two young ladies who have come with their parents. But I warn you, they're already spoken for. Right, Buck?"

"That's right." The pair scrambled to their feet, murmured their thanks and beat a hasty retreat to the door with Cal's mocking laughter following them.

Buster looked as if he couldn't decide to be shocked or annoyed. He swallowed twice then got slowly to his feet. "Seem like real nice guys, they did. Those girls are fortunate to have the interest of such fine fellas."

Seth choked back a laugh at how the young man had said what all of them likely thought and done it in such an innocent way.

Buster seemed a fine fella, too.

Seth would see to getting that belt made soon.

As everyone made their way to Eddie's house, Matt and Buck waited on their horses and called to Seth.

He went to them.

"I almost forgot. Petey said I was to see you got this." Matt handed him a letter.

He stuffed it in his pocket and hurried after the others. Yes, Eddie watched out for Jayne but Seth had given himself the responsibility of assuring her safety, and he couldn't do that if he lollygagged behind.

The women went to the kitchen to finish the meal preparations.

Seth hovered close to the door, alert to any unusual sounds. From where he stood he could see part of the trail that led from town. He watched Matt and Buck ride out of sight. The dust they kicked up would provide a perfect cover for someone to ride close. He waited until their dust died down, his gaze alert to any sign of an intruder. When he saw nothing to alarm him, he leaned in the doorway and pulled out the letter.

The envelope was wrinkled, Seth's name and address blurred. The return address was Corncrib. From Crawford. The pages had gotten wet at some point and many of the words were too blurred to make out.

"Received the money. Just in time as I was

preparing to leave. I've done all I can. Your father —" he couldn't read the next bit. He could decipher only a few more words "— plans to travel . . ."

He folded the smudged paper and put it in his pocket. Seems Crawford meant to leave whether or not Seth returned. He strode toward the open door and looked out. Was he already gone? Seems he must be. How long had Pa been alone? If Seth left immediately, would he get back in time or would Pa die alone and untended? His insides twisted and knotted. Words Pa had said after Frank's body was discovered burned through his brain. *You didn't take care of your brother. Suppose you mean to neglect your parents, as well.*

He'd tried burying the words, vowing to never let them rise again, and yet here they were, mocking him.

A cowboy crossed the yard and Seth jerked to attention. He meant to watch for anyone who meant to harm Jayne.

How could he leave her and go to his pa?

Yet how could he neglect his pa? Pa would be all alone. At least Jayne had Eddie, the ranch hands and all her friends. Not to mention the Mountie.

He turned to the stairs. He took three at a time but halfway up he stopped. Surely

Crawford would have arranged for someone to check on Pa. Made sure he had food and water. He sighed. That made him sound like a pet.

But would a day or two make any difference to Pa except in Seth's mind? Was he letting cruel, thoughtless words spoken by his pa at a time of stress drive his decisions?

He stood on the stairs. What should he do? Be a responsible son or a caring friend who made sure Jayne was safe before he left?

Slowly he descended the stairs, his decision growing firmer with each step. He would never have any peace until he knew the murdering Englishman had been catured and Jayne was safe.

Then he'd ride hard and fast to Corncrib and take care of his pa.

He joined the others and listened to their chatter. He sat at the dinner table and enjoyed the feast, then afterward he joined in the visiting. He rose often and circled the room, looking out the window for any sign of danger. Eddie often checked the windows, too.

There were so many places the man could hide then slip closer without being seen. The yard was exposed from every side to any decent marksman.

Seth had forgotten how to pray. But he

was beginning to think he might need to get back into practice, because only God could see everywhere at once.

Jayne did her best to appear unconcerned about the lurking Englishman but it was impossible to relax and forget it, even for a moment, with both Eddie and Seth prowling from window to window. Bedtime finally arrived, promising relief from the constant reminder until she realized Seth meant to sleep outside her door.

"I'm sure there's no need," she protested.

"How can you be sure? You can't. So Eddie and I have agreed you will be guarded day and night until that man is under lock and key."

She looked past Seth's shoulder to Eddie.

Eddie nodded. "It seems the safest."

She sighed, went into her room and closed the door. She and Mercy and Sybil had chosen to sleep in the small rooms down a short hallway off the kitchen rather than upstairs. Perhaps the latter would have been a better choice.

She lay in bed, acutely aware that Seth was on the other side of the door. She expected to stay awake, eyes wide, listening for any sound, but she fell asleep almost instantly.

She wakened the next morning with a smile on her lips. Remembering Seth guarded her door, her smile widened.

Not wanting to disturb him if he still slept, she tiptoed about getting dressed then cracked open the door.

"Good morning." He sat on a tipped-back chair facing her door. "Did you have a good sleep?"

"I did." She studied him closely. His cheeks were dark with a day's worth of whiskers and his eyes were red rimmed. "Were you awake all night?"

"Off and on."

"Aren't you being overly concerned?"

"Don't think so."

It was on the tip of her tongue to say she wasn't Frank or Sarah and wasn't about to do something foolish like run out into the open, waving her arms, but he yawned and she only wanted to tell him to relax and get some sleep.

"I'm going to feed Thor then help Linette with breakfast." It didn't surprise her when he followed her down the hall. Nor did she object when he pressed her to his side as they went to the barn. There were advantages to his concern.

Breakfast was over when the Mountie rode in.

"Good news," he said to the adults who waited for him in the kitchen. "I believe we have your man." He dug in his pocket and pulled out a ring that he showed to Jayne. "Do you recognize this?"

"Yes. It's the ring Oliver's murderer was wearing."

"You're absolutely certain?"

Jayne nodded. "Completely."

"Good. He'll go to Fort Macleod where the colonel will question him and arrange to have him sent back to England. Miss Gardiner, you may have to go there and give evidence, though the colonel might decide to accept your statement plus the evidence I'll provide."

"What do you have?" Eddie asked.

"In the man's belongings were the stub of his steamship ticket and the copy of a newspaper article concerning Oliver Spencer's death. Pretty conclusive evidence in my opinion, plus he fits Miss Gardiner's description."

Eddie clapped the Mountie on the back. "It's good to know he is no longer a threat to my sister."

Seth didn't add his thanks or gratitude. He simply shook the Mountie's hand. Jayne would now be safe. He could leave with a peaceful heart and go to Corncrib to fulfill his duty to his pa.

As soon as the Mountie departed, Jayne bounced to her feet. "I feel like I've been set free. Now I can go outside without an armed guard."

At least she didn't look at Seth when she uttered those words so he tried not to take them personally.

Jayne rushed toward the door. "I'm going to enjoy the sunshine. Who's coming with me?"

Mercy and Sybil hurried after her. Seth followed more slowly. He really should be on his way. He could get a good start on the journey. But first he had to make sure Thor could handle being out of his pen, as they'd agreed to do for the first time today.

Jayne headed straight for the fawn's enclosure and opened the gate. "I think it's time for this little guy to enjoy some freedom, too. Come on, Thor."

The fawn trotted over to her and followed her past the barn to the open area between the buildings. Billy and Grady raced over. Neil left the chores he'd been doing and came to watch.

Cassie opened the door of their house so she could see. Cookie came out and stood on the cookhouse steps.

As soon as Thor saw the younger boys he started to romp. Soon everyone took turns playing with the fawn. Seth stood back watching but Jayne would have none of it. She had the fawn follow her to Seth's side and darted back and forth behind him while Thor pranced about. Seth couldn't resist and swatted playfully at Thor who danced away and kicked up his heels.

Jayne laughed. "I had no idea a deer would be so playful." She eyed him up and down.

What did she want? What did she think? He didn't have to wait long to find out.

She tagged him. "You're it." She raced away. "Can't catch me." She lifted her skirts and ran for the cover of the trees by the river.

At first he didn't move, overcome with surprise at this playfulness. Then he growled and ran after her. The others had moved down the road, still playing with Thor, and didn't notice the game Jayne had started.

She darted from tree to tree, making it impossible to catch her.

He changed tactics and rather than chase her, started to stalk her. He hid behind some bushes.

She stopped to listen.

He could hear her breathing and silently

moved toward the sound.

"Seth?" She moved into the open to look for him.

He crouched low and used the underbrush for cover as he narrowed the distance between them.

"Are you hiding?" she called.

He waited, holding his breath.

She darted to another tree, bringing her so close he could reach out and touch her. But he waited, biding his time.

As she turned her back to look for him, he took the step that put him right behind her. "Hi, Jayne."

She screamed and spun about.

He caught her arms to keep her from losing her balance.

"Where did you come from?"

"I haven't forgotten how to play." She didn't need to know it had been years.

"So it seems." Her eyes flooded with joy. "Isn't it good to know that man is captured?"

"Relieves my mind greatly." He moved his hands up her arms to her shoulders.

"Mine, too." She scrubbed her lips together. "I owe you thanks for guarding me."

He slipped his hands to her back and pulled her closer. Either she didn't notice or didn't mind because she came readily enough. "Seems you might have resented it a time or two."

She lowered her eyes. "I realized it was necessary but that doesn't mean I had to like it."

She lifted her head and met his gaze. Time waited as they looked deeply into each other's eyes. Behind him the river gurgled by, the sound erasing doubts and cautions and even fears from his mind. All that counted was this moment and the warmth in her eyes.

"I'm glad no harm came to you." Was that husky voice his?

She nodded. Her gaze dropped to his mouth and slowly returned to his eyes.

Slowly, savoring every bit of anticipation, he lowered his head and captured her lips. Sweet as honey. Welcoming as home.

Her hands pressed on his back, holding him, accepting his kiss.

His heart swelled to near bursting.

Pa's voice echoed through his head. He didn't hear the words. Didn't need to. Didn't want to. Only knew he must answer the call of duty.

He ended the kiss but did not release her from his arms. She fit perfectly as if she had been made for him.

The thought scattered through his brain.

Made for him? God made her. Did He mean for Seth to enjoy her presence?

Again Pa's voice called, harsh, demanding.

Seth still did not let her go. The river murmured softly and he remembered a promise to take Jayne and her friends up the mountains. "Do you and the others still want to see a mountain lake?" He didn't even know if there was one nearby but Eddie would.

"I'd love to."

"Then let's plan an outing tomorrow."

After that he would obey his pa's call. But he wouldn't tell her he meant to leave until they enjoyed tomorrow.

They returned to the yard.

Mercy saw them and gave Jayne a startled look.

He glanced in Jayne's direction. No wonder Mercy looked surprised. Jayne had the look of a woman who had been kissed and enjoyed it.

Telling her he meant to leave was not going to be easy.

CHAPTER FIFTEEN

The next morning, Jayne jumped from bed and pulled on her clothes. She decided to wear the same outfit she'd worn the day she shot Seth. It amused her to think her accident had brought him into her life. She brushed her hair, braided it and left the braid hanging down her back. She studied her reflection in the looking glass. Satisfied, she hugged herself. Laughter bubbled up unbidden. She spun around her room, thankful neither Mercy nor Sybil had come in.

Seth had kissed her and held her. Then invited them to accompany him to a mountain lake. A special outing for a special reason? She would make certain she and Seth had time together alone. Perhaps she should warn her friends of her plan.

But when she entered the kitchen they had already gone down the hill to join Seth, who was hitching the wagon.

She joined them.

Sybil and Mercy sat on blankets in the back of the wagon and Jayne perched beside Seth on the seat. "I'll keep you company."

The sun shone in a clear blue sky. It would grow hot before the day was over but the ladies all wore bonnets so they wouldn't get burned. Besides, not heat, nor cold, nor rain or sleet or snow could mar the beauty of this day. But sunshine was the best.

God, please give us a good day full of laughter and love. Her heart flowed with sweetness. Today would be special.

"Eddie suggested we see a waterfall," Seth said as they left the ranch buildings behind them. "He said it was worth the drive."

"Sounds good to me," she said. The trail led across a grass-covered hill. She leaned forward. "It's beautiful country. I love the way the hills roll away in waves of green. And the mountains fold back in blue layers."

"It's fine country."

"I told you this before but I never see the mountains without thinking of how great God is. Powerful, strong, caring. 'In the beginning God created the heavens and the earth.' I've never been more aware of it than I am here."

He nodded. "Seems He is pretty powerful

all right."

She slowly brought her head around to study him, her eyes wide with surprise. "You sound different."

"Do I?"

She looked toward the pair behind them. So did he. The girls strained forward to hear what he and Jayne said. This was not the time to speak of personal things.

He pointed to a tall pine tree. "A bald eagle's nest. Do you see the male bird?" A white-headed eagle circled slowly then descended to the nest. "He's brought food for the eaglets."

Mercy and Sybil pressed forward and they all strained to see the eagle.

He stopped the wagon so they could have a better look but Jayne felt his gaze on her. She turned, not caring about bald eagles, and let her eyes say what her heart felt, let him see that she would welcome anything he said.

"I wish we could get closer," Mercy said.

"We don't want to disturb them," Sybil replied.

"It's impossible to get close in a wagon," Seth told them. "They are magnificent up close, though. So big. So strong."

"Everywhere I look I see evidence of God's majesty and power." Jayne gave him a warm smile. Was he ready to acknowledge God was not only powerful but cared about each of them in a personal way? Ready to acknowledge a faith they could share?

He didn't say anything. Simply smiled.

The smile melted a path to her heart. She could barely keep from hugging herself, hugging him, hugging the world.

He turned his attention to the trail as it climbed a steep hill.

Mercy and Sybil remained kneeling behind them making impossible anything but general conversation.

Jayne didn't mind. This day overflowed with promise and possibility. She meant to enjoy every minute of it.

"The air is sweeter here," Sybil said.

Seth sniffed. "It's the pine trees and mountain air."

Mercy sighed. "It's adventure beckoning. I keep saying we need to go on a camping trip."

Seth jerked about to look at Mercy. "On your own? That would be dangerous. Three young ladies on their own in the woods? Three citified ladies? There are wolves, bears, mountain lions . . . hundreds of different threats you aren't experienced enough to deal with."

All three of them laughed.

Jayne sobered to explain their amusement. "Mercy figures it would take two cowboys each to keep us safe and —" She sought for a word.

"Entertained." Sybil's word carried a good dose of resignation.

Seth laughed. "That's a lot of cowboys. You think Eddie would spare them?"

"No," Mercy said. "I'm just teasing, anyway."

Jayne settled back with a bubble of happiness in her heart. She'd never seen a finer day.

The trail grew more rugged, required more of Seth's attention. They climbed, went past huge rocks, and sheer cliffs rose to their right and fell away to their left. The path eventually narrowed to the width of the wagon and everyone grew silent. Jayne wondered if they all held their breath like she did. Would it merely end ahead? How would they turn around?

They rounded a corner and Jayne gasped as they entered a verdant clearing. Before them water rushed downward in a horsetail of white spray where it gurgled into the river below.

"This is as far as we go," Seth announced and climbed to the ground. Mercy and Sybil scrambled down before he could offer any of them help but Jayne waited for him to reach up and assist her.

She liked the firmness of his hand on hers, the warmth of his fingers at her waist.

Mercy and Sybil skipped away toward the waterfall but Jayne remained at Seth's side as they walked at a slower pace. The roar of the water made conversation impossible.

Mist sprayed from the falls and Jayne pushed her bonnet off, lifted her face to the moisture and laughed. She turned to Seth, saw the wonder on his face and hugged the thought to her.

They poked about the water's edge for a bit, examining the rocks and admiring the tiny flowers. One rock was dark and shiny and somewhat heart shaped. Surely a sign that Seth meant to offer her his heart. She tucked the rock into her pocket.

After a bit they sat on a damp boulder and simply took pleasure in the surroundings.

Mercy and Sybil clambered over the rocks to rejoin them.

"We're hungry," Mercy yelled. "Let's eat." She grabbed Jayne's arm and dragged her and Sybil toward the wagon.

Jayne glanced over her shoulder and called at Seth to hurry, even though she knew he couldn't hear her.

They spread out the quilts, put out the food they'd brought from the ranch and sat down. Seth sat beside Jayne, his legs crossed so his knees jutted out, touching hers.

She turned to him. "Would you ask the blessing?" As soon as she spoke, she wondered if he would feel awkward.

But he gave a casual shrug. "Sure." He bowed his head. "Heavenly Father, thank You for the beautiful scenery, which reminds us of Your power. Thank You for friends to share the day with and for the food. Amen."

Jayne squeezed his hand. "That was lovely. Thank you." She broke off the touch before her friends could comment.

The conversation as they ate was lively and full of laughter.

They barely swallowed the last bite before Mercy jumped to her feet. "I want to explore more." She stuffed the remains of their lunch into the box. "Let's go."

Sybil rose with a long-suffering sigh but Jayne remained seated at Seth's side. "I'll stay here if you don't mind." She hoped Seth would recognize the opportunity for them to be alone.

Mercy opened her mouth to speak but Sybil jabbed her in the ribs, cutting her off.

"Come on, Mercy. Let's go."

The pair sauntered away.

"Don't go too far," Seth called. "I wouldn't want you to get lost. And watch for bears."

Sybil's steps slowed at his warning but Mercy dragged her on.

Jayne folded the quilts and stowed them in the wagon box.

Seth followed, and leaned his back against the wagon. "You sure you don't want to join them?. We could catch up still."

"No, I'm enjoying the view from here." And she didn't mean just the waterfall, though it was magnificent. Seth was a handsome man with his dark hair and hazel eyes. He had a good jawline and eyes that seemed made for smiling.

He met her gaze. His eyes flashed as he looked deep into hers, probing secret places. He bent his head.

She lowered her eyelids, silently inviting the kiss she knew he offered.

His lips touched hers. Firm, cool, tentative.

She tipped her face upward, wanting more . . . more of his kiss, more of him. Her arms stole around his waist. Her hands pressed to his back. Her fingers curled into the fabric of his shirt as a thousand butterflies seemed to take flight inside her and fill her heart, her mind, her every thought.

She'd been kissed before. After all, she'd been engaged to what's-his-name. But his kisses had never caused this soul-searing sensation. As if joy had become a verb and danced in her being.

He broke off the kiss and leaned back to study her. "I'm sorry. I shouldn't have done that."

Sorry? That he'd kissed her? Did it mean nothing to him, while her world spun with happiness? She shifted back, tipping her head and seeking his face for an explanation.

"I have to check on my pa. Make sure he has everything he needs."

Did his eyes say he wasn't anxious to do so? Perhaps because he wanted to spend more time with her?

"Of course. I understand your concern."

"I'll be leaving tomorrow."

Her heart dropped to the bottom of her stomach. Surely he meant to tell her he'd be back, ask her to wait.

She held her breath until her head thundered. But he didn't say the words she hoped for.

"I've delayed far too long. My pa might be in serious condition by now." He patted his breast pocket. "I had a letter from Crawford saying he left. He didn't say if he'd arranged for someone else to care for Pa. I hope he did but Pa is my responsibility and —" He gave her a look so full of resolve that she fell back a step. "I will never shirk my responsibilities."

He moved aside, putting more distance between them.

Not one word of hope. No suggestion that he meant to come back. Or that he wanted her to wait for him. His silence said it all. This was goodbye. He didn't intend to return. "You brought me here to tell me this? Why? You could have told me at the ranch." Where she would have the option to run to her room and bury her head in her pillow.

"No, I brought you here because I promised you and your friends I would take you to a mountain lake. I wanted to do it before I left."

If she'd had a sliver of hope left that he didn't mean this to be forever, he killed it. He did not intend to return.

"Jayne." He reached for her but she moved away. "I didn't mean to hurt you. I thought you understood that I wasn't staying."

"Of course I did." She forced false cheer into her voice. "You stayed longer than you intended simply to teach me to shoot. I'm grateful. I pray you will find your father well." She lifted her skirts and hurried to the path Sybil and Mercy had taken.

How could she have misjudged him so badly? Did he feel nothing when they kissed?

She met up with Sybil and Mercy returning down the path.

Sybil took one look at her and asked, "What's happened? You look like you've had terrible news."

She tried to smile but tears were too close to the surface. "Seth is leaving tomorrow."

"He'll be back." Mercy was quite certain.

"No. He's going to take care of his invalid father. I understand his concern and his sense of responsibility." She hoped her tone conveyed that it mattered not to her that he didn't intend to return.

But the way both her friends hugged her, she knew they weren't convinced. Her leaden feet followed them down the hill.

They jumped into the back of the wagon. She climbed up and sat between them, keeping her back to Seth.

If she looked at him she might forget her pride and demand to know how he could kiss her like that and walk away as if it hadn't happened. She'd gladly fall on her knees and beg him to stay if she thought it would change his mind.

But nothing would shift Seth from his guilt-driven responsibility.

CHAPTER SIXTEEN

The next morning, she prepared a bottle for Thor.

Seth stepped into the kitchen behind her. "I'll help."

She kept her back to him. "I told Grady he could feed Thor. It doesn't require both of us to help him." From now on she'd do it without his help. Might as well start now.

He thankfully accepted her excuse and let her go.

Despite the searing pain in her heart, she laughed at the way Thor bounced with excitement at seeing Grady. It took the fawn a moment to realize his playmate meant to feed him.

Grady laughed. "I think Thor is better than having a dog. Don't you?"

"He's sweet." She'd never see the fawn without being reminded of many precious hours spent in Seth's company. Her hand pressed to her chest as she tried in vain to stop the pain that threatened to burst her heart.

"Can I take him outside to play with?" Grady asked.

"Maybe after breakfast. Just be sure you have permission from an adult who is prepared to supervise. We wouldn't want Thor getting lost. In the meantime, he'll be safe in his pen." The one Seth had built. Everywhere she turned there were reminders of how impossible it was to push him from her thoughts.

Even without reminders she'd never forget him.

Thanks to Mercy and Sybil's understanding, Jayne wasn't forced to sit at Seth's side throughout breakfast.

"I'll be leaving today," Seth announced.

"You're welcome to stay," Eddie said. "I could use another man with the roundup approaching."

"I have to see to my pa."

Sybil sat at Jayne's side and reached out to squeeze her hand under cover of the table.

Jayne felt Linette's concerned look but studied her empty plate.

"Your hospitality has been most generous. Thank you," Seth continued, his words flat. Was he regretting his decision?

She stole a glance at him under protection of her eyelashes. He didn't look in her direction, but the set of his jaw allowed her no hope for a change of mind.

"I'll be on my way directly." He pushed to his feet. "It's been a pleasure. Again, thank you."

Jayne merely stared at a spot in the middle of the table as everyone offered goodbye wishes. When Eddie and Linette accompanied him to the door, she fled to her bedroom. She would not watch him ride away. She would not wave, nor call an agonized goodbye for fear it would turn into a plea to stay. Or at least a promise to return.

Instead, she sat on the edge of her bed, her hands pressed between her knees and whispered, "Goodbye, Seth. May God bless you." Her heart bled empty.

She heard chairs scuff across the floor in the kitchen, dishes rattle in the dishpan, cupboards open and close. Muted voices informed her the other women worked in the kitchen. The outer door slammed. Was it Eddie leaving? Or was it Grady?

She sighed. She couldn't hide here forever but she didn't move, either, not wanting to face the pitying looks from her friends. Nor have her situation discussed.

Her brocade bag, the one she carried her

gun in, sat on a shelf in the wardrobe. She took it and left the room.

"I'm going to practice shooting," she announced. "Unless you need my help with anything." She addressed Linette.

"No, there are lots of people around to help with anything that needs doing."

"I'll be back later." She slipped out the back door before either Mercy or Sybil could voice an opinion. With heavy feet and a lifeless heart she made her way to the spot where the target waited.

She plopped her bag on the fallen log. It landed with a satisfying thud and she sat down beside it and stared at the ground in front of her feet.

She'd wanted to be independent. She'd achieved that.

Strong. Self-sufficient. And alone. Even Smokey didn't follow her, preferring to stay and play with Thor.

Not that she was entirely alone. She had Mercy and Sybil, and Eddie and Linette and a dozen others around the ranch.

But with Seth gone, her heart echoed with emptiness.

A rustle in the underbrush jerked her attention to the side. Had Smokey decided to join her after all?

She squinted into the shadows but

Smokey did not appear.

A dull sound came from behind her, making the hair on the back of her neck stand up. Someone was there. She edged her hand toward the bag and her gun.

"I'll take that out of harm's way."

At the gruff words, Jayne squealed and sprang to her feet. She stared at a man who was supposedly in jail. "You."

The beady blue eyes narrowed and Jayne realized too late that she shouldn't have let him know she recognized him.

"So you do remember me." He smirked.

"The Mountie said you were in jail."

He laughed, a mocking sound. "I was never in jail."

"But —" She wouldn't give him the satisfaction of asking who was in jail.

Seems he didn't need her to ask. "I fooled that policeman good, didn't I? All I had to do was find someone who looked a lot like me, persuade him he wanted my clothes. Sell him my ring and leave a few things in the pocket of my coat." He let loose another burst of ugly laughter.

She edged backward toward the trees as he talked, but he came forward, stepping over the log. "You aren't going anywhere, little lady."

She turned and ran, made two steps

toward safety before his hard grasp on her arm jerked her around to face him.

"You know what I want."

She wasn't going to let him kill her and fought to escape his grip.

He grabbed both her arms and shook her hard. "My key. Where is my key?"

"I have no idea what you mean." He shook her so hard her teeth rattled.

"That's what Oliver said but I saw you with it before I had to run from the coppers. Didn't see it when I'd seen you later."

"You are mistaken." He'd followed her and spied on her? She felt dirty all over.

He grabbed at her throat.

She squeaked. Did he mean to choke her?

He yanked at the neck of her dress and pulled so hard she fell forward. Her dress gave way and she clutched at her throat to protect her modesty.

He pushed her head back to study her throat. "Where is it?"

"I don't know what you mean," she gasped.

His fingers bit into the flesh of her upper arm. "You can stop playing Miss Innocent," he snarled.

"But I honestly don't know." The anger in his eyes made her legs weak. She fought dizziness and tried to squirm free. As his fingers dug deeper she bit back a cry.

"I know you brought it with you. You wouldn't be fool enough to leave it behind."

She sucked in air and released it in a scream that she hoped carried to the ranch. *Please, God, let someone hear me.*

He slapped her face. "Stop that."

She took a deep breath.

Seeing she meant to scream again, he swung her about, pressing her back to his chest, and clamped his sticky palm over her mouth. His clothing smelled of old sweat. Her eyes watered and she clawed to escape his hold.

"You aren't going anywhere until you tell me where that key is."

She fought to free herself.

"Stop it or I'll have to get tough."

She would fight as long as she had strength. With a flash of insight, she realized fighting might be the wrong tactic and she made her body go limp.

"Now that's more like it." He bent to scoop her into his arms.

As soon as his hand released her, she flew from his arms. Her skirt caught her legs. She yanked it out of the way and continued her headlong flight.

The man uttered a curse.

His feet pounded after her.

Please, God. Help me.

He caught her, swept her off her feet. "You little witch. Get it through your silly head. You are not going anywhere until you tell me where that key is." He dragged her at his side like a sack of rotten potatoes.

She skidded to keep her feet under her.

He made it sound like he would release her if she could produce a key but she very much doubted he would.

They reached a dark, narrow break in the trees where a cold campfire suggested he had spent time here. A shadow moved. Had someone come to rescue her? But it was only his horse tethered out of sight.

He pushed her back against a tree, forced her to sit, and tied her hands and legs. His touch, far too intimate, made her skin crawl.

The look she gave him should have blistered his skin but he returned it with a leering grin.

"So what will it take to convince you to tell me where the key is?" He trailed his smelly finger along her cheek.

She shuddered. She only had to delay him. Eddie would discover her absence when she didn't show up for dinner.

Or would they think she wanted to be left alone?

Seth, why did you have to leave when I

Seth had stayed up late last night making a belt for Buster. He'd given it to Eddie this morning. "A thank-you for Buster for taking care of my horse."

Eddie had examined it. "Nice tooling. You do this?"

"My pa taught me." Pa had given both his sons leatherworking tools on their twelfth birthday. Frank had never cared much for the work but Seth had become quite good at decorating leather pieces. Though Pa had never said so. Only those who bought the items had told him.

Seth had stayed long enough to eat a hearty breakfast, knowing it would be the last decent meal he got until he reached Corncrib. At the main road, he'd turned south, leaned over his horse and raced down the road.

He'd delayed his return far too long.

Pa would have every right to think he neglected him.

Only the truth was, he never had and never would. For a few days he'd taken care of a different responsibility. That was all. Pa had no reason to worry. Or condemn.

Why, even when Pa made unreasonable demands on Seth, he hadn't balked. Like the time he'd insisted they needed one more load of wood even though it was almost dark, cold and threatening to snow.

"It will snow before morning," Pa had warned. "Then it will be even harder to get the wood out. You want Ma and me to freeze to death this winter?"

Of course Seth didn't so he'd gone out in the deepening darkness, stumbling over roots he couldn't see. The horse tangled the rigging on a stump and it had taken Seth several hours to get everything sorted out and the wagon loaded. Snow began to fall long before he finished. By the time he got home he was soaked to the skin and so cold the marrow of his bones ached. But he still had to unload the wood, stack it in the shed and take care of the horse.

All Pa had said was, "You got it done? Good."

Not for the first time, he'd wondered if Pa wished Seth had died instead of Frank.

Seth would have gladly given his life for Frank's but he'd been unable to stop Frank from rushing onto the thin ice.

Pa had said so many hurtful things. Expected the impossible from Seth. Seth understood it was because Pa held him responsible for Frank's death.

So many instances came to mind as Seth

rode away from Eden Valley Ranch and Jayne.

As he thought of never seeing Jayne again a groan ripped from the bottom of his insides, like a flash flood tearing up worries and concerns and memories by their roots, swirling them into a quagmire. He hunkered over the saddle horn as if he could block the pain.

Jayne had shared her worries and fears as if she thought he could help her keep them at bay. She had given him sweet kisses.

His fists tightened into knots at how empty his arms were. How barren his future. He longed to hold her next to his heart forever.

But he wasn't worthy.

He reined up and stared at the rocks next to the path.

Why did he think that? It wasn't as if he couldn't provide for a woman. He could work for Eddie. Or start his own ranch.

It wasn't as if he couldn't protect her. He'd shown that. Although, he hadn't really, had he? The Mountie had captured the man without incident. All Seth did was hang around for the sake of his conscience.

But he would have protected her if the need had arisen.

But somehow everything he'd done, or

would have done, wasn't enough.

He continued to stare at the lifeless rock, hoping the answer would somehow appear.

For whom wasn't it enough?

Pa saw Frank and Sarah's accident as proof that Seth could never handle responsibility. He'd expected a lot from Seth and Seth always delivered. But he knew full well Pa was disappointed in him.

"You could never take care of a wife. It'd end up the same way it did with Frank."

Recalling Pa's words shook him to the core.

He'd heard the words enough times, though he couldn't say if it had been a hundred, a dozen . . . or only twice. But they were branded into his thoughts.

He believed them so firmly that he'd secretly vowed he would never take a wife.

But were the words true?

He shifted about, brought his gaze to the trees a few feet away. His throat tightened as he considered what being a husband involved.

There were certainly risks. Illness. Accidents. Wild animals. Childbirth.

Some he could guard against. Others, he would be helpless to do anything about.

Were his pa's words true?

Was his fear of commitment valid?

Was it possible to fulfill his duty to his pa and also be a husband?

And — the biggest question of all — did he dare risk having his heart ripped apart should any of those disasters befall?

What had Bertie said about God having His eye on the sparrows?

Any one of us is worth a whole lot more than a sparrow.

Worth more than a sparrow? Why he hardly gave them a thought.

Wasn't it Roper who looked at his children and said that God saw fit to bring them into their lives so he could surely trust God with their future, their health, their happiness?

Was it possible to trust a God he couldn't see? A God who didn't do things the way Seth thought they should be done?

Or was he simply finding a way to ease his way out of responsibilities that forced him to make a hard, unwelcome choice?

Was he looking for a way to backtrack? To settle into the groove he had dug himself into?

Pa or Jayne. Where did his heart belong?

He jumped off his horse and led him to the trees where he paced from the trail and back again, considering what he should do.

Go to Pa and care for him as was his duty.

Return to Jayne and follow the inclination

of his heart.

Or do both . . . and perhaps fail both parties?

Finally, desperate for an answer, he fell to his knees by a tree. "God, if You care about a little worthless sparrow then I figure You care for me, a worthless man. Show me how to do what is right. Pa or Jayne. Or can I have them both?"

He surely didn't expect a bolt of lightning from the sky pointing the right direction any more than he expected an audible voice.

But he heard a bird nearby and located a nest of little ones. Only they weren't so little anymore. They were fully feathered and flew back and forth freely. Yet they continued to return to the nest where they'd been hatched.

Free to fly. Yet bound to their beginnings.

He had his answer. And he swung to the back of his horse and turned back toward the ranch.

He couldn't wait to tell Jayne his decision.

CHAPTER SEVENTEEN

Jayne's arms hurt from being tied behind her. The ropes around her wrists bit into her flesh. Struggling in a vain attempt to free herself had rubbed her wrists raw. But her captor before her offered no relief. The dark pines pressed close on all sides, filling the narrow clearing with ominous shadows.

Fear clawed at her throat. Made it impossible to fill her lungs. *Be calm. Be brave.*

She swallowed hard. Maybe if she could divert him in some way . . .

"What's your name?" she asked.

"Why you want to know?" The man sat across the small clearing, a space of about eight feet, alternately scowling at her then chewing viciously on his fingernails.

"No matter. Just being polite." But she'd like to be able to tell his relatives — if he had any — when she shot him through the heart.

Her anger lasted but a second. He kept

her brocade bag pressed to his side. She'd have to have wings to get it.

"Guess it don't matter if you know. I'm only keeping you 'till you come to your senses and tell me where the key is."

"Believe me, I'd tell you if I knew."

"Guess I don't believe you." He spit out a bit of fingernail. "Name's Harry Simms."

She didn't know whether to gag at the way he gnawed his fingers or laugh at such an innocuous name for a murderer. Instead, she fixed him with a look that stung her eyes. "Wish I could say it was a pleasure."

He gave a mirthless sound that she supposed was the closest he could come to a laugh. "I'll let you go anytime you agree to show me where the key is." He opened a can of beans. "You hungry?"

"No, thanks."

He scooped the beans out with his knife and ate them directly from the can.

She checked the position of the sun. Directly overhead. Wouldn't Eddie wonder why she hadn't returned for dinner? *Please show him where I am,* she prayed silently.

Harry cleaned out the can and tossed it into the woods. He lounged back, picking his teeth with a thin wooden toothpick. "I can wait all day. Can you?" He pulled his hat over his eyes. In a few minutes, he snored.

Jayne tugged at the ropes binding her. Harry might be a despicable man but he knew how to tie her so tight she couldn't get loose.

She considered her options. Enough time had passed she decided Eddie wasn't looking for her. At least he wasn't finding her.

What would happen if she told Harry she knew where the key was? She played through several scenarios. She could take him back to the ranch, and hope Eddie or one of the other cowboys could stop him. Or lead him to the barn. Or take him . . . Where?

Every possibility ended with her having nothing to show him and by leading him to the ranch, possibly putting others in harm's way.

No. She must find a way to trick him out here where no one would get hurt but herself.

She prayed desperately for God to give her a really good idea. But nothing came to mind. She shuddered to think what would happen to her.

But no matter, she would not reveal her fear.

Nor would she let it control her.

God help me.

She could count on no other help but His.

Seth rode up to the ranch house. Had he arrived in time for dinner? Not that food interested him half as much as the certainty of seeing Jayne at the table.

He went to the back door to knock. Eddie opened it before his knuckles met the wood.

"Seth? Where did you come from?" Eddie glanced past him. "Is Jayne with you?"

"Me? Why would she be with me? I left earlier today. Alone. You know that." He pushed Eddie aside to glance into the kitchen. "Where's Jayne?" Everyone else sat around the table. Mercy's and Sybil's expressions were strained as if the skin on their faces had grown too tight. Linette pulled Grady to her lap and murmured comfort to the boy, although her eyes darkened and she looked worried.

Seth stepped into the room. "Where is she?"

They looked from one to the other.

Mercy answered. "She left right after you did. Said she was going shooting. But she hasn't come back."

Sybil rubbed a hand across her eyes. "We all assumed she just wanted to be left alone, but shouldn't she have come home for dinner?"

"Well, if that's all, I'll go get her." He dashed out the door and trotted up the hill. It would be easier to talk to her in the clearing where they had spent so many hours together. As he headed for the spot, he rehearsed what he would say. "I've come back for you." Hmm. That sounded a bit blunt. "I hope you care enough to —" Still not right. Surely the words would come when he saw her. Or maybe he'd say what he felt with a kiss.

"Jayne." She'd likely wonder why he'd come back and why he sounded so eager. "Jayne." He stepped into the clearing. The target was there, along with the log on which they'd sat to visit, and a few casings of spent shells. But not Jayne.

"Huh?" He turned full circle. Peered into the trees. "Jayne?" Had she heard him coming and been too angry to talk to him? "Jayne, come on. I came back to tell you that I care. I don't want to leave and never see you again." That should bring her out of hiding.

He held his breath and listened for the sound of her approach. The wind rustled leaves overhead. A pinecone rattled to the ground. A magpie squawked and scolded.

Other birds chattered as they went about their business.

His breath whooshed out. "Jayne, are you hiding? Stop it. You're worrying me."

He waited but heard nothing except the sounds of nature. This was past being funny. She should make her presence known. He stepped into the trees and searched the nearby bushes. Where was she and why was she doing this?

No longer did he smile. No longer did he burst with anticipation of telling her what he felt. Instead, he pressed his lips together tightly. When she finally decided to make herself known, he meant to tell her how foolish this game was.

He returned to the clearing and plunked down on the log. Maybe she'd slipped away while he beat the bushes and returned to the ranch.

With a deep sigh, he dropped his hands between his knees.

This was not at all how he'd pictured his return. He scuffed his heels back and forth. Maybe this was a sign from God that he should continue with his original plan and head for Corncrib.

Might as well go back to the ranch. Let her gloat that she'd fooled him.

A bit of pale wood caught his eye. He

picked it from the ground.

A toothpick. A fancy, city-man toothpick. How could it be? Had the Englishman been here days before and dropped it? He ran his finger along its length. The tip was wet. It had been dropped recently. How was that possible? The Mountie had arrested the man.

Had he escaped?

Hot blood boiled from his heart. Had the murderer returned and found Jayne unguarded?

He slapped his forehead. Thrashing through the bushes looking for Jayne would certainly have warned the escapee of Seth's presence and could well have destroyed any trail.

He considered his options. Go back and inform Eddie or go after Jayne? The former would waste precious time but Eddie deserved to know.

He ran to the house as fast as his bowlegs allowed. Thankfully Eddie stood outside the door. Whether he meant to get back to work or waited for news of his sister made no difference to Seth. "I found this." He thrust the toothpick at Eddie. "It's like the one I found where the man had been watching Jayne the other day. He must have escaped. He must have taken her. I'm going to find her." The words came out in a rush.

Eddie slapped him on the back. "I'll get some cowboys together and we'll scour the country. We'll find her. We'll let you take that direction. We'll go there and there." He pointed then ducked into the house.

As Seth swung to the back of his horse he heard Eddie tell the women to pray. Then he turned his mind to what he would do and galloped back to the clearing. He tied the horse at the edge, pulled his pistol from his saddlebag and checked to make sure it was loaded before he tucked it into his waistband.

He searched every blade of grass, every leaf for a hint of the trail. "God, give me eyes to see, ears to hear and a way to protect her.

"Thank You," he murmured when he found the footprint of a man's boot in the soft ground. The imprint was different than the one he'd seen overlooking the ranch but it was possible the man had more than one set of footwear. He followed the direction it pointed, his eyes glued to the ground for another track. He reached a thin strip of grass without finding another track and straightened. His body ached and not from the position he'd held as he crept across the ground. Worry and failure clamored at his bones. There had to be a clue. Where would the man have taken her? He could not afford to waste time searching in the wrong direction. His ribs clamped down so hard it hurt to suck in air. The man had already committed a murder. Another would make little difference to him.

"Oh, God. Protect her." The whispered words ripped from his throat.

He forced himself to take in a slow breath and released it just as slowly. Where would the man go? Where would Seth go if he wanted to kidnap a young woman?

Mentally, he reviewed the surrounding area he had grown familiar with as he guarded Jayne. In a tiny clearing he remembered a circle of rocks that had indicated someone had once built a campfire there. The grass had been undisturbed when he'd found it so it hadn't been used recently. But perhaps someone else had discovered it and now used the spot.

He studied his surroundings to get his bearings. The place would be a ten-minute hike to his left, through some thick bushes. He would have to go slowly in order not to alert the Englishman. And he prayed this was the correct direction.

Parting the branches of the trees carefully, searching for a spongy area to place his foot, he started toward the spot.

He had stopped praying after Frank's death, but had started again since his arrival at the ranch. Now he prayed with urgency. He'd do his best to rescue Jayne and believe God would help.

If she was still alive.

He grabbed the nearest tree and leaned against the rough trunk as the words screamed through his head. Would he fail yet again to protect those he cared about?

Jayne, I love you. Please be safe.

Strength returned to his limbs. He stilled the urgency pressing at him to hurry, and made his careful, silent way toward the spot.

If she wasn't there . . .

He would not think of it.

But should it be true, he'd search to the ends of the earth until he found her.

He must be getting close and stopped to strain for any sound that would let him know if people were at the clearing. A rustle. A snuffling like a horse chewing grass. Satisfied that someone lay ahead he took a moment to plan his next move.

Harry jerked awake and glowered at Jayne. "I'm tired of this game." He lurched to his feet.

Jayne shrank back, her heart tightening.

What would he do to her? She pushed her fear aside. Do something to distract him, she told herself. Think. What could she do? "What's so important about this key?" He had murdered for it. And likely would not hesitate to do so again.

Her mouth dried so much her tongue stuck to the roof of her mouth.

He gave a mirthless laugh. "Don't play games with me."

"It's no game. I don't know."

He sank back on his haunches and studied her.

She met his eyes and hoped she revealed none of her fear or loathing, only curious innocence.

"Huh. Guess Oliver was too smart to tell you."

"Tell me what?" She didn't have to pretend because she had no idea what he talked about.

He snorted. "Your friend was a cardsharp. A cheat. Did you know that?"

She shook her head. She knew Oliver had gambled. He'd made no secret of it. He often commented on how fortunate he'd been and said he'd won big. But would he cheat? At one time she would have instantly defended him but now she wondered. Had she really known anything about Oliver?

He'd never talked about fears, hopes, or even his childhood, apart from the places he'd lived. Likewise, she had never confessed her doubts and fears to him.

Not like she had with Seth.

Oh, Seth. Why did you leave? We had something together.

Had the feeling only been on her side?

Harry shifted and spat and she spoke, desperate to keep him talking. So long as he talked, perhaps he wouldn't act. "I guess I didn't know him as well as I thought."

Harry grunted. "He fooled you, too, huh?"

She gave a half shrug. If she'd been fooled it was only because she was naïve. Or, as Seth said, foolish. She'd been so blind, so trusting, so needy that she hadn't even asked questions.

"So does this key have something to do with what Oliver might have done?"

Harry said a nasty word. Didn't bother to muffle it nor did he apologize. "That man of yours —"

She didn't object, even though Oliver was dead and could never be her man but also because she'd never felt like they'd had that sort of bond.

"He played a dirty hand of poker. Stole every penny I had. I ask you, how am I supposed to keep a household going without any money? Then he had the audacity to lock the money into a strongbox and taunt me with the key. The key he gave you. He said I'd never locate it either. But he didn't know how desperate I was. I should have known he wouldn't keep it on him. But I had to be certain. Surprised me to think he'd give it to you." The smile on his lips dripped evil. "Guess he didn't care much about your safety."

Jayne could not still the shudder that raced up her spine.

"Ha, ha. I see you think as little of him for doing that as I do." He sprang forward until he was practically nose to nose with Jayne.

Fear said to close her eyes. But she would never again give in to her fear because of this man and she opened her eyes wide and glared defiantly at him, ignoring the fetid smell of his breath.

"So, pretty lady, it's time to stop playing games. Where is the key?" He spat the words out, along with moisture that landed on her cheeks.

With no way to wipe off the drops, she ignored them and leaned forward as far as the ropes allowed. "I do not know." She delivered her words with as much force as he had.

His face reddened. "You are a fool."

She would not back down in face of his anger.

He clamped his fingers on her face, pressing her cheeks against her teeth until she tasted blood.

How could she give him something she didn't have? But the man was beyond reason. He believed she had a key to a strongbox and would not be convinced otherwise.

Reaching around her, deliberately pressing into her body, he cut through the ropes at her wrists, having no concern for the fact the blade nicked her skin.

The pain meant nothing to her. She'd face far worse before this ordeal ended but she would not give him the satisfaction of making her beg or cry. As she considered how she'd rip his eyeballs out if she got the chance, the pain disappeared, blocked by the desire to claw his face.

He sat back and looked at her. And laughed. "Don't think there is some way you can make me change my mind. Ha. I'm not giving up until I get that key." He grabbed her hands and dragged them to the front of her.

Pins and needles filled her arms. She wanted to rub them away but he held her in a cruel grip.

"I will find that key if I have to torture you to death."

"Shoot me and get it over with."

He laughed again, a wicked sound that would live forever in her brain. Though forever might be a matter of minutes. *God, I'm trusting You. Either rescue me or enable me to face this with dignity.*

"What good would that do me? Nope. I figure a few cuts with my knife and maybe a little sport with your body —" He eyed her breasts, leaving her no doubt what he meant. "I figure that will convince you to tell me where the key is."

Despite the shiver that passed through her, she clenched her teeth so hard she imagined the enamel cracked but she refused to reveal a shred of fear.

With a quick slash that trapped a scream in her throat, he cut the ropes holding her ankles and jerked her to her feet. "I've run out of patience."

Her legs numb from being bound, she struggled to stay upright as he dragged her across the clearing.

Oh, God. Her silent prayer wailed through her mind. Would He rescue her or take her to heaven? *Please make it swift and painless. Give me courage.*

But it wasn't courage she felt. It was cold, mind-sucking fear that drained her insides of strength. Her knees folded. But he held her by the elbows and continued their journey.

To what? She closed her eyes and did not let the possible answers come.

CHAPTER EIGHTEEN

Seth edged closer, carefully silent.

He heard a man's guttural voice but had no way of knowing if it was the Englishman he suspected had taken Jayne. But who else would it be? When the voice came again, he detected an English accent.

No female voice came to him. Where was Jayne?

The man shuffled and grunted as if dragging something heavy across the grass. Something like a body.

Seth's limbs froze. He couldn't go on. Was it Jayne's body being dragged? Then fire burned through his veins. He would tear the man from limb to limb if he'd hurt Jayne.

His first instinct told him to beat through the bushes in a mad rush, but good sense told him surprise was his biggest weapon. So he checked each step before he lowered his foot.

A minute later he saw movement. A man's back. When the man shifted, Seth saw her. Jayne, her hair loose and tangled about her face. Was she alive? He couldn't tell from where he stood.

He edged closer, keeping a shield of trees before him.

Jayne's eyes were wide, flashing anger, her jaw set.

His legs wobbled. She was alive. *Thank You, God.*

Her determination would serve her well.

The pair shifted. Jayne's pretty blue dress was torn, exposing her neck. Had he molested her? Harmed her? Bile rose in his throat and he choked back a growl. Any man who hurt Jayne would pay at Seth's hands. His fists curled. He would exact justice. Though hanging would be the man's due. His fists relaxed. He would let the law mete out justice.

How was he to get Jayne away? *God, help me.*

He edged to one side. If no one noticed him, he stood a chance of getting to the trees close to the man. From there he would burst forth and press his gun to the man's head. He palmed his pistol in preparation and began the slow circle to his left. He dared not rush. Any sound would alert the man and ruin the element of surprise. He sucked back a breath and held it as he slid through the trees.

The horse whinnied.

Seth jerked to a halt. If he didn't move the man might not notice him.

The scoundrel pulled Jayne to his chest. A metallic flash caught the sun's rays. Seth's heart slammed into his ribs as he saw the man held a knife to her throat.

"Who's there?" he called. Slowly he circled, his arm so tight about Jayne she clearly struggled to breathe.

Seth prayed the man would not see him.

"You. In the trees. Step out where I can see you."

So much for hoping for invisibility. He shoved his gun into his back waistband. If he got any sort of chance he would use it.

"Hands in the air."

The man had a voice of evil. But then Seth might have a prejudiced opinion.

He stepped into the clearing and smiled at Jayne. A tight smile he hoped offered encouragement.

Something flickered across her eyes. Her gaze darted to the side. He shifted slightly so he could look without being too obvious. Her brocade bag. No doubt she wanted the gun but he didn't need hers. He had one he meant to use.

"I wondered if you'd come looking for your lady friend."

"You wondered right. What do you want with her?"

"She knows and she's playing dumb."

Jayne managed to croak, "He thinks I have a key but I know nothing about one."

Seth glanced about. Pretended not to understand. "You think the key is here."

"I'm not stupid. She has it somewhere. I expect she brought it with her. Maybe brought the strongbox, too." He jerked her tighter against him and brought the knife closer to her throat. "Stop stalling and tell me where it is." He grunted as if an idea had embedded into his brain. "Better yet, show me." He shoved her forward, still gripping her arms.

Seth growled when she stumbled. "You're hurting her."

"Yeah. So what? It might convince her I'm serious."

"Harry, I believe you but I can't help you," Jayne managed to say. "You're mistaken about the key."

"I know what I saw."

"Harry, is it?" Seth asked. "Maybe you should listen to her."

"She's lying." He noticed that Seth has

edged closer. "Stop right there. You must have a gun. Toss it aside."

Seth didn't move. Harry had no way of knowing he had a gun at his back and Seth didn't intend for him to find out.

Harry pressed the knife tighter to Jayne's throat. A drop of crimson blood dripped from the blade.

A reeling sensation as big as the heavens swept over Seth. He had never before considered throwing caution to the wind. But he wanted nothing so much as to launch himself at Harry, wrench his knife from him, press it to his throat and apply enough pressure to bring out a few drops of the man's own blood.

Only the knowledge of how little it would take for that knife to end Jayne's life kept him from springing forward.

Seth kept his hands up. "You see any guns?"

"Don't toy with me. Turn around. Unless you'd like to see your lady friend bleed."

If the knife went any deeper, Jayne's life would be in danger. Seth turned slowly, knowing Harry couldn't miss his gun.

"So you think you can toy with me. Take it out slowly and toss it to the side. And no funny stuff."

What choice did he have? He couldn't

hope to swing his gun into position without risking Jayne's life. So he gingerly pulled the gun from his waistband and tossed it to the side. But if he got the chance he would retrieve it and shoot the man.

Or if the man lowered the knife, he would snatch Jayne away. Let the man use the knife on Seth if he wanted but Seth would not stand by and watch Jayne hurt if he had it in his power to stop it.

"I might know what you're looking for. If you let her go, I'll take you there." If Harry would release Jayne . . .

"I don't think you're in a bargaining position. Where's the key?" He spilled another drop of Jayne's blood.

"Look. Take my gun. You've got a knife. What chance do I have against you? But I won't take a step unless you let her go."

"You like to see her suffer, do you?"

"No. Stop." Harry would kill her if Seth kept it up. "I lied. I don't know anything about a key. I only hoped to trick you."

With a growl, the man shoved Jayne to one side, his hand holding her like a vise. "You think you can toy with me?" He lunged toward Seth.

Seth brought both hands down as hard as he could on Harry's arms. The man shrieked and loosened his grip on Jayne. Seth shoved her to the side. "Run. Get away."

Harry's knife slashed toward Seth's heart. He wrenched to one side. The knife caught him in the ribs. So this was what a knife wound felt like. Burning. Searing.

But the burning didn't slow him down. He had to protect Jayne. He threw reason and caution aside. His anger burned so fierce that if he'd been made of wood, he would have ignited and set both of them on fire. A satisfying picture.

"Seth, you're hurt."

Why was she still here? "Jayne, go get help." At least she'd be out of danger's way if she went after Eddie. Though he didn't expect help would arrive in time to do any good.

The knife came at him again. Seth grabbed Harry's wrist. Harry growled and tried to twist away. Seth would not release his arm. Out of the corner of his eye, he caught a flash of blue. Jayne! How could he protect her if she didn't use her common sense and leave?

Jayne's throat closed off as she watched Seth struggle to get the knife from Harry's hand. Seth expected her to leave. Run and get help.

But all thought of escape fled when she

330

noticed blood trickled down Seth's side.

She had watched one man bleed to death. She would not let it happen again. She gritted her teeth. She would not run and leave Seth. There must be something she could do. Seth's gun. Where was it? There. Not two feet from where she stood.

Just as it had been when Harry had shot Oliver.

Only this time Jayne didn't intend to stand by and let it happen.

As the men struggled for the knife, their attention away from her, she rushed forward and scooped up the gun. She hadn't known Seth to carry a loaded pistol but prayed, *Lord, let it be loaded this time.* Without consciously considering Seth's step-by-step instructions, she took her stance and aimed. Her arm lowered. If she missed, she might hit Seth. Might kill him this time.

The pair shifted. Seth had Harry's knife-wielding hand by the wrist.

She aimed at Harry's head, refusing to think what might happen if she missed. She had to take her chances. She sucked in air, steadied her hand and squeezed the trigger.

The blast battered her eardrums. An acrid smell tainted the air.

Harry screamed. "You shot me."

Obviously not in the head or he wouldn't

be yelling like that.

Harry held a bleeding hand. "Lady, you're crazy."

"Crazy enough not to stand by and let you hurt another person."

Seth pushed the man to the ground face down and planted his knee in the middle of his back. "Nice shot, Jayne," he said.

"I meant to hit him in the head," she admitted.

"You put him out of commission, that's the main thing. Grab a rope off his saddle."

She hurried to do his bidding.

He trussed the man up solidly then rushed to her side. He took the gun from her hand and stuck it in his waistband. He lifted up the front of her dress, pulled a handkerchief from his pocket and pressed it to her throat.

"Are you okay?" he asked, though his voice cracked.

"I'm fine." She touched her fingers to his ribs. "But you're hurt and I'm again responsible."

"No, he is." He nodded toward Harry Simms. "You saved us both."

"You'll never get away with this," Harry yelled.

They ignored his muttered complaints.

"I'm okay," Seth said.

Jayne's knees folded. Her vision blurred.

Seth sank to the ground, taking her with him, and held her close. Shivers raced through her, rattling her teeth.

Seth rubbed her back. "You were very brave."

She clutched his shirtfront. They'd both end up stained with each other's blood. She should likely care and do something about it, but instead she merely held on to him.

He pressed his cheek to her hair.

"Where did you come from?" she asked. "I thought you left."

"I did. But I came back."

She didn't want to leave the shelter of his arms but she must see his face when she asked her next question. "Why did you come back?"

"Because of you."

That didn't provide any information.

Harry thrashed about. "You can't do this to me."

Now was not the time and place to ask questions. She pushed to her feet. "We need to get you to the ranch and tend that wound."

"My horse isn't far away."

"I'll get it." He must feel worse than he cared to admit because he sat there as she headed for the place he indicated.

But she had gone only a few yards when

Eddie, Slim and Roper rode into view.

"I heard a gunshot," Eddie said when he saw her.

She nodded, her voice suddenly gone.

Eddie dropped from his horse and raced to her side. "You're hurt." Blood from Seth's wound blotched her dress. Perhaps a drop or two of her own had spattered on her bodice.

"I'm okay. Seth has a knife wound." She led them back to the clearing.

Seth struggled to his feet. "Good to see you."

Eddie jerked Harry to his feet. Slim brought his horse forward and they swung him into the saddle. No one paid attention to Harry's continued protests except Eddie.

"You kidnapped my sister. That's a capital offense."

Harry glowered. "She's got something of mine."

"I don't want to hear it."

Roper led Seth's horse forward and Seth swung into the saddle. Jayne noticed his lips were white and suspected he was in a lot of pain.

His gaze met hers and he smiled in a slow, intimate way that touched her heart. Whatever his reason for returning, they could wait until the business with Harry Simms was over and done with to discuss it.

Eddie pulled her up behind him and they rode for home.

As soon as the women saw them, they rushed forward. Linette immediately guided Seth upstairs. She would tend his wound and make sure he would live. But Jayne's heart followed him up the steps. She couldn't wait to have him to herself so he could explain why he'd returned.

Mercy and Sybil took Jayne under their wings and helped her change into a clean dress. They demanded all the details of what happened.

Sybil tenderly washed Jayne's neck. "It's only a nick."

"You really shot him?" Mercy asked again.

"I had no choice. He meant to kill Seth."

"You're a very brave woman," Sybil said.

"And a good shot." Mercy's voice was filled with awe.

Her strength returned. She could finally look at the situation fully. "I'm not a good shot. I meant to shoot him in the head but somehow managed to hit his hand."

Mercy and Sybil stared at her. Mercy started to laugh. Then Sybil joined her.

Jayne stared at them both. "I might have hit Seth."

"You already did once and he survived,"

Mercy managed to gasp out.

"But at least you did what you could." Sybil choked out the words in between laughter.

Poor Seth. She truly might have injured him again.

What must he think? He'd taught her all he knew and she still couldn't hit what she aimed at.

A tickle began beneath her ribs and raced upward to escape as a burst of laughter.

The three of them fell on her bed and laughed out their tension and fear and relief.

After a moment, Jayne sobered. "I hope the knife wound isn't too serious. Let's see if Linette is done yet." If she was and Seth felt up to being on his feet, Jayne meant to have a talk with him.

The three returned to the kitchen where Eddie waited for her. "Sit down. Tell me what happened."

Mercy and Sybil sat beside her. Before she began, Linette returned. "I want to hear. too."

"So do I." A deep, familiar voice drew her attention to Seth.

"Are you okay?"

"I've been hurt worse. I was shot once, you know." His grin said he meant it to be teasing.

"I'm sorry. Somehow I feel I am to blame for this time, too."

Mercy moved over and made room for him at Jayne's side.

"You likely saved our lives."

She nodded. He'd said it before. All she had to do was believe it.

She turned to her brother and began her account of the day's events. "Harry Simms is his name. He was never arrested." She told how Harry had set up some poor man to appear to be him.

She told every detail. "He wants a key that I don't have." She ended by relating how she'd missed her target.

"I meant to shoot him in the head."

Her friends muffled a laugh but Eddie smiled at her. "My little sister can take care of herself."

"She sure can," Seth answered.

Their praise gave her food for thought. She had taken action rather than cowered in fear. She'd missed her intended target but nevertheless had disarmed the man.

Yes, she could take care of herself.

But she'd learned a second, equally valuable lesson.

Taking care of herself could be a lonely business unless she had a partner.

Why had Seth come back?

CHAPTER NINETEEN

Jayne hoped she and Seth would get a chance to talk but Linette had supper ready and after the meal, everyone continued to hang about.

Mercy and Sybil didn't leave her side, as if afraid she would disappear again.

"You aren't leaving again in the morning?" Jayne managed to ask Seth as they all clustered about the table, reading the newspapers brought back from town. It grew increasingly obvious that no one intended to leave Seth and Jayne alone. Whether intentional or not, she couldn't say.

He shook his head. His eyes promised they would talk. And with that she had to be content.

Around the table Sybil covered a yawn and Linette's head bobbed.

"We've kept you up long enough." Sybil patted Linette's arm.

Jayne's sister-in-law had weary lines about

her eyes, from hard work and her pregnancy. Jayne sprang to her feet. How selfish to be thinking only of getting a chance to talk to Seth. "Yes, it's time for bed."

Mercy rose and the three friends headed down the hall to their bedrooms.

Jayne paused just before she ducked out of sight and called "Good night." She meant it for all of them but her gaze went only to Seth who stood in the hallway that went in the other direction.

His smile blessed her as he lifted a hand in a tiny wave.

Until tomorrow, she promised herself as she went to her room. He had come back. Surely that meant good news for her.

She didn't have the strength to think of other reasons he might have returned.

The girls had made her put on the dress she'd worn when Seth had taken them to the waterfall up the mountain. When she'd taken it off she hadn't planned to wear it ever again. It reminded her of his announcement that he meant to leave. He'd given her no reason to hope he'd come back or that he cared for her in the slightest.

Now she willingly hoped and believed he'd changed his mind.

She lifted the skirt to her nose and breathed deeply of the memories. The cool dampness of the spray of water, the sweet pine scent. She touched her fingertips to her lips, recalling the warmth of his kiss. How she'd thought it so full of promise.

Perhaps there would yet be a promise. She jammed her hand into the pocket. Her fingers encountered something hard. She dug deep and pulled out a little stone.

Her heart swelled with hope as she cupped it in her palm. Smooth and heart shaped, it had lain hidden in her pocket, forgotten until now.

A tremble filled her heart. The promise of that day had disappeared as Seth rode away. But now he had returned.

Hope danced across her nerves.

Clutching the rock, she went to her trunk and dug through the contents until she found her little treasure box. In it were items of sentimental value. She set it on her bed. A smile caught her lips as she opened it and lifted out a tiny gold locket. Mother and Father had given it to her when she was six years old. Perhaps one day she could pass it on to a daughter. Her throat tightened, as she pictured a tiny girl with hazel eyes like Seth's and a smile that turned her heart to liquid honey.

She set aside the locket and picked up a valentine card her sisters, Bess and Anne, had made for her. For days they had labored over their secret. Bess was only about twelve years old and Anne nine at the time. The card they'd crafted was a little uneven in places but every time Jayne looked at it she remembered the way they had smiled as they presented it to her.

Next were four picture cards from the trip when Father had taken them to Paris. She sat back on her heels. Life had seemed so simple then. She would never have believed so much tragedy would hit her in a few short years.

She put the cards on the bed beside the other things and put her heart-shaped rock on the bottom of the box. Right beside the locket Oliver had given her. She touched the heart and key. Stirred them across the bottom.

The key didn't match the heart for proportions. It was too large and heavy. Oliver had said she needed a big key because he had a big heart. At the time she'd put it down to Oliver's likeness for doing things in a large way.

Where's the key? Harry had been sure she had it. Insisted he'd seen it. Was this what he meant? Could this be the key he sought?

A key to what? She studied it for a long time, searching her mind for a clue. What had Oliver said when he gave it to her? Nothing that seemed to indicate anything unusual. But several times he'd caught the charms as they hung from her neck and then said something cryptic. *You have the key to my heart and so much more.*

Another conversation surfaced in her mind.

"Of course." Now it all made sense.

She returned to the kitchen. It was dark. But she saw light in the hall. She found Eddie in the library, entering figures into a ledger.

He set aside the pen as she entered. "How are you doing?"

She shrugged. "Fine. I found this. Oliver gave it to me on a chain with a locket."

Eddie examined it carefully. "It seems rather large to hang on a chain about your neck."

She nodded. "I thought so, too, but it seemed sweet of Oliver to give it to me." And then Oliver had died and she couldn't bear anything that made her remember the details of his death so she'd put it in her treasure box and forgotten it as she tried to forget about Oliver's murder.

"Oliver used to joke about a box he'd asked to store in a garden shed on our property. Said he didn't think his parents would value it as they should and might even destroy it. He said someone had given it to him. He valued it for some reason, though he never said why." She'd never thought to ask him. Or if she had, she'd quickly dismissed her curiosity. Oliver did not like her to ask too many questions. "I asked the gardener if he minded and of course he didn't. I think this is what Harry was after."

"I think you're right. I'll send the key to Father to check out."

"If the box is full of money as Harry said, who does it belong to?"

"I really don't know. I guess Father will have to get his lawyer to sort things out. I don't think you need to worry about it, though." He leaned back and studied her. "I guess that solves the mystery surrounding Harry."

"Now I can rest in peace. Not that I think he'll ever be a threat to me again."

"What about Seth?"

She blinked. "Seth was never a threat to me."

"Not physically. But I think emotionally he can hurt you very badly. Did he say why he came back?"

"We haven't had a chance to discuss it." She tipped her chin in a gesture of determination. "We will in the morning."

He laughed at her little show of firmness. "Let me know how it goes."

She rose, bent to kiss him on the forehead and pat his shoulder. "I'll tell you what you need to know."

He grinned. "Getting real independent, are you?"

She smiled down at him. "Not so independent I don't need friends and family." And a husband.

He opened his mouth, likely to add the same words she'd added silently.

She patted his shoulder again, not giving him a chance. "Good night, big brother."

"Good night, little sister. Though not so little as you used to be."

Nor so weak or fearful, she added silently.

Seth's injured side did not pose a hindrance to his sleep. But his thoughts did. He still didn't know what he meant to say to Jayne.

Not that her friends and family had allowed him a chance to talk to her. Maybe they purposely prevented it. After all, he had left her. And they'd all seen her hurt.

But he would speak to her alone and he'd do his best to find the words to explain why he'd returned.

He rose early the next morning and made

his way to the kitchen. Jayne was there preparing a bottle for Thor as he'd hoped.

"I'll help you feed him." Did she understand he wouldn't accept any excuses to avoid him?

She nodded. "Come along, then."

They traipsed down the hill toward the barn. Out of habit, he reached out to pull her to his side but the danger of a murderer watching her was over. And he didn't want to cloud his mind with the joy of her pressed close. He dropped his arm and allowed a few inches between them.

Thor greeted them and bunted against Jayne in his eagerness for the bottle.

He didn't say what his heart felt as the fawn sucked. It was too easy to be distracted by Thor's playfulness.

"I found the key," she said. She must have noticed his confusion. "The one Harry wanted."

"I thought you didn't know anything about it." His blood thundered against the top of his head. Had she put them both in mortal danger for a lie?

"It was a key Oliver had given me with a heart-shaped locket. I'd forgotten all about it. I found it last night when I was poking through my stuff." She ducked her head as if to check on the fawn but maybe also to hide her face from him. Did she regret his return? Maybe she'd been relieved to have him leave.

No. He would not entertain doubt. He would explain his reason for coming back and let her respond.

The fawn finished and turned to play with Smokey.

Jayne faced him, her eyes dark, allowing him to read nothing. "Seth, why did you come back?"

"I came to ask you to go with me."

Her mouth dropped open. She closed it and swallowed hard. "Why?"

"Because I have to take care of my pa."

"You don't need me for that."

He wasn't explaining himself well. "On my ride south I started to recall things my pa said to me. Hard things."

She nodded.

"He blamed me for Frank's death. He had taught us to watch out for each other and I failed."

"You didn't fail." She brushed her hand along his arm. "You tried to stop them. The choice was theirs."

"I know that but I still feel Pa's accusation." He found strength in the look she gave him. "He said I would likely fail to take care of my parents, too."

She squeezed his arm.

"There's more." His throat tightened so his voice cracked. "Pa told me I could never take care of a wife. I guess I believed him."

She waited, a curtain closing her thoughts to him.

"Until yesterday."

Her eyes looked hopeful and guarded at the same time.

He hated that he was responsible for the latter emotion. "Yesterday I stopped and thought of all that Pa said. I realized that just 'cause he said it didn't make it true."

She nodded. "That's so."

"But even if it isn't true, marriage is a risk. So many bad things can happen."

"And so many good things."

"Yes. I made a decision to trust God with the future and enjoy the present."

"I'm glad." Her voice was quiet, overly controlled.

"I want you to come with me. Meet Pa. I will have to stay and care for him. It's my duty and I would never neglect him."

"I wouldn't expect you to."

"Will you come?"

She lowered her head so he couldn't see her eyes or read her expression.

"I can't bear to leave you behind."

"It wouldn't be proper for me to go with

you. An unmarried woman." She shook her head.

"But what if we're married?"

Her head came up. Her eyes widened. "Married? What are you talking about?"

He furrowed his brow. "Isn't it obvious? I love you and want you to come with me."

"Whoa, there, cowboy. Back up a minute. What did you say?"

He slapped his forehead. He'd forgotten the most important thing he meant to say. He tipped Jayne's chin up and studied her eyes, her beautiful skin, her firm little chin.

He jerked his thoughts back to the words he wanted to get just right. "Jayne Gardiner, I love you with my whole heart. I want to spend the rest of my life with you, sharing the good times and the bad. Growing old and gray. I want to hold you next to my heart." He patted his shoulder. "Right here where you belong. Jayne, will you marry me and make me the happiest man in the world?"

Her eyes filled with such warmth and joy he could hardly meet her gaze. "Yes." She laughed. "Yes, yes, yes, yes, yes."

He caught her to him and kissed her. When her arms pressed into his back he sighed. He'd come home where he belonged.

He ended the kiss and smiled into her welcoming gaze. "Does that mean you love me?"

"Seth Collins, I love you so much I wonder my heart doesn't explode."

"Is that good?" he teased.

"Oh, it's very good." She tilted her head to the side. "How long have you known you loved me?"

"I don't know. I guess I knew it when you stood in my arms, insisting you would learn to shoot even though you were scared to death of guns."

"It took you long enough to say it."

He nodded. "I had learned to shut my heart to love and focus only on responsibilities."

"I'm sorry your father said such unkind things. I expect he spoke out of his own grief and pain." She pressed her palm to his cheek and he turned to kiss it.

He nodded. "I guess so. But if I ever say anything that hurtful please remind me of the power words have."

"You mean like this? Seth, I loved you when you pulled that wad of money from your boot so intent on caring for your pa you would have bled to death trying to get to him. I loved you when you made sure I knew how to shoot. I especially loved you when you held my hand steady when I couldn't keep my eyes open. I knew then that you were the kind of man who would walk at my side, helping me and supporting me." Her voice fell to a whisper. "I thank God He brought us together."

"About God. I have stopped shutting Him out, too. I prayed when you disappeared. I believe God led me to you and helped us escape." He laughed. "Though you shooting Harry's hand certainly made it possible."

She shuddered. "I dare not think how close I came to shooting you."

He shook his head. "I was never in danger. You're a better shot than you know. Jayne, what about coming with me to see Pa?"

She pressed her head to his shoulder. "That's something we need to discuss. It takes time to plan a wedding and make arrangements."

"Time is something I don't have. Pa has been alone for days. I don't know if he's being taken care of or not. I have to do my duty." Not that it was duty alone that drove him. He had always planned to take care of Pa. That hadn't changed.

She clutched his shirtfront. "I know. I can't bear to let you go. But waiting for me will only delay you longer."

He did something he hadn't done in a very long time. "Jayne, let's pray about it and trust God to provide a way." He took her hands, pressed them to his chest and bowed his head until it touched hers. "Our Father in heaven. First of all, I want to thank You for Jayne. For bringing us together and for making her strong and brave. I don't want to leave her but my pa needs me. Could You bless our love by providing a way for us to stay together? Amen." It was the longest prayer he'd ever prayed and the most sincere and urgent.

"God will provide," she whispered. "Now I promised Eddie I'd tell him anything he needed to know. I want him to know about us."

Eddie, Linette and the others were gathered round the table for breakfast when they returned.

"Finally," Mercy said. "Eddie was about to send out a search party."

"No need," Seth said. They stood side by side, facing Eddie. "Jayne has agreed to marry me."

Eddie stood and grabbed Seth's hand. "Congratulations. You've made a good choice." He hugged Jayne.

The others clustered around them, offering congratulations.

"You're getting married?" Grady asked.

Jayne hugged the little boy. "Yes."

"Are you going to live here?"

She lifted her face to Seth. Her coffee-brown eyes promised so much he wanted to shout with joy. "I don't know where we'll live. We haven't figured that out yet."

Where were they going to live? What about Pa?

The questions hammered the inside of his head. If only he could stay here and forget his responsibilities. But he couldn't.

Was their love strong enough to survive the uncertainty of their future?

CHAPTER TWENTY

"Have you made any wedding plans?" Linette asked.

"No," Jayne said. It had been only a few minutes since they'd confessed their love. She wanted to twirl down the hall, laugh with joy and stand out in the sunshine to shout to the heavens. She gave Seth a slow, deliberate look. He met her gaze, his forest-green eyes full of longing.

Mercy nudged her. "Ahem."

Jayne blinked, smiled distractedly and tried to remember what the conversation involved.

But she couldn't focus on anything apart from the questions burning her mind. When would they marry? Where would they live? So many things to work out. And so little time.

As soon as breakfast was over and she'd helped with the dishes, she hurried outside to find Seth.

He came around the house. "I've been waiting for you."

Her heart swelled with sweetness to know he wanted to spend the rest of his life with her.

He held his hand out to her and they walked to the clearing where they'd spent so much time, and sat on the log.

"I will always think of this as our special place," she said.

He pulled her close. "But this is your special place." He pressed her head to the hollow of his shoulder.

"My place. I like that."

For several minutes they didn't move. She would gladly have spent the day there.

"We need to make plans." His words disturbed her peace.

"I suppose we do." She sat up and turned so she could watch his face as they talked.

"I love this country."

Her heart leaped within her. Was he going to stay here after all? Dreams filled her head. A little home for the two of them. Visits with Linette and her friends. Keeping house.

He sighed. "If I had time I would look about for a piece of land to start my own place."

She began to decorate a house — a big

table in the kitchen so she could do lots of baking and canning like Linette did and entertain visitors. Maybe she'd make a quilt for their bedroom. Light flooded a secret place behind her heart. A place that until now had been unknown.

"But I doubt Pa will want to move."

Her dreams disappeared in the blink of an eye. "What will you do in Corncrib?"

"I'll work for ranchers. Do odd jobs. Whatever I can find that will allow me to be home every day to care for Pa."

She touched his freshly shaven cheek. "I'll help you."

He nodded, his eyes flooding with so many things — determination, love, surprise, as if he didn't believe that love possible. "I don't want to leave you."

"You go. Look after your pa. I'll wait until you sort things out." A lump in her throat cut off her flow of words.

He pulled her close, cupped his hand to her head. "It kills me to think of leaving you but I must."

Perhaps it was only because her ear was pressed to his chest that his words seemed more like a growl.

They clung to each other, till finally a sigh rippled from him. "I'll stay the day."

Did the thought of only one day hurt him

as much as it did her? She hoped so, yet she didn't want to add to his distress.

"A day will be wonderful." She would do her utmost to make it a day of sweet memories that would make him never forget how much he loved her and she loved him. Her decision made, she kissed him soundly. "Let's go on a picnic."

"I'll enjoy whatever we do. So long as we are together." He pulled her to him and kissed her. She sighed and leaned into his embrace. Maybe they could stay here and forget everything and everyone but this moment and each other.

But she wanted to know everything about him. She loved listening to the beat of his heart but wanted to listen to the words of his heart, as well.

So they returned to the house where Linette helped Jayne prepare a lunch to take with them. Jayne explained Seth would be leaving tomorrow and she wanted to be alone with him.

"I'm sorry you only have today," Linette said. "Enjoy it to the fullest."

They set out with no destination in mind, talking as they walked. They reached an open area that let them see the rolling hills that flowed away from the mountains.

"This looks like a good place." Seth

spread the blanket Jayne had brought and they sat side by side looking out at the vista before them.

For a moment, they didn't say anything.

"What kind of house will we have?"

Seth leaned back on his elbows and tickled her neck with a blade of grass. "Pa's house is small. Two bedrooms upstairs but he sleeps in a bedroom on the main floor. We'll have our privacy."

"I wasn't worried about that. I'm simply trying to imagine your home."

He sat up. "If I could start my own ranch, I'd build a solid house, frame or log. I'd start small and add on rooms as our family grew."

She turned on her side to face him. "Family?"

He touched her cheek. "Don't you want children?"

She brought his fingers to her lips and kissed them. "I want a little boy with dark brown hair and hazel eyes and the sweetest face in the world."

"Jayne." His voice thickened and he drew her in for a kiss. Then he smiled at her. "I want a little girl with coffee-brown hair and brown eyes that would make it hard for me to be stern."

"Only two?" she asked.

"More would be nice."

She sighed and lay back to look at the fluffy clouds overhead. "Tell me about your childhood."

"Before Frank's death?"

Sensing that his childhood ended after the accident, she murmured agreement.

He told of a stern father and a gentle mother who taught the boys responsibility and hard work but who also engaged in outings to church gatherings, town fairs and who played board games with their sons and read to them.

"But there was no more of that after Frank died."

She opened her arms and pulled him close, holding him like he'd not been held since that awful day. If only she could kiss away all the pain of his past. She vowed she would try her best to do so.

Her eyes filled with tears, and she blinked them away. She would bravely face his departure and leave him only the memory of this day and her smile.

Her tears would be shed in the privacy of her own room.

His heart so heavy it pressed against the soles of his boots, Seth saddled his horse the next morning. Every heartbeat squeezed out shards of glass, tearing his veins to shreds.

He must go but it would be the hardest thing he'd ever done.

Jayne waited for him outside the barn. He led the horse out and stopped. What did he say to describe his reluctance to leave her? He simply pulled her into his arms and hoped she understood.

She clung to him so hard the knife wound in his side hurt but he welcomed the pain. It would serve as a diversion in the days to follow.

"I can't promise when I'll get back." They had decided he would make arrangements for someone to care for Pa so he could come back. They would marry then return to Corncrib. He glanced past the ranch buildings. How he'd like to start fresh with land of his own. Perhaps God would allow it in the future.

For now he was grateful for the blessing he had and he pulled Jayne closer.

"I'll be here waiting and watching." The words grated from her throat, and he knew she found this parting as difficult as he did.

He would be brave for her sake.

He tipped her head up and gave her a kiss so full of hunger and missing and loving that she gasped then returned the kiss with equal emotion.

He tore himself away. "I must go." He'd already said goodbye to the others. A groan threatened to escape as he turned toward his horse and swung into the saddle.

His smile barely moved his lips but it was the best he could produce and he took Jayne's outstretched hand and held it a moment. Regret dulled her eyes. His likely revealed the same emotion. "Until later."

She nodded.

Looking to neither the right nor the left he bent low and raced from the yard.

"Whoa!"

He jerked up at the word, fought to control his mount and stared at a covered wagon he'd almost run into. He squinted at the older couple driving the rig. It couldn't be. . . .

"Hello, son."

"Pa!" Not another word came to his befuddled brain.

"You look surprised."

"I guess I am!"

"But Crawford wrote you. Told you I was marrying and headed out here to visit you."

"Married?" He looked at the woman at Pa's side.

"Meet my wife, Edna."

He doffed his hat.

"Howdy," she said, grinning at his confusion. "Looks like you didn't get the letter."

"I did but most of the words were smudged. I only knew Crawford had left. I figured you were home waiting for me to finally show up."

"Nope. I been busy with my own affairs." He patted Edna's arm.

Eddie signaled from the house to bring them in.

"Come and meet the Eden Valley Ranch crew."

Jayne had climbed the hill and stood at Eddie's side, her hand shading her eyes as she watched him.

Pa was here. He was well enough to drive the wagon, though his face drooped on one side. Seth didn't know what it meant but one thing was certain: He didn't have to go to Corncrib. His heart bounced from rib to rib in joy.

"Take the wagon to the door," he called to his pa then turned his horse, raced to Jayne's side where he jumped to the ground and swept her into his arms. He swung her about in a big circle.

"Seth, are you crazy?"

"Crazy about you." He kissed her nose.

When the wagon reached the house, Pa and Edna stepped down. Seth kept Jayne at his side as he went to Pa's side. "Jayne, this is my pa and his new wife."

She looked up at him in wonder and surprise. "You mean —"

He pulled her close to his heart. "I don't have to go to Corncrib."

Her eyes said she understood what this meant as clearly as he. He led her to Pa and Edna. "I'd like you to meet my intended, Jayne Gardiner."

Pa gave Jayne a quick study then shook her hand.

Edna gave Pa a scolding look. "Pshaw, what's wrong with you, Murdo? She's family." She hugged Jayne.

Seth swallowed a lump then turned to the others.

He waited until introductions were made and Linette invited the guests inside before he took Jayne's arm and drew her down to the river. Pa surely had a story to tell but it could wait.

Once they were in the shelter of trees he turned her into his arms. "When can we get married?"

She kissed him. "I love you, too."

They returned in time to partake of dinner. Afterward, Pa said he wanted to talk to Seth. "Bring Jayne along, too."

362

"Feel free to use the front room," Linette said.

They retired there.

Pa leaned forward. His right arm still didn't move a hundred percent correctly.

"I can't believe how improved you are." Seth shook his head. "I expected to find you an invalid."

"Crawford did a world of good. But it was Edna moving in next door that did the most for me." He took her hand as he talked. "She lost her husband and son in a horrible accident. Her husband had been cleaning a gun and accidently shot their boy. When he saw what he'd done he turned the gun on himself. He left Edna to deal with it on her own."

"It was difficult," Edna said. "But I've discovered what doesn't kill you makes you strong."

Seth grinned at Jayne. "I think we're also learning that. And that God is always there to help us."

Pa continued. "As Edna told me what she'd dealt with and I saw how she shone like gold despite her trials —"

Edna made a dismissive noise but gave Pa a grateful smile.

Pa nodded. "I realized I had allowed bitterness and blame to become my way of life." He reached for Seth's hand and held it in his own.

What was this all about? Did Pa mean to clear his conscience by laying the blame firmly at Seth's feet? His heart ticked in steady, warning beats.

"Seth, I said cruel and untrue things to you. I don't know if you recall them or if you believed them. I regret them. It wasn't your fault Frank died. And despite the things I said, and the times I failed to show appreciation, you have been a fine, upstanding person. I'm proud to call you son. Can you forgive me for the wrong things I've said and done?"

Seth's lungs emptied in a rush. "Pa, I forgive you." The power of Pa's words had started to fade when he met Jayne. They had grown fainter as he grew to love her and lost most of their power when he stopped on the trail and decided to throw off their chains.

Pa's apology forever erased them from his heart.

When Pa and Edna left them a few minutes later, Seth turned to Jayne. "We can start with a brand-new, clean slate. How does that feel?"

"It's wonderful." She kissed him then they

moved to the window to look out on the ranch.

He looked past the buildings to the promise of a bright future in God's generous plan.

EPILOGUE

Three weeks later

Jayne looked at her reflection in the mirror.

"You look lovely," Sybil said. "The new dress was a good idea if I do say so myself."

Linette and Sybil had offered to make her a wedding dress to remember. She'd refused. "I'm to be a rancher's wife. I prefer something plain so I can use it again."

"A nice dress can never go amiss," Sybil had said. "Allow us to do this."

"I'm glad you persuaded me." Jayne loved the dress. Made of ecru satin with seven rows of green piping at the wrists and a row of green-covered buttons down the front, it was dressy enough to be special and yet she would be comfortable wearing it to church and other special events in the future. The waist dipped in the front. The neckline ended in a small stand-up collar. "It's lovely." She faced her friends. "So are you."

Mercy wore a dark blue dress that brought

out her beauty. Sybil shone in a golden dress.

Eddie appeared at the door, handsome in his dark jacket and white shirt. "Are you ready?"

She nodded. Mercy and Sybil left the house ahead of her and Jayne took Eddie's arm for the walk to the clearing where she and Seth had decided to get married — the same clearing where they had spent many happy hours. "Still no word about the box Harry Simms was after?"

Eddie smiled down at her. "It's too early to get a reply from across the ocean but Father will take care of it. You needn't give it another thought."

"I won't." Her life was too full of joy and love to be concerned with the past.

They paused to let Mercy and Sybil walk down the grassy aisle ahead of them.

Then they stepped into sight. The assembled people turned. She felt their smiles. Their love.

She spared a glance about. She and her friends had spent hours preparing the clearing for this day. They'd gathered wild flowers and placed them in containers around the circle, and Sybil had hung pink, red and white ribbons from the trees. Jayne smiled. It was perfect.

This day was perfect, blessed with sunshine and a breeze that rustled the leaves overhead enough to prevent the air from becoming too warm.

She scanned the crowd. Everyone from the ranch was there, and Seth's pa and Edna, who had decided to live in Edendale.

Buster looked like a new person. He'd taken his first month's pay, gotten a haircut, a new shirt and pair of trousers. He wore the belt Seth had made him.

Her heart swelled with pride at Seth's skill and generosity.

Eddie had arranged a preacher from Fort Macleod to perform the ceremony. He stood patiently at the front.

She had resisted looking at Seth until now because she knew once she saw him, nothing else would register.

His smile blazed at her.

His hair had been trimmed. He wore a white shirt and a dark gray vest that emphasized his coloring.

She drew in a breath and held it.

"I can't believe I'm marrying such a handsome man," she whispered to Eddie.

"He's marrying a beautiful woman."

"Thank you." Her eyes on Seth, she walked at Eddie's side until he released her to Seth.

"To have and to hold from this day forth."

The words rang in her mind as they went through the rest of the ceremony then returned to the ranch to a beautiful meal the women had prepared. They ate outside.

Then at some invisible signal, likely from Linette, the people filed by Seth and Jayne to congratulate them and say goodbye as they made their way to their own homes.

Seth smiled down at Jayne. "Dear wife, it seems we can finally go home."

"Husband, that sounds real good."

They went to the small cabin across from the cookhouse where Linette and Eddie had spent their first winter.

Seth swept her into his arms and carried her over the threshold. He kissed her soundly before depositing her on her feet.

"Our first home together," she said, her voice filled with joy.

"Next spring I will find land and build a house on our own ranch."

She wrapped her arms around his neck. "I don't care where we live so long as we're together. You are mine to have and to hold for the rest of my life."

He kissed her. It was the beginning of their lives together.

God had blessed her beyond measure.

Dear Reader,

In my mind this story began with a man suffering from an injured leg and needing care. At first I had the heroine stumble into his life while seeking shelter and a place to rest for her sick companion. But that version simply did not want to be written. Which left me with the lingering thought of an injured cowboy. I struggled a long time trying to work out how to injure him and how that injury would involve the heroine. In the end, I simply had Jayne shoot Seth. It seemed the only way to get this pair together. I hope my solution worked for you, the reader. I loved dealing with how a big, independent cowboy would deal with his injuries and how an uncertain, yet courageous lady from a pampered background would help him.

I hope you enjoyed this story as much as I enjoyed writing it.

I love to hear from my readers. You can contact me at www.lindaford.org where you can also see what's coming next for the Cowboys of Eden Valley.

Linda Ford

QUESTIONS FOR DISCUSSION

1. Jayne wanted to learn to shoot a gun. Why was it important to her? Do you think her reasoning made sense?

2. Jayne was raised in a rich home. What sort of challenges does she face living on a ranch? How is she handling the challenges? Which do you think would be the hardest for you to deal with?

3. What did you think of the friendship she had with her two friends? What strengths did she add to the mix?

4. Seth feels his duty lies in caring for his father. Do you find his reasons for doing so understandable?

5. Do you think Seth should have sent the money without actually visiting his pa? Why or why not?

6. Did you suspect the deeper reason for his reluctance to open his heart to love before he recalled his pa's words?

7. In the end, Seth found emotional healing. Did only one event accomplish that? Or more? What was the event or events?

8. When Seth returns, he has a plan, or does he? What do you think his plan was? How did it get side-tracked?

9. Who saved whom in the end? Was this act what healed them? Or was it a culmination of events?

10. How did Jayne prove she was capable? Was it enough? What more did she discover she wanted?

11. Do you think Jayne will be able to go from being a rich man's daughter to a poor rancher's wife? On what do you base your answer?

12. If you could write a chapter five years from the end of the story, what would you include?

ABOUT THE AUTHOR

Linda Ford lives on a ranch in Alberta, Canada. Growing up on the prairie and learning to notice the small details it hides gave her an appreciation for watching God at work in His creation. Her upbringing also included being taught to trust God in everything and through everything — a theme that resonates in her stories. Threads of another part of her life are found in her stories — her concern for children and their future. She and her husband raised fourteen children — four homemade, ten adopted. She currently shares her home and life with her husband, a grown son, a live-in paraplegic client and a continual (and welcome) stream of kids, kids-in-law, grandkids and assorted friends and relatives.